ALWAYS A HERO

BAYTOWN HEROES

MARYANN JORDAN

Always a Hero (Baytown Heroes) Copyright 2024

All rights reserved. No part of this book may be reproduced or transmitted in any form or by any means, electronic or mechanical, including photocopying, recording, or by any information storage and retrieval system without the written permission of the author, except where permitted by law.

If you are reading this book and did not purchase it, then you are reading an illegal pirated copy. If you would be concerned about working for no pay, then please respect the author's work! Make sure that you are only reading a copy that has been officially released by the author.

This book is a work of fiction. Names, characters, places, and incidents are either products of the author's imagination or are used fictitiously. Any resemblance to actual persons, living or dead, events, or locales is entirely coincidental.

Cover by: Graphics by Stacy

ISBN ebook: 978-1-956588-60-6

ISBN print: 978-1-956588-61-3

❦ Created with Vellum

ABOUT THE AUTHOR

I am an avid reader of romance novels, often joking that I cut my teeth on historical romances. I have been reading and reviewing for years. In 2013, I finally gave in to the characters in my head, screaming for their story to be told. From these musings, my first novel, Emma's Home, The Fairfield Series, was born.

I was a high school counselor, having worked in education for thirty years. I live in Virginia, having also lived in four states and two foreign countries. I have been married to a wonderfully patient man for forty-two years. When writing, my dog or one of my cats can generally be found in the same room if not on my lap.

Please take the time to leave a review of this book. Feel free to contact me, especially if you enjoyed my book. I love to hear from readers!

Facebook

Join my Facebook group: Maryann Jordan's Protector Fans

Sign up for my emails by visiting my Website!

Website

Author's Note

Please remember that this is a work of fiction. I have lived in numerous states as well as overseas, but for the last thirty years have called Virginia my home. I often choose to use fictional city names with some geographical accuracies.

These fictionally named cities allow me to use my creativity and not feel constricted by attempting to accurately portray the areas.

It is my hope that my readers will allow me this creative license and understand my fictional world.

I also do quite a bit of research on my books and try to write on subjects with accuracy. There will always be points where creative license will be used in order to create scenes or plots.

1

Ten Years Ago

No frills. Just the way Sam liked it. The inside of the bar was simple, with exposed brick on the walls. A longstanding bar dominated the length of the left side. The barstools had seen better days but were comfortable. The center and right side were dotted with tables, giving patrons plenty of room to drink and gather. There was an intentional absence of a pool table, dance floor, or corner for musicians. If a patron was looking for an exciting night spot, they'd be disappointed in this choice. But the owners were happy with its proximity to the Newport News police precinct, offering a steady stream of officers looking for a place to drink and gather after a day on the front lines.

Sam sat at the bar, savoring the well-earned aftershift beer with one of the best men he'd ever known.

Edward Brooks. Their bond was forged at the Virginia Police Academy training, having both previously served in the military. Both were offered jobs in Newport News and while not partners, their camaraderie was steadfast. They often worked the same shifts, and once or twice a week, they would end a shift with a drink before heading home.

"Did you say Hayley was coming?"

Edward's face gentled as he smiled and nodded. He and Hayley married two years ago, just before Sam met Edward. For him, she was not just a life partner but truly the love of his life. As far as Sam was concerned, Hayley was a perfect match for Edward, and as happy as he was for them, he felt a small twinge inside at not having the same.

Sam had tried... and failed at marriage. He and his ex-wife had been too young to face any difficulties. "You're one lucky bastard to have landed a woman like Hayley."

Edward chuckled, still nodding. "You're not telling me anything I don't know. She's absolutely the best." He looked over and said, "It'll happen, man. Just gotta find the right one."

"I sure as hell didn't the first time around."

Edward shook his head. "Then she wasn't the one. If she couldn't handle being a soldier's wife, she'd never make it as a cop's wife."

"Yeah, but it wasn't all on her. We married too damn young. Hell, we got married when I was only twenty."

"Fuck, that was young," Edward agreed.

He shrugged. He hated admitting defeat at anything,

and his divorce at twenty-three had been a bitter pill to swallow. He eventually realized that the idea of a failed marriage hurt more than actually not being married to her anymore. And that was a sobering thought. "Oh, well, maybe one day."

He glanced over Edward's shoulder and watched Hayley gracefully enter the bar. Since he and Edward always sat in the same two seats at the bar, her gaze immediately found them. Her smile widened, and her blue eyes twinkled in the lights reflected in the mirror behind the bar. Hayley was beautiful, smart, and able to handle her husband's chosen career. *Edward was a lucky man.*

Sam wasn't jealous, but he sure as fuck was envious. He wouldn't mind having someone in his life like Hayley, but wondered if that was in the cards for him.

She winked at Sam, her smile widening as she slipped next to Edward, wrapped her arms around him, and kissed his cheek.

"Hey, darlin'," Edward said, pulling her close. He turned his head to plant a kiss on her lips.

"Hey, back." She looked toward Sam, and her smile stayed bright. "Hi, Sam."

"Hayley," he greeted, dipping his chin. He looked for the bartender and lifted his hand to signal for another beer to come their way when Hayley shook her head and waved her hand in front of them.

"Sorry, no beer for me."

"Do you feel okay, sweetheart?" Edward asked, his brow instantly furrowing as his gaze moved over her face.

"Actually, I feel great. But I just don't want a beer."

"Do you want a glass of wine?" Edward pressed.

She threw her head back and laughed, the soft sound resounding in the noisy bar. "No, actually, I don't want any alcohol at all. But I do need to tell you something."

A flicker of understanding hit Sam, and he darted his gaze toward Edward, amused to see his friend was still clueless. Biting the corner of his lip, he looked down at the bar, trying to suppress his grin. It slipped out nonetheless, and his shoulders shook as his laughter began.

His bewilderment palpable, Edward asked, "What's going on?"

Hayley's hand landed on her hip. "Honestly, honey, I thought you might guess it when I said no alcohol. Let me put it this way... I can't drink for the next seven months. Well, actually longer than that, but definitely for seven months."

Sam watched the scenario play out in front of him, enjoying his front-row seat.

Edward slowly filtered through Hayley's hints before a gasp flew out of his mouth. "You're pregnant?"

Hayley rolled her eyes and laughed, a pretty blush gracing her cheeks. "Way to tell the whole bar, sweetie!"

Edward wrapped his arms around his wife, lifted her feet off the ground, and twirled her around. Sam couldn't help but laugh, seeing two people he cared about experiencing such joy and allowing him to be a part of the good news.

When Hayley's feet touched the floor again, Sam clapped his friend on the shoulder, then leaned over and kissed Hayley on the cheek. "Congratulations to you two. That's great news, and it couldn't happen to a nicer couple."

Hayley placed her hand on her stomach. "I'm only about two months along, so I'm not going to share it with too many people yet." She glanced around, seeing several other police officers lift their beers and call out congratulations. She sighed, shook her head, and turned her attention to Edward. "I guess this wasn't the place to tell you if I wanted to keep everything quiet, right?"

"You gotta know that I'm over the moon, babe." Edward's already proud-papa smile spread across his face. "It'll be hard for me to keep it quiet."

"We're not going to tell our parents until I get a little bit further along, and we can be sure everything's okay."

"Whatever you want," Edward promised just before he kissed her again. "Let's go home and celebrate."

Sam knew they were ready to be alone, so he offered his congratulations again, gave a hearty handshake and back slap to Edward, and then pulled Hayley in for a light hug and another chaste kiss on the cheek. "Your kid will be the luckiest with you two for parents. Can't wait to spoil him or her."

She looked up, her eyes shining with both excitement and unshed tears. "Thank you, Sam. You'll be the best honorary uncle."

Edward reached for his wallet, but Sam threw his hand out. "No way, man. Drinks are on me tonight." With that, he waved goodbye and watched as they walked out of the bar, arm in arm, their joy palpable.

The bar noise faded away as he continued to sit alone in a sea of people. He lifted his beer mug in a silent salute to his friends before draining the last of his drink. When he caught a glimpse of his reflection in the mirror, the dim lighting reflected his contemplation... as well as the crinkles at the sides of his eyes. Not quite thirty, he felt much older.

The weight of the tours as military police while spending countless nights earning his Associate's degree in police science. He had a few more years as a civilian police officer while taking more classes. Throw in one failed marriage and enough one-night stands to make it painfully obvious that finding love... true, long-lasting, partner-for-life love wouldn't be easy.

He shook his head, dislodging the maudlin thoughts creeping in. Other police officers and patrons filled in the spaces around the bar that Edward and Hayley had vacated. Still surrounded by friends, he was ready to head home. Tossing money on the bar to cover his and Edward's drinks, he offered a chin lift to the bartender and others as he made his way out the door. The cool air hit him in the face, and he pulled it deeply into his lungs.

Once home, the quiet was almost tangible. His apartment was functional but lacked any semblance of warmth. He didn't own many worldly possessions when he was married, and even though his wife wanted the divorce, he also couldn't deny that they weren't meant to be. When they divorced, he'd given her most of the furniture since he was heading out for another military tour.

Once he landed his law enforcement job in Newport News, he bought just the necessary pieces of furniture.

Sofa. Comfortable chair. Small dining table with two chairs. A bed. A chest of drawers. He thought about the house Edward shared with Hayley, filled with warmth and personality. There were throw pillows on the sofa, colorful kitchen curtains over their windows, and a coffee machine on the counter that made to-die-for coffee. Chuckling, he looked over at his kitchen counter with his single-cup pod coffee maker.

He didn't hurt so much for the loss of his short, youthful marriage as it was for the loss of what he'd hoped life would be.

Lying in bed that night, he tried to read but cast his thoughts, once again, to Edward and Hayley. Tossing the book onto the nightstand, he slid down, staring at the ceiling. A bittersweet grin slipped over his face as he made a silent vow. If he were never going to have children of his own, he would be their best honorary uncle. *And maybe that will be good enough.*

One and a half years later

"Can you please explain why we must do this now?"

Sandra's strident voice from the passenger seat grated on Sam's buoyant mood. He flicked a sideward glance at her, noting the hard set of her face and her arms crossed over her chest. "I don't know why this is so hard for you to understand, Sandra."

She threw her hands up as an exaggerated huff flung from her lips. She turned her glower toward him.

"Maybe because it's a freaking birthday party for a one-year-old! Jesus, it's not like he'll even know if you're there!"

"I told you about Eddie's birthday party weeks ago. I don't see why it's such a big deal to you now. If you didn't want to go, you should've said so."

Another sharp exhalation burst forth, and her face flushed. "So you can remember it's his one-year birthday, but you can't even remember it's our anniversary?"

His grip tightened on the wheel as his eyes cut back to her. "Anniversary?"

"Jesus, are you that dense, Sam? Yes, our anniversary. We've been dating for *four* months. We met exactly four months ago. When you told me you had plans for today a few weeks ago, I thought it would be to celebrate us. Then when you told me it was for that kid's birthday party, I couldn't believe it. I thought surely you were joking. In fact, I was certain that you were just pretending so you could surprise me with a romantic gesture."

Sam looked in the rearview mirror, glad to see no one behind him. He flipped on his blinker and eased his SUV to the side of the road before parking. He mentally counted to ten as he shifted in his seat to face her more fully, but it did little to ease the clench in his jaw. He rarely lost his temper, but his ire had been building with each demand Sandra had been making over the past month.

He would agree that they'd been going out for about four months. *But who the hell celebrates a four-month anniversary?* And it wasn't as though he sprang this birthday event on her. He'd explained two weeks ago that he was going to Edward and Hayley's house to celebrate little Eddie's first birthday. He'd taken her out last night for dinner, spending more on food than a cop's salary would normally allow, all because she pouted about him spending more on *that* kid than he did on her. Knowing she wouldn't enjoy it, he hadn't planned to take Sandra to the party, but she'd insisted. *And now I know why.* Her insistence wasn't about the party– it was about her. *A-fuckin'-gin.*

Because just like everything else with Sandra, she wanted it all about her. Now, he wondered what he'd ever seen in her. She was beautiful, and the first couple of months had been fun. But lately, it became painfully obvious that she wanted their relationship to revolve around her expectations.

Now, looking at the hard set of her face, pouting lips, and glare in her eyes, he wished he had insisted on going by himself. He would have turned around and taken her back to her house before showing up at the party if he'd had time.

"Sandra, I'm sorry you thought when I said we were going to Eddie's birthday party, it was code for something else. I can't imagine why you thought that. And it doesn't matter that he's only one and won't remember this party. His parents are my closest friends, and I won't miss this occasion." His voice was firm, and he braced himself for an explosion, but wasn't going to change his mind.

She opened her mouth and snapped it closed, pressing her lips tightly together as though forcing the words she wanted to spew to remain muted. Finally, drawing in a deep breath and letting it out, she said, "Fine. We'll go, but I expect to be taken out tomorrow somewhere very nice. If I have to spend the afternoon with *your* friends and their baby, then you better plan on making it up to me!"

The urge to end things right then was strong, but Sam battled back, refusing to act on emotion. He'd be forced to address the brewing tension later. *One thing at a time, and right now, it is for Edward, Hayley, and little Eddie.*

For the next several hours, he ignored Sandra's straight-back, stick-up-her-ass posture as she perched on the edge of the sofa, barely speaking or smiling. Instead, he focused on the one-year-old little boy, snapping pictures of smeared birthday cake on chubby cheeks and sitting on the floor as Eddie stood on wobbly legs and helped him open presents.

The house was filled with family, friends, and a few other toddlers running around, as well as Edward's and Hayley's parents.

"I'm almost out of baby wipes for sticky hands," Hayley exclaimed, standing and walking down the hall. "I have extra ones in his room."

Edward looked up as his wife started up the stairs and called out, "I think they're on the top shelf."

Eddie was hanging on his dad, so Sam jumped up. "I'll go get them for her."

Finding Hayley in the nursery, he pulled the large multipack of baby wipes from the top closet shelf. "I see you guys buy in bulk!"

"We've learned that's the only way to do it." She laughed. Stepping closer, she whispered, "It doesn't look like Sandra is having a very good time."

Her face was filled with concern, and the stark difference between Hayley and Sandra couldn't have been more obvious. He shook his head and heaved a sigh, his hands on his hips. "I think it's time to end things. In truth, I never thought she was right for a long-term relationship anyway. But, lately, I'm not even enjoying myself, and she certainly doesn't seem to be either."

"Thank God!" Hayley gushed. "Edward and I have been wondering when you'd come to that decision."

He jerked slightly. "You two never said anything."

She placed her hand on his arm, her eyes warm as they held his. "Because it's a decision you had to make. If you thought she was the right person, then we'd want you to be happy. We just never thought she was the right person."

"Yeah, you called that right." Chuckling ruefully, he added, "Looks like my dinner tomorrow will be unpleasant."

Holding the baby wipes in one hand, she looped her other hand through his arm. "Well, we're grateful that you're a part of our lives and gave up time today to be with us for Eddie's first birthday."

"How could I not? After all, you did name him Edward Samuel Brooks. He's the closest I'll come to a namesake!"

As they walked out of the nursery, she shook her

head. "You'll find somebody, and when you do, Edward and I will be so happy for you."

They returned downstairs, and he spied Sandra still fuming. Walking over to Edward, he plucked Eddie up, gave the squirming birthday boy a hug, and kissed the top of his head. Looking into Edward's proud gaze, he said, "Fatherhood looks good on you. I'm happy for you."

Edward looked at his son in Sam's arms and grinned. "Thanks, man. And thanks for coming today."

"Nowhere I'd rather be than with you and your family."

Saying goodbye, he collected a brittle Sandra and escorted her to his SUV. As he rounded the vehicle to climb into the driver's seat, he looked back at the house, spying Edward, Hayley, and Eddie through the big living room window, and realized his parting words to Edward were true. *"Nowhere I'd rather be than with you and your family."*

2

ONE YEAR LATER

The neighborhood park was filled with other cops and their families as they celebrated the retirement of their captain.

Sam and Edward walked off the baseball field, having just finished a friendly game with fellow cops. Walking straight toward the picnic tables, they were met by a smiling Hayley. She held out two cold sodas in her hands, and he thanked her, turning it up and chugging it down. Edward hefted Eddie into his arms, and Sam grinned. He'd heard Hayley mention the other day that Eddie looked more like a toddler, and seeing him running around, Sam understood. He was still a chubby-cheeked, adorable little boy, but his features had already taken on the distinctive characteristics of both his parents.

"Want to race?" he asked Eddie.

Before he had a chance to say, "Go," Eddie squealed and started running toward the ball field. Laughing at the little boy's head start, he began to jog, staying right with Eddie, step for step. When they finally collapsed onto the grass, Eddie was panting, claiming, "Me won! Me!"

"You sure did! I can't believe how fast you are!"

Hayley headed toward them, snapping pictures with her phone and carrying his toddler soccer ball in her other hand. "Just wait till you see what he can do with this."

Eddie squealed again as his mom dropped the ball onto the ground. He began to run, kicking the ball perfectly and only falling a few times. He managed to keep the ball going as he headed back toward the picnic table where his dad sat.

"Holy shit!" Sam said, shaking his head as he plopped his fists onto his hips. "He's amazing."

"I think so too, but then I'm biased."

He smiled at Hayley. "That's okay. You're allowed to be. Special mom privileges."

Laughing, they walked back to the picnic table together. Soon, their paper plates were filled with food that everyone had brought. They shared a picnic table with another family, but Sam managed to snag a seat next to Eddie, giving Hayley and Edward a chance to eat unencumbered with a two-year-old for a few minutes.

After lunch, Hayley took Eddie home for nap time, and he and Edward sat with the others from their precinct, shooting the shit and enjoying time with the retiring captain. The conversation rolled to the challenges of law enforcement in the area. More hard-core crime. More drugs. And a fuck of a lot more gangs.

Sam leaned back in the lawn chair, crossed one ankle over his knee, and dangled his water bottle between his fingers. "Do you ever think about moving somewhere different?" he asked Edward.

"Hell, yeah. All the time, actually. My parents are in South Carolina. Hayley's parents are out in Arizona. Her brother and his family are in Ohio. I mean, damn, it's not like we have family tying us here."

Both sighed, then sat in silence for a moment before Edward continued. "And now that we have Eddie? I think about the kind of place where I want him to grow up. The school system. The playgrounds."

"Yeah." Sam nodded and focused on Edward. "What's holding you back?"

"Christ, it just seems so overwhelming. We'd have to decide where to go. Sell the house. Find a new house. Pay for movers. And that doesn't include doing all that after finding a new police job."

"I hear you, man."

"What about you?"

"Same thing. Of course, it'd be a lot easier on me. No wife, kid, school system, house." He chuckled, hearing himself. "Now that I say it out loud, I'm not sure what's holding me back."

"You know, once you pass your detective exam, then it might be a better time for you to make a change if you want." Edward kicked Sam's foot and laughed. "But then you'd have to give up your Eddie babysitting, and I don't know if we could handle that!"

Sam grinned in return, but the sting was felt deep in his heart. Not being around Edward and Hayley or seeing Eddie grow up was all the reason he needed to stay right where he was for now.

Four months later

Sam's gaze lifted toward the sky, his thoughts as heavy and dark as the brooding clouds barely waiting to unleash the rain threatening to fall. Thankfully, the heavens held back their tears, something no one else in the gathering below had managed to do. He'd thought nothing could make this horrible day worse, but even he had to admit that standing in the pouring rain would have made the day's events crash straight from unbearable into absolute hell.

His chest ached with a pain so vivid he wondered if he were having a heart attack. It wouldn't have surprised him. His heart, overburdened with gut-wrenching sorrow, was close to simply giving up, ceding to the toll the week had taken on him.

The tremendous number of mourners assembled was not unexpected. Their presence was a testament to the love, care, and sorrow everyone wanted to express. Sam's eyes flickered momentarily to the left, spying the tear-streaked faces of extended family members. Behind them stood a sea of uniforms—officers, captains, and lieutenants from their precinct and law enforcement from neighboring towns and cities. Street cops, special ops members, administrative staff, detectives… the whole precinct had turned out.

Despite his awareness of the throng surrounding him, his focus was constricted to the woman and child beside him. Hayley's arms were wrapped so tightly around her son that Sam could see her embrace was more of a vise of grief than a cuddle. Eddie began to squirm, no longer satisfied with his confinement.

Sam shifted slightly on the seat, reaching out to take the eager-to-move toddler onto his lap. He caught Hayley's gaze, hoping she didn't mind the change, but her eyes registered little other than an abyss of heartache.

Sam was certain that his eyes would mirror the same grief.

Because right in front of their chairs, the epicenter of their world of loss, was the flag-draped casket, now the final resting place of the best man he'd ever know.

It should've been simple, although nothing for a cop is simple. A traffic stop for an automobile whose taillights were not working. Edward followed all protocol, but the two gang members inside the car transporting drugs and guns panicked, certain they would be searched. One pulled a gun, then shot wildly out the window, striking Edward in the neck. They took off, fleeing in cowardice while Sam's best friend bled out quickly on the street.

Sam had received the call from the captain, giving him the news. His knees had nearly buckled, and if it wasn't for his partner and another officer, he was sure he would have hit the floor. Pain sliced open his chest, threatening to rip out his heart. Then, the captain asked him to accompany the chaplain to talk to Hayley. And as much as he wanted to rush out to find the killers, he knew he had to be with Hayley.

For the first time, driving up and parking outside the home she and Edward shared, he hated the idea of walking in and blowing her world apart. A surreal fog enveloped them as she gave in to the trauma slicing through her.

The women and wives from the precinct stepped in and immediately brought food, babysat Eddie until the family could arrive, and gave him and Hayley a chance to take care of all the business needed when someone died. The fucking business. The funeral home employees had a job to do, but as he sat with Hayley, he understood they were trained to say all the right things, speak softly, and maneuver the grieving to make decisions. He respected them and hated them all at the same time.

Hayley was a robot. Truthfully, he wasn't functioning much better than she. But he forced himself to do everything he knew Edward would want him to do, and thank God, Edward and Hayley had their affairs in order, saving her from having to make some of the more painful decisions.

The first night, he slept on her sofa, listening to her sobbing upstairs. By the second night, her parents had arrived, soon followed by Edward's parents. Sam no longer spent the night but found his apartment was a black hole of aloneness. Sleep didn't come, so he drank whiskey while sitting on an uncomfortable kitchen stool. During the day, he filled his time to keep his grief at bay by being with Hayley and Eddie.

The chaplain had stopped by and asked if he was taking time to grieve. His chest still sliced open and laid bare, he shook his head. "I'll grieve later. Right now, I need to be strong for Edward's wife and little boy."

And now, sitting with them in the white folding chairs that the cemetery sets out under the awning, he bounced Eddie on his knee and squeezed his eyes tightly to keep the tears from falling.

A little bit longer. I need to hang on a little bit longer. At the end of the service, he assisted Hayley in standing, holding Eddie to his chest with an arm around Hayley's shoulders. As the others started to walk away, he stood as Hayley slipped from the security of his arm and placed a single flower on the head of the casket. Bending, she whispered words for no one else to hear, then turned back to Sam.

Her face was a landscape of raw emotions, with dark circles under her eyes that stood out in stark contrast to her ghostly white complexion. Gaunt cheeks marred her beauty. Her hair was brushed back into a simple ponytail, and while her black dress was stylish, he knew she gave no thought to her appearance.

"Are you ready to go?" he murmured softly.

Their closest friends were heading to the local American Legion Hall for the wake. He wanted to take her and Eddie home, wrap them safely into a cocoon, and keep the world at bay. But, knowing Hayley, she would do everything expected of her, if just to honor Edward's memory.

She looked over her shoulder, and he felt her full-body shiver. He wrapped his free arm around her again, keeping hold of Eddie, who was now resting his head on Sam's shoulder.

Her eyes found him, and she whispered, "I just keep thinking that when I walk away from here, I'll never be able to see him again. Even if it's just his coffin, it's still something tangible. And after today, I'll only have the headstone." Her voice was barely a whisper, the words laced with fragility.

"Hayley, you've got a thousand memories in all the pictures you've taken over the years. Those will never be buried. No one can take them from you."

Eddie let out a little squeal and wiggled in Sam's arms.

Just as he was going to suggest that they head to the car, Hayley sucked in a shuddering breath, then swallowed deeply. "Sam, I... I have something to tell you. Something I haven't told anyone. I'd only told Edward a few nights before he was... he died."

Sam waited patiently, knowing whatever was agonizing Hayley, he wanted her to feel free to talk to him in her own time.

"I..." Her hand dropped to her stomach. "I... I'm pregnant."

Rocked by her words, he was stunned. The air rushed from his lungs so quickly that he felt lightheaded. Locking his knees in place, he stared as the tidal wave of emotions hit him. Knowing he should say something, he opened his mouth, but no words came forth, leaving them blanketed in silence.

"He was so excited..." she whispered, then her voice

broke. Her face crumpled, and fat tears rolled down her cheeks.

"Oh God, Hayley," he finally managed to utter. With Eddie still in his arms, he tried to pull her even closer so the three of them were forced together. For a long moment, they shared heartbeats, grief, and tears.

Then he said the only thing that came to mind. "I promise to help with everything I can. Edward was my best friend, and I won't let you go through this alone."

As her tears soaked his shirt, his gaze stared over the top of her head to the casket, now being readied to lower into the ground. "I promise." He whispered his vow as much to Edward as it was to Hayley and Eddie. And the new little one, yet to be born.

3

ONE YEAR LATER

The roar of the lawnmower created a monotone white noise, albeit loud, that allowed Sam's mind to wander as he walked back and forth over the small yard. The flower beds in the front remained weeded but only contained a few flowers from bulbs that came up each year. He hadn't wanted the space to become unruly with overgrown weeds, but there had been no time or inclination to plant more flowers. He remembered how the planters had once been a riot of color. But now, Hayley was busy with a baby and potty training a three-year-old. And continuing to grieve.

At first, Hayley's tears had been hourly, then daily, and slowly, more time passed between breakdowns. Much in the same way as he, their grief journey seemed to mirror each other. They talked a lot about grief in the early days, acknowledging that it would hit both of them at different times and in different ways. But interestingly enough, he and Hayley seem to be in sync.

Maybe after all the time he spent with her and Edward, that wasn't too surprising.

He'd accompanied Hayley to an array of prenatal doctor's appointments, feeling every heartbeat on the ultrasound as if it were echoing inside him.

Hayley had wanted him present for the birth even though Hayley's mom had acted as her coach. But she had fervently insisted she needed him there, and even though he knew his role was a surrogate for Edward, he wouldn't deny her anything. So he'd sat with Eddie in the waiting room until a nurse came to get him. He'd stood and placed Eddie in the capable hands of Hayley's dad and Edward's parents and walked down the hall toward the birthing room. His footsteps on the tiled floor were drowned out by his heartbeat.

He donned the paper gown, moved to Hayley's head, and tried to comfort her through the process that left men humbled and in awe. Men might believe they were the protectors providing the sturdy fortress around their families. But seeing Hayley's resolve, birthing her baby without Edward, and knowing that her heart was broken over Edward never having the chance to know their daughter, Sam was certain he'd never witnessed anything more inspiring.

When she'd insisted he hold the tiny newborn, his hands had trembled until the bundle was placed in his arms. Then, he'd battled back the tears as an emotional avalanche engulfed him. *This should be Edward's place to hold Hope first.* But staring at the tiny button nose and pursed pink lips, he fell in love—the profound, soul-shaking kind of love. And once again, he offered a silent vow to take care of Edward's family.

Hayley, in the utilitarian hospital bed and ugly gown with sweat-slicked hair and a tear-streaked face, suddenly smiled and radiated tranquility. Sam thought she was more beautiful at that moment than he'd ever seen. His heart had jolted with an emotional swell as he leaned over to kiss the top of her head.

He'd quickly handed Hope back to Hayley and, when he spied the question in her eyes, blurted, "I'm going to get Eddie. He'll want to meet his sister." Her smile let him know she was anxious to hold her son again.

He'd disappeared down the hall, breathing deeply to clear his mind. Entering the family waiting room, he felt a smile hit his face at the sight of Eddie bouncing in excitement. "Come on, everyone. Come meet Hope."

Eddie had raced forward, grabbed his hand, and the two walked back to Hayley's room with the four grandparents following. Once inside, Sam had stayed busy, giving Eddie plenty of time to say hello to his mom and new baby sister while making sure the exuberant boy didn't inadvertently squish anyone.

When it came time for pictures, he'd stepped back, allowing the grandparents to snap photos of Hayley holding Hope with Eddie pressed tightly to her side. Hayley looked over and said, "Sam, come on."

Eddie's eyes lit up as he clapped his hands in enthusiasm. "Yeah, Sam. Come be with us!"

He'd sat on the edge of the bed, and Eddie leaned away from Hayley, now pressing against Sam. His heart filled as he smiled for the cameras, then caught a shadow pass over Edward's parents' faces. He'd swallowed deeply, acknowledging their grief during this time of joy. In truth, he felt it deeply, too.

The day he drove Hayley and Hope home, he'd stayed just long enough to see them settled. Her mom planned to stay for a couple of weeks to help, and Sam felt like he needed to step back. He tenderly kissed Hayley's cheek once she was on the sofa with Hope in her arms and Eddie playing on the floor with his trucks.

Hayley's hand on his arm stopped him as he started to stand. Looking down, he waited.

"Thank you, Sam," she'd murmured, her eyes searching his as she blinked back the moisture. "I couldn't have done this without you." When he started to protest, she interrupted. "I *wouldn't* have *wanted* to do this without you."

Her words anchored deep within him. With a soft smile, he'd looked at Hope's downy head, his love real. "My pleasure, Hayley." Kissing her cheek again, he'd headed back to his lonely home.

Now, he spent more time with Hayley and the kids than at home. Glad he finished the mowing before Hope's nap, he cleaned off the mower and rolled it into the garage.

"Sam!"

He turned at the familiar voice and grinned. Eddie ran toward him, waving a piece of paper in his hand. Sam recognized the paper and laughed as Eddie thrust it at him.

"I got ten stickers in a row!"

Hayley had tried different ways to potty train Eddie

and had even checked out the mom groups on social media, finally turning her back on everything except positive reinforcement. And the sticker chart was on the bathroom wall… well, now it was in Sam's hand.

"Way to go, buddy," he enthused as he knelt to Eddie's level. "So, what reward are you going to pick out?" Thoughts of treats, a toy, or an outing to the park ran through his mind.

"I told Mommy I wanted a daddy."

Sam's body locked as his breath halted in his lungs, and his heart threatened to pound out of his chest. Eddie stared up at him with such innocence and a touch of seriousness in his big eyes. "Uh…" he uttered. This was one of those times he knew to tread carefully and battled between needing Hayley to come outside to take charge of the situation and overwhelmingly being thankful she wasn't. "Well… uh…"

Seemingly unaffected by Sam's inability to speak, Eddie continued. "I want you to be my daddy."

He nearly choked as he swallowed past the lump in his throat. He couldn't imagine what Hayley's response would have been. "So, uh…" Jesus, he'd never had such a hard time figuring out what to say. The weight of Eddie's request sat on his chest like a boulder.

"Mom said that I had a dad. He's in heaven. He's proud of me, too."

Finally, the air rushed out of Sam's lungs, and he managed to nod. "That's right, buddy. You have a dad who is so proud of you."

Eddie grinned, all happy in his world, while Sam tried to find steadiness as his world skidded off its axis.

"I want ice cream. And a truck."

Gathering his wits, he nodded. "I think we can take care of that. We'll get your treat once your sister wakes from her nap."

Eddie nodded, then turned and started running toward the house, his sticker sheet still gripped tightly in his little hand. Suddenly, he stopped, turned abruptly, and raced back to Sam, throwing his arms around Sam's neck as he still knelt on the ground.

"I have Dad and you!"

Standing with the little boy clutched in his arms, Sam held him tight. "Yeah, buddy. You do. You have a dad and me."

Lifting his gaze, his breath hitched as he saw Hayley standing behind the sliding glass door of their house. Her fingers pressed against her lips, and even from this distance, he could see the tears in her eyes.

4

TWO YEARS LATER

Sam's desk was nestled amid the organized chaos of the precinct's large detective workroom. He leaned back in his chair and scanned the case files and laptop piled on his worn desk. He had taken and passed his detective examination several months after Edward died, but the captain had been slow to throw him onto major cases right away. For that, he wasn't too proud to admit he was grateful. His promotion to detective was a triumph he'd once envisioned sharing with his best friend.

The two gang members who had killed Edward had been found before he was even laid to rest. So Sam spent his energy and focus on ensuring Hayley and Eddie were taken care of.

Eddie was now in school, and Sam was the backup guardian angel, listed for pickups and emergencies. He shoveled snow on the few occasions they had accumulation and continued to mow their grass during the summers. Every few weeks, he popped the hood of Hayley's small SUV to check her engine, wanting her to be safe on the roads. He'd gone with her to pick it out, honestly not caring if it felt heavy-handed, but grateful when a relieved expression settled across her face as they approached the dealership.

He relished the detective responsibilities, occasionally remembering how he and Edward planned to become detectives together. Sam wore suits to work, grinning at the memory of the first time he stopped by Hayley's house after work, and Eddie looked up with bright eyes, exclaiming that he wanted a *big boy* suit, too.

Hayley's laughter had filled the air, a melody Sam loved hearing more and more. She shook her head, saying, "I remember when he used to see you and Edward in uniforms and wanted a cop outfit like Daddy and Sam."

As soon as the words left her mouth, Sam had braced, the sentence hanging between them. It spoke of a cherished memory and a painful reminder. He waited for the onslaught of tears to begin at her admission that Eddie now focused on Sam more than his dad. She looked stricken for a moment, then sighed heavily, but no tears came. Her resilience struck him, as it always did, leaving him in awe.

After his last conversation with Edward, Sam had never discussed his desire to move elsewhere. While the idea of moving to a new location would have been hard in the past, he would've taken comfort in the fact that Edward and Hayley and their children would've had each other. But now, his life was intrinsically intertwined with Hayley, Eddie, and little Hope. At the crossroads of duty and devotion, he was a guardian at heart, anchored to them by a promise he intended to keep. A promise he *wanted* to keep.

He chuckled, looking at the photographs he had on his desk. The three pictures were in a tri-fold frame. One was he and Edward in their police uniforms with smiles on their faces during happier times. The other was a photograph of Hayley and Edward holding Eddie as a baby. The third photograph was taken a few months ago of Hayley holding Hope and Eddie standing in front of Sam, with Sam's hand resting lightly on the little boy's shoulders.

His attention was drawn back to the present when his partner, Leon Portillo, sat in the chair at his desk facing Sam's. They had been partners for the past year. And while Sam didn't consider Leon a best friend like Edward, he couldn't have asked for a better partner. They complemented the other, each developing ways of questioning suspects together that ended in results.

"I'm going to type up our interview from the pawnshop robbery," Leon said. "I thought about putting it off until tomorrow, but I'd rather stay late and get that done before I forget anything. Why don't you head on out, and I'll see you tomorrow."

Sam's dedication would have him stay with Leon, but he also had something pressing he needed to do. Of course, looking at the stack of open case files on his desk, he also always had something work-related to do. He didn't mind putting in long hours on days when he didn't have anything after work planned, but on a day like today, he had somewhere else he wanted to be.

"Thanks, man. I'll probably get in early tomorrow and review the notes from the carjacking down on Johnson Street. I have a couple of people who I think might be able to point us in the right direction."

"Good deal," Leon said, offering a chin lift before looking back down at his laptop, his fingers tapping over the keyboard.

Grabbing his suit jacket from the back of his chair, he slid it on and headed out to the parking lot. Last year, he bought a new SUV based more on safety ratings than sporty looks. And in the back seat were two car seats. At first, Hayley thought it was excessive and hated him spending the money, but he wanted to be prepared to take both kids somewhere, either in an emergency or just for fun.

He drove straight to one of the town's recreational parks and walked across the lawn to where the parents sat on the side. He easily spied Hayley's ponytail and the little girl she bounced on her knees. Hope was now a toddler with bright eyes that didn't seem to miss anything and a smile that lit up when she saw her mom, Sam, or especially her brother. She had been a very calm baby, making life much easier for Hayley during those early months. Now, she eagerly sought after each new adventure with excitement. And she was beautiful. He knew he was biased, but she was a gorgeous little girl, holding the promise that she would be just as beautiful as her mom.

"Hey there," he called out, walking around before settling into the camp chair Hayley had set up next to her.

Hayley's head jerked around, her ponytail swinging. Her eyes lit up as she smiled at him. "Hey, back."

His heart had stuttered the first time she'd said those simple words. As soon as she'd said it to him, he feared she would become upset at the realization that she'd used a simple phrase with him as she had with her husband. But now, it just seemed to be what she said, and he accepted it with gratitude.

Hope screeched and threw out her arms as she lunged toward him. He barely had a chance to catch her, then held her steady as he lifted her, made a scrunchy face, and listened to her giggles. As he brought her back down to his chest, he kissed her cheek and blew raspberries on her neck, eliciting more giggles.

He dangled his keys, which she loved to play with, as his eyes darted out to the field where little five- and six-year-olds played soccer. Or rather, for most of them, playing *at* soccer. But his gaze quickly found Eddie, whose face was serious as he ran down the field with a soccer ball bouncing between his feet and very little opposition from the other team. In fact, as Sam watched, Eddie was more likely to run into opposition from his own team.

Chuckling, he looked over at Hayley again and smiled. "I take it the game is going well?"

She laughed and shook her head. "I'm not sure you can actually call it a *game*. Some of the kids are picking dandelions. Others run in the wrong direction. Some keep picking up the ball and throwing it. But a few are like Eddie and know what they're doing."

"Yes, but it doesn't look like any of them have his level of focus and tenacity."

"I know," she said softly, her smile dropping.

Her tone surprised him, sounding slightly off. Or maybe wistful. Or maybe worried. Hell, he didn't know, but he didn't like anything with her or the kids being a mystery.

"Is everything okay? Are you worried about Eddie?"

A short bark of laughter erupted. "What parent isn't worried about their child?"

Her gaze stayed on the little ones as they ran around the field, and then she finally said, "He does seem very serious, doesn't he?"

Sam hesitated, wanting to choose his words carefully while trying to think of Eddie objectively, which was hard, considering how much he loved that little boy. "I think he is serious, but I think that's part of his personality. I don't see it as a bad thing, Hayley."

She turned to him. Her gaze dropped to Hope sitting in his lap and then back to his eyes. "I don't know. I keep trying to remember how he was before Edward died and see if he's more introspective now."

He nodded as his heart ached for the woman beside him, who was an amazing mom occasionally plagued by insecurities. "I'm not sure you can look at it that way. He was only about two and a half when Edward died, and what I remember was a happy, bouncy toddler. But even then, he would focus on kicking a ball. He started talking early. So I think there was always a seriousness about him. But you'll never be able to truly know exactly how the circumstances may have changed his personality."

He held his breath, hoping his words didn't upset her. But he should've known. Hayley accepted everything with a gentle nod.

"You're right. I guess I just worry so much about him growing up without his father. I know his memories really only come from looking at pictures. So whether he truly remembers Edward or not, I don't know." Once again, her gaze dropped to Hope, and her smile tinged with sadness. "And, of course, Hope will never know her father."

"She'll know him, Hayley. Every day, you bring part of Edward into their lives."

"Sometimes I wonder if it's enough."

Hope wiggled in his lap, and he scrunched his face again and pulled her close to inhale her sweet toddler scent as he kissed her forehead. "And I promise I'll do everything I can to help you know your daddy."

Turning toward Hayley, holding her gaze, he stared into her beautiful, expressive eyes. "Believe me, it's enough. We'll make sure it's enough."

"I don't know what I would do without you, Sam. You're—"

Their serious discussion was interrupted by children yelling as they charged off the field. He stood and waited as Eddie ran first to his mom, his eyes bright as he excitedly recounted the tale of his goal. Then Sam passed Hope over to Hayley so he could high-five Eddie.

"I wasn't sure when you got here! Did you see me?

Did you see me running with the ball?" Eddie jumped up and down with excitement.

"You bet I did," Sam said, his smile wide. "I think you're the best one out there!"

Eddie grinned and ducked his head as he looked side to side. "Well, I don't want the other kids to feel bad, but I think I was one of the best ones out there, too!"

"Does anybody think celebratory ice cream is in order?" Sam asked.

Hayley laughed as Eddie raced around them, throwing his fist in the air and shouting, "Yes!"

"How about if we hit Taco Town first, eat dinner, and then run by Cool Chucks Ice Cream?"

Once again, his suggestion was met with approval and delight. Hope bounced and cheered, clapping her hands, picking up on her brother's enthusiasm. The sweet little girl was happy to be with her mom and brother, and Sam hoped that happiness carried to him, too.

"Help me pack up the chairs, Eddie," he said while Hayley grabbed the snack bag. Once put together, Sam slung the chair carriers over one shoulder, the tote bag on the other, and held Eddie's hand as they stepped out into the parking lot. Hayley and Hope followed.

5

TWO YEARS LATER

Hayley stood in the cemetery, surrounded by trimmed green grass and neat rows of white headstones underneath the blue skies. For a long time, she never noticed anything but the single spot that drew her like a cruel magnet. Now, finally, she could look around and appreciate the place of calm, quiet respite away from a whirling, sometimes overwhelming world.

Staring down at Edward's headstone, she repeated the same actions she had for five years. She lay a small towel on the grass, then sat in front of the marble slab and traced her fingers along the letters.

Edward John Brooks
Beloved Husband and Father
Faithful Friend and Protector

In the years since he'd died, she cried until no more tears fell, screamed until her voice was hoarse, railed against the universe, and finally managed to just talk to her husband the way she used to. When he was alive, he would pull her against his chest, kiss the top of her hair, and listen to whatever she needed to talk about. Looking back, she wondered how he managed to be so patient. But then he loved her. *And oh God... I loved him.*

"Hey, Edward." She pressed her lips together, and a soft sigh escaped. "It's been over a month since I came to visit, but never doubt you're always with me." She looked down at her lap, her hands clasped together. "I can't believe it's been almost five years since you were taken from us. Since you were taken from me. I didn't know how I would go on. I guess the kids... our kids made it possible. You'd be so proud of them, Edward. Eddie is so smart and thoughtful and feels things so deeply. And Hope is bright and happy, and her world is full of rainbows and unicorns."

She stretched her legs in front of her and leaned back with her palms on the towel. When she looked upward, the fluffy clouds floating along the blue sky captured her gaze. "And every day, I'm thankful for Sam. He has stepped in and helped me so much. Sometimes, I feel as though I've kept him from moving on. I'm sure he's gone on dates, but he hasn't had a girlfriend since you passed away. And I wonder if that's because he feels such an obligation to us. As much as he *loves* us, I wonder if we're a burden. Oh, Edward... I wish I knew what to do. Sometimes, I look at him and feel things I wasn't sure I'd ever feel again."

A little gasp slipped out, and her heart raced. "I can't

believe I just said that." She leaned forward and covered her face with her hands. "Edward, I don't know what I feel. I look at Sam, and I feel alive with him for the first time in so long. But nothing can come of those feelings, so there's no need to explore them."

She shook her head. "Maybe if I could move on, then he could, too. Of course, seeing him with someone else would cause my heart to crack. But I had my heart broken in the worst way when you died, Edward, so I think I can handle a little crack."

She closed her eyes and tried to keep her tumultuous thoughts from overtaking her. A breeze ruffled her hair, startling her from her musings. Looking at her watch, she realized it was almost time for the kids to get home, so she stood quickly, grabbed the towel, and shook it out before folding it. Sometimes, she gained peace from coming to the cemetery. Other times, like today, she left with more questions tumbling in her mind.

As she always did, she bent and lightly kissed the top of the headstone. The cold marble was a poor replacement for the real thing, but it had become a habit, and she had no desire to stop doing what gave her a modicum of peace.

On her drive home, her phone rang, and she answered it through her car. "Hi, Mom. What's up with you?"

"Oh, the same old, same old," her mom said.

Hayley grinned at the familiar response from her mom.

"Are you in your car?"

"Yes, I'm just leaving the cemetery."

"I hope you had a nice visit," her mom replied.

Hayley knew that many would consider that a strange comment, considering she had been visiting her husband's gravesite. But her mother knew her well. She took comfort in having that time alone with her thoughts as she talked to Edward. "I did. But you might be surprised to find out that I started thinking about going out with someone."

"Sam? Did he finally ask you out?"

"Mom, you know that's not going to happen."

"I don't see why not. I see how he is with you and the kids. That man cares a great deal for you."

Her heart squeezed just a bit. "He cares for us because we were all friends before Edward died. I'm afraid he feels obligated. Having Sam in our lives has been wonderful, but I need to stop relying on him so much. Mom, he can't move on with his life if he's so indebted to ours." There were a few seconds of silence, and she wondered what her mother was thinking.

"Well, you know best, Hayley, but it would be better to have that conversation with him before you just assume he needs to move on with his life."

"You're right, Mom." After another few minutes of chatting, she disconnected as she arrived home. Hayley walked into her house, glad she had a little time before she needed to pick up the kids from school and preschool. She stood in the living room, then slowly turned, taking in the space. It had changed a little from the time that Edward had died.

The furniture was the same. Sam had bought an

upscale television, but it stood in the same place as the old one.

She walked over to the fireplace and looked at the framed pictures on the mantel. A few new ones were added for the kids, but the last family picture with Edward was still there. She couldn't imagine ever having a house where his picture wasn't prominently displayed. To the side, she'd placed a picture of the kids with Sam and remembered when she did so, having a twinge of guilt that their lives had moved on when Edward's had ended.

But the truth was, she could now go days without Edward being foremost on her mind. At first, whenever a decision needed to be made, she immediately thought of how Edward wasn't there to assist. But now, it was Sam that she thought of first whenever she had something she needed to do.

"Am I holding Sam back?" she asked the empty room, not surprised when the empty room gave no answer. She made her way into the kitchen, looking at what she could fix for dinner, but her mind wasn't on the upcoming meal.

The marketing firm she worked for had been supportive when Edward died and extra generous with her maternity leave. She had started working from home when Hope was born. When she decided she couldn't part with putting Hope in daycare, she was more than grateful for everything they had done for her. Recently, one of the employees had shown an interest in her.

Dave knew about her loss and had only recently

begun to linger after a work video call. He'd asked her out for drinks one day, but she had to get Eddie to soccer practice, so she turned him down. He was the first person to ask her out since Edward had died. She'd recoiled slightly, giving him her excuse. Then he said he hoped she'd consider going out to dinner with him when her schedule allowed.

She had wondered if she'd feel guilty or horrified at going out with someone else but found that the only thing she thought of was if she went to dinner, she would have preferred Sam's company. With Sam, there would've been no awkward conversation. No history to explain. No private jokes to avoid.

But Sam would never ask me out, and I can't expect him to.

She glanced at her phone again and realized it was time to pick up the kids. *Maybe I should take Dave up on his offer. Maybe if I tried to go out with someone else...*

She didn't want to bring anyone else into the kids' lives, preferring to keep their world simple and straightforward. And she wasn't about to introduce them to anyone who might come and go. *Another point in Sam's favor.*

She climbed back into the car to drive to the school and thought about an argument the kids had the other day. She told them to play together and not be selfish. *Is that what I've been with Sam? Selfish? For four years, I've allowed Sam to devote his time and energy to us. It's time for me to make sure he knows he'll always have a place in our lives, but he doesn't need to sacrifice his life for us.*

The kids had gone to bed, and Sam wandered Hayley's house like Hamlet's ghost. He was shocked when she first told him that she had accepted a date from someone she worked with. In hindsight, he shouldn't have been. Hayley is beautiful, and he knew he was not the only one who noticed. Yet in the years since Edward had died, she'd never once talked about wanting to date again. And now, he wasn't sure what bothered him more... the fact that she was going on a date or the fact that the date wasn't with him. Wincing, he sighed heavily. When Edward was alive, Sam never looked at Hayley as anything other than a friend and the wife of his closest friend. For a few years, his only thoughts for her were caring for her and the kids, wanting to do everything he could to honor Edward's memory by helping his family survive after his death.

He couldn't even remember when things had changed.

One day, he had taken Hayley and the kids to Virginia Beach, and they enjoyed their time on the Chesapeake Bay, hunting for shells and playing in the water. As the sun set, they sat on beach towels, staring out over the bay. Eddie turned to him and said, "It's weird. If you stare at the setting sun, you can barely see as it slowly goes down. But if you look away for just a moment and then look back, it seems like it's dropped fast."

As that memory hit Sam, he realized how appropriate the description was of his feelings for Hayley.

Being with them so often, he never realized when his feelings slowly transformed and couldn't even truly define the change. But now that he looked back, he realized he cared for her much more than friendship.

He sat on the sofa, leaned back, and sighed heavily. She certainly never indicated she'd felt the same for him. *That's why, now that she's ready to consider going on a date, she's with someone else. I need to accept that friends are all we'll ever be.*

When she mentioned she was going on a date with a friend, he'd volunteered to babysit. He had done so many times, but she expressed surprise and a small dose of angst this time. Sam had a feeling that she didn't want him to be around when another man came to the door. And he noticed when she mentioned the outing to her kids, she simply said she was going out with a friend from work. The kids didn't seem surprised since they wouldn't understand the concept of a date. She was going to meet the man—Dave—at the restaurant. Sam also knew she was not willing to expose her children to anyone she wasn't ready for them to meet. Suddenly, the garage door opening caused him to leap to his feet. By the time he walked into the kitchen, she was already coming through the door.

The fitted but modest red dress played up her curves and dark hair. She even wore heels, which she'd always complained about in the past. Her eyes lit when her gaze met his. "Everything okay?"

"Kids are great." She smiled at his response, but he couldn't help but stare, trying to decide whether her smile was a little brighter or if her eyes sparkled a little more from having been on her date. Unable to keep from asking, he blurted, "So how was it? How was your date?"

Her teeth chewed on her bottom lip, but she didn't stop smiling. "It was a little weird. I mean," she rushed, "just weird in that it felt strange to be out with someone as a potential date. But he was very nice, and we had a good time."

Her answer was simple, but he found that he wanted more. *Did you enjoy his company as much as mine? Did you let him kiss you good night?"*

He jammed his hands into the pockets of his faded jeans. The material felt as rough as his raw vulnerability at that moment. "Do you see yourself going out with him again?" Hoping the answer was no, his heart plunged when she smiled and nodded. "I think so. I think I'd like to go out with him again."

The axis of his world suddenly tilted. The sensation was painfully familiar, mirroring the day when Edward had been taken from them, though admittedly, that ache had held more desperation. Still, the realization that his life was shifting threatened to rearrange everything he'd grown to cherish. The sensation was visceral, and he stood on the precipice of uncertainty, caught between the agony of unrequited love and the solemn promise made years ago.

"I'll just go up to check on the kids," she said, then lifted on her toes to kiss his cheek. "Thanks again for always being here."

He was glad her attention was diverted. She would have seen his pain if she had looked into his eyes. He walked outside after making sure the house was secure and climbed into his SUV. Driving to his lonely apartment, he was engulfed with emotions. Circumstances were changing and might never be the same again. And he felt his heart rip.

6

THREE MONTHS LATER

Sam sat in the worn chair in his living room, his gaze transfixed on the letter in his hand, the life-changing decision weighing down on him. It was the offer for a detective position in a rural county. It had been his dream to leave the city police force and seek a position in a more remote area where residents knew each other, and neighbors became friends. At least, that had been his goal years ago—before Edward died and before Hayley and the kids needed him. *Before I needed them.*

But now circumstances had changed. Hayley had been dating Dave for the past three months. The relationship had unfurled slowly, and she had been hesitant to allow him around the kids. To Sam's knowledge, Dave had never been in her house when the kids were there, but he had shown up to a couple of ball games, and they'd had pizza out together a few times.

So far, Hayley had only referred to Dave as a friend, but Sam knew it was only a matter of time before she took their relationship to the next level. *And I'm fucking in the way.* He knew it. He accepted it. But other than moving away, he had no clue what to do about it. Leaving Hayley and the kids would rip out his guts. But staying and seeing her with someone else would do the same.

His gaze moved over the words on the paper even though he had them memorized.

"North Heron Sheriff's Department is pleased to offer you the position of detective. Contact the human resources administrator to finalize the paperwork to begin your employment. As sheriff of the department, it is my pleasure to welcome you to North Heron County." The signature was Sheriff Colt Hudson, and under it was a handwritten note. *Glad to have you with us, Sam. Good luck with the move, and let me know if you need anything.*

He'd driven to the Eastern Shore of Virginia the previous month after sending in his application. He'd met with Colt, impressed with the large, stoic man who ran an efficient sheriff's department with an outstanding record. Seeing the rural county bordered on one side with the Chesapeake Bay and the Atlantic Ocean on the other, he'd grown more excited. North Heron was one of two counties in Virginia that wasn't connected by land to the rest of the state. Bordered on the north by Maryland, the only connection to the rest of Virginia was by the Chesapeake Bay Bridge-Tunnel that ran seventeen miles between North Heron and Virginia Beach.

It was a different world from Newport News. Colt had taken him to lunch at a local diner, where he met

Colt's wife, Carrie. She was vivacious, friendly, and pretty. The sheriff was a lucky man. And from the expression on Carrie's face, she considered herself to be just as fortunate.

When he'd asked about housing, Carrie immediately jumped in to suggest purchasing a duplex. When Carrie first met Colt, she lived in a duplex with her son, and they shared the other side with an elderly gentleman. They all moved in with Colt when an arsonist struck, and both duplexes suffered fire damage. "If you bought the whole duplex, then you could live in one side and rent the other. You can choose your neighbors and then get the rental money!"

He had to admit, her suggestion had merit. After talking to Colt, he'd contacted a real estate agent and discovered a few duplexes were for sale. And now, with the formal acceptance letter in his hand, he inhaled deeply, letting the air hiss out of his lungs between clenched teeth.

It seemed like everything was falling into place… except for one blaring heartstring entanglement. He still needed to talk to Hayley.

At first, he kept the news of his possible new job locked up within because he'd hate to see her pity him if he didn't get accepted. But when he'd visited the Eastern Shore, she asked why he'd chosen to spend a vacation day there. He'd told her about the sheriff's office needing a detective and casually commented about wanting to check out the area. In Hayley's perceptive way, she'd dug for more information, but he'd still downplayed the possibility.

His mother used to say that everything worked out for a reason, and he believed that until Edward died. From that moment on, life seemed like a complex mix of chaos where plans and decisions were tangled in unpredictable knots.

Just yesterday, he had been reminded of the complexities of life. He'd arrived at the park a little late, hustling to get to Hayley's side so he could catch Eddie's game. But when he approached, Dave sat in the lawn chair beside Hayley. The one that was always there for him.

He hesitated, but his feet moved forward as if they had a will of their own, taking him forward until he stood next to them. Dave looked up and smiled, but Hayley's expression jolted into a wide-eyed expression of uncertainty. Her mouth opened, but she froze before words could be spoken. He could read her face like a book and instantly knew that she hadn't invited Dave to sit in the chair that had always been for Sam. Yet there he was, and until her eyes had landed on him, Hayley had seemed comfortable talking to Dave.

There were a few occasions over the years when Sam could not make a game. *Hayley probably assumed I wasn't coming.*

Before anyone had a chance to comment on the seating, there was a break in the game, and most people took to their feet. Hope ran over, threw her arms around Sam, and he picked her up, nuzzled her neck, and gave her a kiss. "I love you, sweet girl."

"Love you too!"

Eddie ran over and gave Sam a high-five before

speaking to the others. But then both kids greeted Dave. Albeit was not with the same exuberance as they had with Sam, but definitely as someone they knew.

Sam had left early, making an excuse about having something to do, but just drove home. Torn between frustration, heartache, and even a form of grief that came when a relationship changed, he'd gone to bed that night wondering about the job on the Eastern Shore.

If I get it, then that must be a sign.

And now, the letter had come. He looked at the clock and remembered that the kids were at an after-school activity, and knowing he couldn't put the conversation off anymore, he drove to Hayley's house.

Her gaze searched his face as soon as he stepped inside, and she could read his expression as easily as he read hers.

"You got the job, didn't you?" she asked, her voice barely above a whisper.

The words caught in his throat, so he handed her the letter, watching as her eyes moved back and forth over the words on the page. When she looked up, the moisture had gathered in her eyes, threatening to spill over her cheeks.

"Congratulations, Sam. I'm so very proud of you."

He jammed his fingers into the pockets of his jeans, suddenly uncertain what to say.

"I can't believe, though, that you're moving away. I know it makes sense. I know it's good for your career. And I know it's not far. But it just seems…" She sighed heavily, and a tear dripped down her cheek.

Hating their distance, he stepped closer and wrapped his arms around her. He pressed his lips to the top of her head—a simple gesture he'd often made in the past several years.

"It's time, Hayley. I can't stand in the way of you moving forward, but I don't want a front-row seat as another man takes my place."

She gasped, and he recognized that he'd just given voice to what he'd tried to hide. She leaned back and looked up, shaking her head.

"Oh, Sam, no one is taking your place," she rushed, and another tear fell.

He offered a little smile. "I know. But it's right for you to start looking to the future, and maybe me as well."

He lifted a knuckle and placed it under her chin, keeping her gaze on his. "But it isn't forever. I'll only be an hour away. I'll be back for lots of ball games and special occasions. And I expect you and the kids to visit often. The beach at Baytown is perfect."

"Promise me this isn't the end of us… uh… our friendship, Sam." Her voice trembled, fragile as glass.

Staring into her eyes where he'd often found solace, he said, "I can give that promise easily. This is not the end of us. And it sure as hell is not the end of the relationship I have with Eddie and Hope. This is just about work."

The final sentence left his lips smoothly but was a lie. He couldn't bear for her to shoulder any guilt about the seismic shift his decision was causing in their lives. It was time to pick up the kids. She asked him to join her, and he eagerly agreed. They then went out for ice cream, to the delight of everyone. He told the kids he would move to a new house closer to the beach. They easily accepted the news since they had no concept of where it would be.

It wasn't until he was saying goodbye that Eddie asked if he'd be at his next game. He kneeled to be at Eddie's eye level and carefully chose his words. "I won't get to be at every game anymore since my house is a little farther away. But I'll come to all I can and have you visit me, too."

Eddie's face filled with serious intensity, staring as though trying to understand the mysteries of the universe. Staring into the face of the child who was so wise beyond his years, Sam waited, his heart aching.

Finally, Eddie asked, "Are you leaving us?"

The little boy's question hit Sam like a physical punch. "No. I promise I will always be here for you, your sister, and your mom."

Eddie held his gaze for a long moment as though measuring each word, then nodded. "Okay, Sam. I trust you."

At that moment, seeing Eddie grapple with the beginnings of adult-sized emotions, Sam felt his own feelings splinter into a thousand pieces. The heartbreak that Sam knew was coming began in earnest. And just like he knew it would— it hurt like a bitch.

7

SIX MONTHS LATER

Sam walked out of his two-story duplex, his lip curling in disgust as he spied the overflowing trash can near the front door. *Christ, I need to get these people out of here.*

He had moved to the Eastern Shore and found what he thought was a tremendous property. He'd taken the recommendation from Carrie, and when the real estate agent showed him a duplex, he eagerly made the purchase.

The house was set on an acre of land at the end of a lane with other houses and duplexes lining the former farmland. A forest of trees was at the back of his property, providing more privacy. It was perfect.

Well, almost perfect. His current tenants had turned out to be a thorn in his side. At least they only had another month on their lease, and he wasn't renewing it. The thought of replacing them loomed large. The idea of advertising and interviewing was daunting.

Shaking off the rental concerns, he steered his SUV into the parking lot of the sheriff's station, immediately struck once again with how much contentment filled him each time he arrived at work. The modern building was set in the county seat town of Easton. The new courthouse, administrative offices, sheriff's office, and the county jail maintained in the red-brick facade as the historical courthouse that stood nearby for visitors to view.

As he stepped out of his vehicle, he lifted his hand to greet his colleagues walking toward the building. Seeing his partner, Aaron, he waited as the young man caught up to him, and they entered the building together.

"I hear we're going to be put on the Malroney case," Aaron said, unable to hide his enthusiasm.

Sam nodded, understanding Aaron's eagerness. There was something about being handed a new case. The chance to investigate, search for clues that weren't obvious to others, and then start moving the pieces of the puzzle around until the evidence began to solidify. He'd loved being a cop but loved being a detective even more.

They navigated the corridor, the waxed floor echoing their footsteps. Just before they turned toward the room shared by other detectives, they met Carrie as she walked out of Colt's office, holding a little boy's hand. Colt followed, carrying a little girl. Both children's almost black hair gave evidence to their heritage, and Sam grinned at the picture the sheriff made with his family.

"Hello!" she called out, her smile wide and welcoming.

It was said that the dark-haired, outspoken beauty

had softened the rough demeanor of the sheriff without taking away any of his intensity. Considering most people found Colt a force to be reckoned with, Sam couldn't imagine him being even more so before Carrie. Being a husband and father was a good fit for the iconic law enforcement leader.

"Hey, Carrie. How are you?"

"Happy as a clam." She laughed. "The more important question is, how are you doing? Colt mentioned that you were having trouble with your renters, and now I feel horrible for recommending you purchase a duplex."

They moved to the side of the hall so others could pass by, and he shook his head. "Don't feel bad. They're on their last month, and I've already told them that I won't renew their lease. Of course, they'll probably try to skip out, but I have their security deposit as collateral for any damage."

"You might want to do an inspection," Carrie said, her eyebrows knit together in concern. "And take pictures. I just hope they don't trash the place!"

"You and me both. I'm eager to find new renters, and considering I inherited these guys when I bought the place, it'll be nice to choose my own renters from now on."

With pleasant goodbyes offered, Sam headed down the hall and into the detectives' workroom. Settling into his comfortable, swivel chair, he faced his desk directly across from Aaron's. They finalized their schedule for the day then headed back out to talk to some of the people on their cases.

"So the Malroneys have five rental properties, and two of them have been hit recently, right?" Aaron asked.

"That's right. There are two in the historic district of Baytown and three bay front properties south of town. The two in the historic district haven't been hit, but two that are more private have been. The first robbery was called in at about a quarter after midnight, and Deputies Johnson and Walker responded. Then Harry Malroney called in the second one this morning just before we arrived."

"The man's got money, and from what I hear, he's tight with the mayor of Baytown."

"That just makes our job all the harder," Sam said. "The high-profile cases I used to have in Newport News were always a pain in the ass."

"Well, I can tell you from working with Colt for a couple of years that he will not put pressure on us to dump other cases just because someone with money or political connections is squawking. As far as he's concerned, all the citizens in the county will be treated the same."

"That's good to hear. I've been in the county for five months and seen how he supports his staff. Not a day goes by that I'm not thankful I moved here."

The instant the words left his mouth, a thick silence enveloped Sam as they headed to the parking lot and climbed into Aaron's vehicle. Aaron continued to navigate the road ahead, unaware of the emotional turmoil swirling within his partner. On the surface, Sam was thankful for his change in employment, but every day he didn't see Hayley and the kids, it was a little stab to his heart. For the first four months, he'd made the trip to visit every other weekend. Those days were his lifeblood, sustaining him through the gaps of time and distance. However, this past month had been a whirlwind of complications—dealing with house repairs, irresponsible tenants, and a heavy load at work—so he hadn't returned to Newport News. He was overdue and miserable, missing them with every heartbeat.

He'd bridged the chasm by video-chatting with Hayley and the kids and staying involved in their lives. But he wondered if this diluted connection was the best they could hope for. As heartbreaking as it was to think that was what their relationship might become, he'd do anything to make sure Hayley was happy. And if that meant staying away so Dave would become what Hayley needed, then Sam would bury the pain.

Before his thoughts became more morose, they pulled up to a large house on a dune overlooking the Chesapeake Bay. They both looked out the windshield, and Aaron whistled in appreciation.

"Holy shit. I wonder how much that cost?"

Sam chuckled. "Depends on when they bought it, but chances are Malroney paid well over a million for this one house. It's got to be close to four thousand square feet and is beachfront property."

"I was looking at it this morning before we came out here," Aaron continued. "He gets some serious weekly rental money for all his houses."

"Yeah, and there's nothing like getting bad reviews on vacation websites to kill his rental business."

They walked up to the front door and barely rang

the bell when the door was thrown open by a man whose gaze moved between the two men on his stoop. He had a poor dye job of solid black hair that did little to hide the thin hair on top styled in an unflattering comb-over. With a hawkish nose, thin face, and wiry body, his weasel appearance was unwelcoming with the narrow-eyed glare he threw their way.

"Mr. Malroney, I'm Detective Sam Shackley, and this is Detective Aaron Bergstrom from the North Heron Sheriff's Department. We're investigating the reported robberies from two of your properties."

"They're not just reported!" Harry blustered, his arms shaking out to his sides. "They really occurred!"

"We're not questioning the veracity of the report, sir. That simply means a report was made, and we are investigating."

"Harumph," Harry grumbled but stepped back, allowing them inside the house, where they were met with another man and woman.

Introductions were made, and Aaron wrote in his notes that Cheryl and Marcus Holloway were the vacation renters for the week.

"I woke up about six o'clock this morning to go for a run," Marcus said. "I realized then that the kayaks and canoes stored underneath the back deck were missing. We hadn't used them yet but had planned to go out on the water today."

"Were they yours or Mr. Malroney's—"

"They were mine!" Harry barked. "That's one of the things my exclusive vacation rentals offer– bicycles, kayaks, and canoes."

"Were they secured with locks or just stored underneath the deck?" Sam asked.

"During the winter months, when I don't have as many vacationers, they're stored in the garage. Once we get into the spring, I bring them around and have a kayak and canoe rack underneath the deck. They're not locked, but someone would have to either make their way around the house to get them or come from the bay, which makes no sense."

"Mr. Holloway, if you show Detective Bergstrom where they were located the last time you saw them, I will get the information from Mr. Malroney on each item and their value."

Aaron shot Sam a look of gratitude, and Sam merely offered a subtle chin lift in response. While Aaron had been in the county longer, Sam had seniority based on years in service. He had no doubt that Aaron would rather leave the curmudgeon owner for Sam to deal with.

"May we offer you something to drink?" Cheryl asked.

As he was about to decline, Harry groused, "He's here to find out who stole my kayaks, not drink lemonade!"

Cheryl tossed a pinched-lip glare toward the owner, then turned and walked away.

"What have you found out about the other house that was hit in the middle of the night?" Harry asked.

"I know the deputies questioned the renters, and we'll be going back over as soon as we leave here. I can also get that now if you have the information on what was taken and the value."

Harry continued to grumble but finally sat down in the living room and pulled out his phone. "I have pictures of the insides of my rental houses, the landscaping, and any equipment I have. That all comes under my insurance, but I have it in case of a problem with a renter. I won't have someone come here for a week of enjoyment and leave my place trashed."

It ran through Sam's mind that he wished he had the same in place for his renters. As soon as those people moved out, he'd be better prepared for the next ones who moved in.

"I'd like you to send those photographs to my tablet. Here's the address." He showed the address for his tablet and was glad Harry was busy doing as he asked without more commentary. "Do you have a value for each item?"

"Of course I do! What do you take me for? I'm not some local yokel who doesn't know how the hell to run my vacation rental business!"

Choking back his sigh of exasperation, Sam nodded. "Of course, Mr. Malroney. If you send me that as well, then it will be easier to identify if whoever took them attempts to sell them."

"Ought to be able to outsmart the goddamn crooks," Harry said. "I have identification numbers on every one of my kayaks and canoes. I bet you want that, too, don't you?"

Surprised he managed to keep his eye roll to a minimum, he nodded. "That would be perfect."

"I know every member of the board of supervisors,

and I'm friends with the mayor of Baytown. I expect this to go to the top of your list of cases you're working on. Although you probably don't have much to do in this backwoods county, do you?"

Sam kept his head down as he continued to type into his tablet. Refusing to rise to the bait of the man whose frustration caused him to be even more combative than his normal blustering personality, Sam looked over as Aaron walked back into the room. The unspoken communication moved between them, and Sam appreciated the ease of their partnership. He didn't expect to have such camaraderie with the first partner he was assigned to, but for the five months he and Aaron had worked together, they easily fell into sync.

Back in Aaron's vehicle, they drove to the other property and talked to the renters there. Just like the Holloways, they heard a noise, but by the time they convinced themselves that someone might be around and looked over the deck, the kayaks were already gone. There were no tracks from dragging the watercraft or from vehicles in the yard around the house. Even though the tide had washed away what was close to the shore, it appeared that the kayaks had been taken away by water, just like at the other house.

"You think someone in a boat tied them together and dragged them behind like a chain?" Aaron asked.

"That's what I was thinking. Came in by a small boat, go straight to the kayaks and canoes that aren't locked up—"

"Because they've scouted the area," Aaron interjected.

Sam nodded. "Yes. They've scoped it out, came in at night, hauled them to the water, tied them up, and floated them away behind them."

"They wouldn't have gone far," Aaron surmised. "That's a total of seven kayaks and two canoes for the night. There's no way they would've gone far with all of that."

"They would've needed accomplices who would have come by land, probably with something as innocuous as a U-Haul truck or trailer. Once everything's loaded, then they could go anywhere."

"Do you think they would've gone far?" Aaron asked. "Of course, they could've gone up or down the coastline, but if they know this area so well to hit two of Mr. Malroney's houses, that just feels more local."

"I agree. So we need to check pawnshops and put out something to the deputies to keep their eye out for anyone offering kayaks to sell."

"Hell, around here, people will open up the back of their pickup truck and sell things on the side of the road."

"That's what I'm thinking. That would be the easiest way to get rid of things in an untraceable way."

"Let's hit the local pawnshops and get the message out to the deputies. We'll find out if someone's trying to sell them in this county."

"And Accawmacke County?"

Only two Virginia counties were on the Eastern Shore. North Heron was at the peninsula's southern tip, and Accawmacke was just north. The two sheriffs, Liam and Colt, were good friends and members of the local

American Legion, as were the other law enforcement leaders in the area, including the police chiefs of the smaller towns. Sam had been invited on his first day on the job and had attended each monthly meeting since then.

He nodded at Aaron's suggestion. "I'll send something to Liam, and he can disseminate it among his staff."

They spent the rest of the day making the rounds of the pawnshops, giving out the information and alerts to the patrol deputies, and sending the information to Accawmacke County and the Maryland county just north of them.

By the end of the day, Sam dreaded going home to an empty house and seeing what havoc the renters may have wrecked. He eagerly accepted a chance to head into Baytown for an after-work beer with Hunter Simmons, one of the other detectives.

Hunter had been with the sheriff's office for several years, having transferred from working undercover with the Virginia State Police. His wife, Belle, was a nurse at the local nursing home. The few times Sam had been in her presence, he was struck with her soft-spoken, almost delicate nature, but then had seen her at a county meeting, stepping up to talk about the needs of the elderly. He realized then that she was a force to be reckoned with and the perfect match for Hunter.

Once in the pub, he greeted the others he knew, then slid onto a barstool next to Hunter. They talked quietly about a few cases for several minutes, and he appreciated Hunter's input.

"Do small-town politics play a big part around here?" he asked. "I haven't seen much of that yet, but I have a feeling the Malroney case I'm working on just might come down to that."

"Not as much as you might think. Half the board of supervisors stays more than one term, and as long as Colt is sheriff, he'll take the political heat and keep it off us. I've got to tell you that man is a saint in my book."

Sam chuckled, unable to imagine that Hunter called many people a saint.

Hunter held Sam's gaze, taking a swig of his beer, then shook his head and sighed. "I might as well warn you that some of the wives have seen you at the American Legion activities and wonder why you don't have a girlfriend or a wife." He threw up his hands quickly. "Believe me, I don't give a fuck. Your life is your life, but I'm just giving you a friendly warning that meddling might be brewing."

Sam shook his head, then took a long swig of beer as he thought about his response. Opting for honesty, he said, "I was married once. Too young and too stupid to know any better. She thought being married to a soldier would be a lot of fun, and come to find out, it wasn't what she wanted. We only lasted about two years, and we were apart for months of those years. It was for the best when she decided to leave."

Hunter nodded slowly. "Yeah, a lot of women can't handle being married to someone in the military. Hell, they can't handle being married to someone in law enforcement either."

Just then, Sam's phone vibrated in his pocket, and he

looked down to see a message from Hayley. His heart leaped. He had come to expect that response every time her name came up on caller ID. Before he had a chance to tap on the message, Hunter chuckled and shook his head.

Looking at the big man who had a grin on his face, Sam tilted his head to the side and lifted his brows in silent question.

Hunter explained, "For all I know, that message came from your mom. But I swear, with that grin, I have a feeling you're already taken."

"Afraid not, although not because I wouldn't want to be. The sender of this text and I are just friends."

"Friends can become more. Not a bad way to start."

"Talking from experience?"

Hunter chuckled and nodded. "Yeah."

Sam tossed some money onto the bar, slid out of the seat, and clapped Hunter on the shoulder. "I hear you, but some things just aren't meant to be more."

Hunter lifted his chin, his smile still in place. Sam hustled out of the bar and down the road to his SUV, anxious to see what news Hayley had.

8

"Mrs. Brooks, I can't express how sorry we are that this happened, but of course, we have to consider everything."

Hayley stared at the elementary school principal, anger racing through her veins. He was new this year, had no history with her children, and she was tired of hoping for a change in his attitude.

"I don't understand why you're not taking any action. My son is being bullied. It took him a long time to finally tell me what was going on, and when I talked to his teacher, she admitted that she has to focus on a couple of students in the class because their behavior is negative to other students. And since she's been paying more attention, she's monitoring the situation in the classroom, and it's better. However incidents can still occur in music, art, PE, recess, and lunch. And that doesn't even include when they're walking in the hall. But the latest from the PE class is inexcusable. And when the PE teacher tells me that my son just needs to toughen up, I'm ready to take my complaints to the school board."

He threw his hands up and shook his head. "Now, now, Mrs. Brooks. Let's not lose our heads. We certainly take bullying seriously, but no one witnessed what happened in the PE class."

"Witnessed? How about the two students who were brave enough to come forward and say that they saw three boys gang up on Eddie? How about what my son has said? He would have no reason to lie."

"At this age, Mrs. Brooks, boys will often act out—"

"Don't you dare make ludicrous assumptions or accusations!"

"I will certainly talk to the PE teacher, and we will monitor the situation."

"I don't think that's good enough. I'll talk to a friend who is in law enforcement and see what else can be done." She purposely omitted that her law-enforcement friend no longer worked in the area, but her comment seemed enough to make the principal sit up straight.

"I'm sure we can come to a reasonable solution for this situation," he said.

Standing, she pulled her purse strap over her shoulder, looking down at him. "I have no doubt that I will be able to have a satisfactory solution. Whether it's the same one you're thinking of or not, I doubt it."

With that, she marched out, battling the urge to slam his door while equally fighting the urge to cry as soon as she saw Eddie and Hope sitting in the adult-sized chairs in the school office, their legs swinging back and forth with nerves. Eddie's expression didn't hide his anxiety. His lips were pressed tightly together, but Hayley could see the tremor and the rapid blinking to keep the tears from falling. Hope glanced between her brother and mom, her eyes wide as she chewed on her bottom lip.

Walking straight to them, she plastered on a smile. "Come on, sweethearts. Let's head home. And maybe tonight is a good night for pizza. What do you say?"

A spark lit in Hope's eyes, but Eddie remained wary as he stared hard into her face as though he would be able to see all her emotions if he kept looking long enough. The way she felt, she was sure her perceptive son could probably ferret out her wild-swinging mood.

By the time they had pizza and finished their homework, it was time for bed. Eddie took a bath while she and Hope picked up Hope's room, which was scattered with dolls, stuffed animals, and toys.

"Mommy, I think you look sad," Hope said.

Tears were so close to the surface that Hayley couldn't believe she kept them from falling in front of her daughter.

"I'm not sad, sweetheart. How could I be sad with two such wonderful children as you and your brother?"

Hope smiled just before a giggle burst out.

They continued picking up toys, finding a place on the shelves or in the toy chest for most of the mess in Hope's room before her daughter turned to her again.

"I miss Sam."

"I do, too," Hayley admitted. The children often asked if Sam would come back for longer than just a visit, and she tried to explain that his job was now elsewhere. They understood the concept, but for Hope, Sam being unable to just be there at a moment's notice was still something she struggled with. Eddie understood maps and time much better, but he also struggled with not having Sam around as much. And now, more than ever, she wished a quick phone call would bring him to her door.

With Eddie out of the bath and in his pajamas, she sent Hope in, and they quickly got the little girl clean and in her pajamas, too. Thankful that Hope went to sleep quickly, she walked back into Eddie's room, finding him with one of his favorite books in his lap. While he was lying in bed, she could tell he wasn't reading. Sitting on the edge of the bed, she asked, "What are you thinking? Anything you want to talk about?"

"I'm sorry you got called into school today, Mom."

She shook her head quickly. "Sweetheart, you did nothing wrong. Those other kids were bullies, and you tried to talk to them and get them to leave you alone."

"De-es-calate."

Cocking her head to the side, she blinked. "De-escalate? Where did you learn that word?"

"That was something Sam told me to do. He always said I should stand up for myself and my family and stand up for what I think is right, but he also said that I should try to talk through a problem or talk to someone. I'm making it better by de-escalating."

She nodded and smiled at her sweet son. Hearing Sam's advice to Eddie only made her feel the absence of his influence even more. In the aftermath of Edward's death, her world had crumbled into a heap of ashes. The prospect of being a single mother had been so daunting that it had stolen her breath in fear. But she'd never truly walked that difficult path alone. Sam had always been there with his steady, reassuring presence that cast a warm glow in the cold places of her heart. He'd provided cohesion to her family, and she'd never taken it for granted but hadn't realized she'd relied on him so much.

Even if he wasn't physically there now, the traces of his emotional support lingered, still giving guidance to her children. And at that moment, she understood how profoundly she missed his solid grounding force. Truthfully, she simply just missed him.

She cleared her throat. "Well, Eddie, I'm glad you remember what Sam taught you."

"Well, he told me that again tonight."

Hayley blinked, her chin jerking back in confusion. "You must be confused, honey. You didn't talk to Sam tonight."

Eddie pressed his lips together and, with his head slightly down, looked up at her from the corners of his eyes.

"Edward Samuel Brooks, what did you do?"

"Um… I used your phone and sent a text to Sam. I told him I had a bad day, and he called."

Stunned, she jerked again. "First of all, Eddie, you know you're not supposed to use my phone unless it's an emergency."

"Mama, I heard you yell at the principal. You were really upset, and I thought Sam should know."

Torn between being proud of her son for wanting to

stand up for her, she wondered what Sam thought when he got the message, and she sighed heavily. She didn't have it in her to fuss at her son. He'd called the one person in their lives they could count on. Now it was her turn to press her lips together as she stared at Eddie, noticing he seemed calmer than he had earlier.

"What did Sam say? Besides to de-escalate."

"He said he was really sorry that happened and wants to see us. And he said he's going to call you once we went to bed."

Shaking her head slightly, she leaned over and wrapped her arms around her little boy, who was growing up without a father but still had a wonderful father figure in his life. "Do you think you can sleep?"

Eddie nodded as he scooted into bed and pulled the covers to his chin. "Yeah, Sam made me feel better, and I know he'll take care of you."

Deciding not to touch that comment, she kissed the top of his head. She had to admit that he was much calmer than he'd been all afternoon and evening. Saying good night, she closed his door and walked across the hall to her bedroom. She snagged her phone where Eddie had found it on her dresser. Quickly checking, she saw where Eddie and Sam had talked for about five minutes and snorted as she shook her head. In those five minutes, Sam had calmed her son, offered him advice, and congratulated him.

Carrying her phone back downstairs, she moved into the family room and plopped onto the sofa. Putting her feet up on the coffee table, she settled in for what she knew would be an important phone call.

The phone barely rang once before it was immediately picked up. "Hayley?"

With only him calling her name, the deep tenor of his voice wrapped around her, filling the emptiness and lonely spaces. "Hey, Sam."

"Are you okay?"

"Not really, and I just found out that Eddie sent you a text, and then you called him. I had no idea he was doing that."

"You know I've told the kids they can call me anytime. I'm just glad that Eddie did."

"He enjoyed talking to you, and it was probably better for him to talk to you than for me to rehash everything."

At the sound of Sam sighing, she could easily imagine what his expression looked like.

"Hayley, I want to know everything that's going on. As soon as I got off the phone with Eddie, I was ready to jump into the car and come straight there. I'm still not convinced I'm not gonna come."

"No, don't do that," she begged, rubbing her forehead. "Honestly, I'm exhausted, and I'm sure I'll be thinking clearly in the morning."

"Tell me what the hell happened at school today."

Hayley reclined against the plush cushions of her sofa, propping her feet onto the coffee table. She closed her eyes, inhaling deeply before slowly letting out the air, trying to center her thoughts before delving back into the details of her day.

She had already talked to him about some of the bullying going on at school but retold what happened.

While the incidents might seem trivial to some, they gnawed at her soul. She was furious for her sweet, sensitive son. Hayley understood the difference between children saying and doing things that weren't nice as they grew and learned what was acceptable behavior. She often had to referee between Eddie and Hope when they were tired and grumpy with each other. But the one bully had targeted Eddie, and while the teachers took the situation seriously, she felt the principal blew it off.

Sam's muttered cursing under his breath was audible, and once again, she was struck with how wonderful it was to have someone in her corner, ready to fight the battles for her children. She could easily imagine his face as though he were right in front of her... brows lowered as he glowered at the perceived threat to her or the kids.

"I want you to come here. Tomorrow is Friday, and you could drive here right after school. I'll be off by four, and you guys can spend the weekend with me. It'll give the kids a chance to get away, give me a chance to get a pulse on how everyone is doing, and I don't give a fuck if Dave doesn't like it."

Her eyes clamped shut, and her lips pressed tightly together. She had held back, not telling Sam anymore about her relationship with Dave. Clearing her throat, she plunged ahead. "The kids would love to come, and so would I. And... um... for the record, Dave isn't a consideration anymore. Um... he's no longer in the picture."

A thick curtain of silence fell between them after her

last statement, and she was uncertain whether he was still on the line. "Sam? Are you there?"

"Yeah, I'm here, Hayley. I'm glad you guys are coming because we have a lot to hash out this weekend. Starting with why the hell didn't you tell me that you weren't with Dave anymore?"

Her mind churned with the thousand reasons rattling inside her brain, and she couldn't think of anything that would make sense now. Uncertain what to say, she now found no words coming.

Sam jumped into the silent chasm. "You know what, Hayley? It doesn't matter. You and the kids come because it sounds like all of us need a chance to talk, and have some fun, and everybody can just relax."

Hayley let out a breath, her chest deflating like a released balloon. Each exhalation was calming, and she was once again reminded how wonderful it was to have Sam to lean on. Wincing at that thought, she knew she could not return to pretending he didn't mean anything to her. *It doesn't matter how he feels about me or how I might be heading toward heartache. The fact is, my kids need him. I need him.*

Making their final arrangements for the next day, she disconnected, tossed the phone on the sofa beside her, and smiled. It was the first deeply felt smile she'd had other than with her children in weeks. A smile of hope, of comfort, and of a love she had kept locked away for too long.

9

"Sam! Over here!"

Nestled in a low-slung beach chair, Hayley watched Sam pass a football back and forth with Eddie, both having to watch out for Hope, who darted around them, chasing something in her vivid imagination.

She and the kids had arrived on the Eastern Shore midmorning, and they hadn't stopped going and doing since they pulled up to Sam's duplex. He'd taken them out for a huge breakfast at a local diner, agreeing with the kids that twirling on the tall counter stools would be more fun than sitting in a booth.

With Eddie and Hope sandwiched between them, she and Sam had little opportunity to talk, but that was fine. What mattered most was the joy radiating from her children's faces when they were with Sam.

Now, she finally relaxed as the sun warmed her and the gentle breeze from the bay washed over her. Lifting her hand to shade her eyes, she naturally gravitated to watching Sam as he tossed the ball. Seeing him ignited a smile that warmed her from the inside out. His eyes shimmered with kindness and strength. The lines on his face etched a captivating pattern. *How did he get more handsome in just a month?*

With their big breakfast and then snacks on the beach, the prospect of an early dinner seemed perfect. She didn't doubt that the kids would fall asleep quickly this evening, and once alone, Sam would want to turn the conversation to what had happened with Dave. *And maybe what's happening between them.* A sigh escaped her lips. *What the hell will I tell him? I can't say, "I broke it off because my heart belongs to you!"*

The autumn breeze began to feel less like a caress and more like a nudge for Hayley to push herself out of the sand chair and call out to the kids and Sam. "I know you're going to grumble, but let's get ready so we can have dinner."

The idea of grilled burgers and hot dogs was all it took to encourage the kids to rush around, helping to gather their toys. The kids carried their tote bags to the SUV. Sam leaned in and whispered, "I'll grill outside, but if the neighbors are around, I'll have you keep the kids inside. I can't trust the neighbors not to be a problem."

"I'm so sorry you have to deal with them." She hated for the reason he whispered, but couldn't deny she loved his breath so close to her ear.

"Well, it's not for much longer. Their lease ends in a month, and I've already talked to them. I wasn't going to renew their lease, and they told me that they were going to leave anyway. In fact, they may be packing up now."

Turning her worried gaze to him, she asked, "Will that be a problem if you lose that rental income?"

He barked out a laugh. "Not at all. They already know they're not going to get their security deposit back. While the place hasn't been trashed, I'll still have to do some repairs."

Her stomach dropped. Sam had taken care of her place as well as his own for years, and now he hated that he had more responsibilities piled onto his plate. She placed her hand on his arm. "I'm so sorry about that."

Their conversation ended as he pulled into his driveway and spied the old pickup truck and trailer backed up to the door of his renters. "Thank God they're getting out of here," Sam mumbled. He turned to Hayley. "You take the kids inside and do whatever you need to do. I'm going to check on what's going on next door, and then I'll be back."

She nodded, and as the kids unbuckled from their booster seats, she corralled them from running in the yard and hustled them inside. She had a feeling that some not-very-nice words might take place between Sam and the renters when he went inside to check it out.

"Okay, kiddos, let's take a bath and get clean before Sam fires up the grill." She looked down at Eddie and smiled. "I know you don't want to miss any time with Sam when he's grilling."

Those magic words sent Eddie racing up the stairs. Hope turned and crinkled her nose as she looked up at her mom. "I don't like the smoke getting in my eyes."

Tapping her forefinger on the tip of her daughter's

nose, she laughed. "How about we stay inside and fix the yummy things to go along with the hamburgers and hot dogs?"

Hope threw her hands into the air and shouted, "Yay!" as she ran up the stairs after her brother.

Wishing she had the kids' energy, Hayley followed. It had been a great day. In fact, it was one of the best she'd had in a while. At the top of the stairs, Eddie stood just outside the room he shared with Hope when they visited. "Mom, can I take a shower like grown-up men do?"

"Well, you can, but you have to wait until I have Hope in the bathtub."

He nodded his agreement easily, and she ran the water in the hallway bathroom for Hope's bath, threw in the bubble bath Sam had bought for her, and then left the door cracked so she could hear her daughter if she needed her. She went back over to Eddie. "If you get your clean clothes, then as soon as Hope is finished with her bath, you can take a shower."

"I thought maybe I could take a shower in Sam's bathroom. He's got a separate shower in there. That's really cool."

Considering her son had only seen showers as part of the bathtub, she imagined a separate bathtub and shower stall would be different. "Honey, that's Sam's bathroom. We need to use the guest one—"

"Not on my account." Sam's deep voice came from the bottom of the stairs.

As he walked up the steps, she searched his face to ascertain his mood after having spoken to the renters.

His face appeared relaxed, but she asked, "Is everything okay?"

He nodded and smiled. "Better than I thought. They took care of a few repairs themselves. I told them after I thoroughly inspected it, I would see what percentage of their security deposit I could return. They're pulling out right now, so I can take a look at that this week. I have two ladies who said they'll come in and clean for me, and I think most of the repairs will be something I can handle or can call in a few buddies to help."

She breathed a sigh of relief, her smile matching his. "Good. I'm really glad."

"Sam, can I use your shower?" Eddie interrupted softly, shifting from one foot to the other as he looked up, eagerness written on his face.

"Absolutely. And if your mom says it's okay, she can stay and help with Hope's bath, and I'll be around in the master bedroom to make sure you're okay and help you get the water temperature right."

Eddie's face lit up like a sunburst. His adoration for Sam was evident with the stars in his eyes. Hayley felt the bittersweet ache settle in her chest, struck by how much her kids had come to rely on him and how much they missed him when they were separated. It never got old. A part of her heart would always belong with Edward, and she never wanted the kids to forget who their father was. But the incomprehensible reality was that Edward had been gone now longer than they'd been married. It didn't seem possible that the years had passed so quickly. Her heart would always mourn for Hope, who never knew her dad, and for Eddie, who barely remembered him. But through the years, Sam had so naturally stepped into the breach, making her life and, more importantly, her children's lives easier.

Seeing the two male faces looking at her, she nodded, tossing out a wink. As she went back into the bathroom to check on Hope, she could hear the low rumbling of Sam's voice, the laughter coming from Eddie, and the sound of the shower water spray. She imagined Eddie was getting hit by the water in his face.

Once the kids were clean and in fresh clothes, they all worked together to fix dinner. Sam was so much more relaxed in his backyard, not having neighbors directly on the other side of the small privacy fence that divided the two patios. With no one else around, the kids could chase each other and giggle as loud as they wanted without Hayley feeling like she needed to shush them so they wouldn't bother anyone.

Once the grill was heated, Eddie stayed right by Sam's side like a pint-sized sous chef as they cooked the meat. She disappeared into the kitchen, fixing french fries, mac & cheese, sliced apples, and a big salad. They sat on the old picnic table Sam had bought from a friend, and she loved that at this time of year, no bugs tried to get after their food. The sun set early, and by the time they finished eating and cleaned up, they piled into the living room to find a movie on TV that would keep the kids entertained.

Hayley took in the domestic scene around her. The feeling of family surrounded and filled her. Yet the idea of Sam eventually finding someone to fall in love with pierced her bliss with a jagged, sharp knife. But like Sam had when she started seeing Dave, she would give him the freedom he deserved. And that thought caused her heart to ache with a grief she hoped she would never feel again. Blowing out a breath, she refocused her thoughts on the movie and the laughter coming from her children.

"Okay, time for bed," she exclaimed when the movie ended. She knew the kids were tired when there was no grumbling or begging to stay up longer.

After brushing their teeth, both climbed into the guest room's bunk beds. Eddie was on the top and Hope on the bottom, her bed shared with the multitude of declared necessary stuffed animals she'd brought. Sitting in a chair near the beds, she read a story. Sam appeared in the doorway, a gentle smile on his face.

"Come on, Sam!" Hope called out, scooting over a little.

He sat on her bed, ducking his head so it wouldn't bump on the top bunk. His arm wrapped around Hope as they listened to the rest of the story. Hayley climbed on the ladder to kiss Eddie good night, and she and Sam traded places. She hugged and kissed Hope, tucking her in tightly with her favorite teddy bear, but couldn't help but hear Sam talking to Eddie.

"You did real good calling me when you were upset, Eddie. You can call me anytime. You know that, right?" Sam whispered.

"Yeah, Sam. Thank you," the little boy replied, his adoring gaze never leaving Sam's face.

Sucking in a breath to keep her heart from pounding

out of her chest, she walked out of the room with Sam following, flipping off the light as they went.

"Keep the door cracked," Eddie called out.

"No problem, buddy," Sam said. "You'll always be safe here."

Once the kids were finally put to bed, Sam grabbed a beer and poured a glass of wine for her. Holding her gaze while they stood in the kitchen, he said, "It's time, Hayley. I want to know what's been going on. It guts me not to be with you and the kids when things go wrong. But I consoled myself in thinking you had someone else you could rely on. Sweetheart, let's talk."

She nodded and led the way back into the living room, where she sat in a comfortable chair, and he took a place on the sofa. She'd chosen not to sit on the sofa with him, wanting to see his face as she explained everything that had been happening. But she hated the distance, feeling he was too far away. Refusing to be self-conscious, she stood and moved over to the other end of the sofa, twisting her body so she could still face him while only being a foot apart.

Sucking in a deep breath, she let it out slowly. "There's not much more to tell you about what's going on with Eddie at school than what I've already told you, Sam. There's one kid in his class who's a little bit bigger and a whole lot meaner than anyone else. Eddie is not the only child who has felt the sting of this bully's nasty comments. But it seems this kid has figured out Eddie's weak spot, and it makes him really angry. And, of course, like with most bullies, they'll dig in more once they find your weak spot. I guess one of the other kids who knows Eddie's background mentioned that Eddie's father had died. And suddenly, this kid is making nasty comments about that."

"What the fuck?" Sam bit out. "He's only nine!"

"Oh, Sam. You work with the public and with the criminal element. You can't possibly be surprised at something like this."

He shook his head, still scowling. "You're right, and I'm not really surprised. Maybe just more pissed off. Eddie told me he had someone in his class he didn't like, but I didn't know it was this bad."

"You and me both!" She heaved a great sigh and continued. "Yesterday, I got a call from the principal because Eddie had finally had enough, lost his cool, and yelled back at the kid. So the principal hauled Eddie into the office and then called me—"

"Who is this guy?" Sam growled.

"Believe me, honey, there's nothing you can say that I didn't already say when I got there." She rubbed her forehead and felt the tension in her shoulders.

"Turn around."

Her gaze jumped back to his. "I'm sorry?"

"Turn around. You look like you need some tension relief."

She couldn't argue with him about that point, but her thoughts jumped immediately to the tension relief she'd like to get from Sam. Pushing those thoughts away, she shifted around on the sofa, giving him her back.

His hands curled over her shoulders, and his thumbs dug into the tense muscles covering her shoulder blades. She groaned and dropped her head forward. She couldn't remember the last time she had a neck massage, but as she thought about it, she realized it was something Sam did in the past when she'd had a particularly bad day. His skillful hands continued to work the knots out of her muscles, and even the tension in her headache eased.

"Move here."

She heard the two words uttered in his deep voice, but since she was so relaxed, it took a few seconds for them to sink in. Twisting around quickly, she furrowed her brow as she looked at him. "Huh? What did you say?"

10

For Sam, spontaneity was a rarity. He knew there were times in life when a person's mouth worked ahead of their brain. He'd seen it often when interviewing suspects. But, for him, that rarely happened since he thought through almost everything, sifting through information, pros and cons, before putting words to his thoughts. It was evident from Hayley's expression that she assumed he'd uttered words he hadn't fully processed.

But Sam had said exactly what he meant. He didn't just blurt out the two words—the idea had formed in his head weeks ago. On a particularly good day at work, he'd missed not being close to Hayley and the kids to celebrate by running out for ice cream. Then he'd come home and had to deal with his renter's garbage in the front yard, the motorcycle they had taken apart and hadn't put back together yet, and the sound of their visitors coming and going. He was sure that the smell of pot stopped once he moved in because he flashed his badge the first day. He was equally sure that was why they were moving out before the end of their lease. Having a detective as their landlord cramped their style.

And the idea of Hayley and the kids renting the place next door had popped into his head and hadn't left. He'd hated that it wouldn't come true, considering she and the kids were settled into their lives and the house they'd had before Edward died. Add in that she had a new man in her life, and he didn't see a way for him to have his dream.

Now, knowing that Eddie struggled at school, Hayley was stressed, and Dave wasn't in the picture anymore, the idea resurfaced with such a force he could no longer keep it at bay. He threw the idea out, no longer hesitating. *Nothing ventured, nothing gained, as Dad used to say.*

"You heard me right," he reiterated, locking eyes with her. "Move here."

She swiveled her body toward him, reducing the gap that had separated them. Tilting her head to the side, her gaze scoured his face. "I'm sorry, Sam. I don't understand."

He chuckled and shook his head. "I'm not sure I can make it much plainer, but I realize this has caught you by surprise."

"And not you? It hasn't surprised you that you've just blurted out something major?"

"Have you ever known me just to blurt out something?"

Her nose crinkled, and he grinned. Hayley's expression was a mirror image when both she and Hope were confused.

"Listen," he said, scooting a little closer. "I realize what I said has caught you off guard and doesn't make any sense to you right now. So let me explain. Hope and Eddie are both in elementary school. I know that it's important to have stability, but I also know that they're still young enough that a move to a new place in a new school would not be devastating. You work from home, so you would be able to work anywhere. Baytown Elementary has a good reputation and a phenomenal gifted program. And there are private schools in the area if that's what you think is best."

Hayley hadn't refuted any of his points so far, and he took that as a good sign. But they had a lot to go over and consider.

"I don't make this offer lightly. The house you live in is the house that belonged to you and Edward. It's the house of your memories of him. Hell, it's the house of my memories of him, too. And I would respect you if you told me that you never wanted to move from that house. And I know you've lived in Newport News since college. Again, I'd respect the hell out of you if you told me that you never wanted to leave."

At that comment, she snorted, and he lifted his brows.

"Sam, believe me, nothing about the city of Newport News has a pull on me."

She didn't mention the pull of the house or her memories, which didn't surprise him.

He continued, "If you wanted to keep the kids in the

same school, I get it. There are a lot of reasons for you to stay right where you are and not make a change. And you and I will keep on being what we are, no matter what."

They were both quiet, and he wasn't in a hurry to rush her thoughts. After a moment of comfortable silence, he asked, "Is this a good time to find out how things stand with you and Dave?"

She nodded slowly and sighed. "When he first asked me out, I refused because I wasn't ready. But after a while, I agreed to dinner. I had a good time, and then we started going out more often. I found him easy to talk to, and it crossed my mind that maybe I was ready to consider dating again. On paper, he seemed wonderful. Patient with both me and the kids. Never attempted to rush anything. Never attempted to step in and be anything more than what he was, which was just someone I was going out with. But eventually, after a couple of months, it became very apparent to me that he was not someone I saw as a permanent fixture in our lives. The kids accepted his disappearance quite easily. In fact, so much so that I realized that as much as they were okay with him being around, they never saw him as anything more than their mom's friend."

"And that's it? Was there a problem when you stopped seeing him?"

"If you're asking me if he was overly disappointed, angry, or upset when I told him I didn't feel more than friendship, the answer is no. He was very polite. He hugged me and said he was sorry that I didn't feel as though we had a future but that he understood." She dropped her gaze to her lap and fiddled with the bottom of her shirt.

He knew all of Hayley's tells—when she was stressed, nervous, or upset. Her fiddling fingers told him there was more. "What else?"

Her gaze shot back to him, and she quickly shook her head. "That's it. Since I work from home, I don't see him any more except for an occasional meeting. He's very polite and friendly, so he's not a factor in my decisions."

Sam knew there was more to what she was telling but didn't want to derail their conversation by pressing too hard.

"Here's the thing, Hayley. I've missed you and the kids so much that I'd give anything for you all to live right next door." He skipped the part about how he wished they were all living together. That would be too much for her, and if he could just have them next door, he'd be grateful. "But I don't want to guilt you into anything. You and I agree that the kids are the most important thing to consider. Where they live. Where they go to school. What would make them happy. You all have visited enough to know that there is a beach, parks, and recreational activities, but I know it might not be enough. I know you'd want to check out the schools. And as I said earlier, I wouldn't blame you if you didn't want to leave the house you and Edward shared. So let's just say that if you *are* looking for a change, I hope you'll keep this in mind."

Her top teeth landed on the side of her bottom lip, and she chewed nervously. "You're right. There is a lot to think about. But *if* I was willing to make a change like this, are you sure about renting the other side of your duplex to us? That seems awfully close, and I'd hate to think that you'd... oh, I don't know... come to resent us."

He shook his head and snorted. "Before I moved here, you and I spent a ton of time together after Edward died. We know each other's moods. We know each other's families. We've seen good days and bad days together. I've been with the kids when they were sick, and you brought me soup when I was ill. I held your head when you threw up with morning sickness. What makes you think having you and the kids next door would be a problem?"

Her lips started to curve, and then a small laugh bubbled out. "You're right again. We have seen each other at some of our worst times, haven't we?"

He leaned forward and placed his much larger hand on her much smaller one. Holding her gaze, he asked, "Besides the house and the school, what are you really concerned about? I have a feeling there's something you're not mentioning. Hayley... we are too good at being friends to keep something hidden."

She dragged her tongue over her bottom lip, and he felt her hand quiver in his.

"It's just that... well... I realize it was a little difficult for you when I went out with Dave. I thought it was the right thing to do—to give you a chance to have your own life since you devoted so much to me and the kids."

He was startled at her comment but forced his hand

to remain steady on hers, needing her to finish whatever she wanted to say.

"If you started dating someone, they might not like how close we are. Or... if I were to meet someone, they also might not like how close we are."

There was a hell of a lot to unpack in those few statements but now was not the time. Or, at least, not the time to ask all the questions he'd really like to ask. "Hayley, you and the kids mean the world to me. And if I ever start dating someone, they would have to understand from the beginning that you, Eddie, and Hope are my family. And I have a feeling that you would be the same. Dave seemed like a good guy, but I'm sure he was happy when I moved away."

Her shoulders slumped, and she nodded slowly. "Yeah. I could tell he was, too. And I think it surprised him when I broke things off before they started progressing. I think he thought that having you out of the way would open things up for us. But I was just more morose not being close to you."

Those words sent Sam's heart soaring. "Then you've got some things to think about, sweetheart. And it's a lot, and I'll go over anything and everything you want to. If you want to stay an extra day and visit the school, I'll get one of my friends to watch the kids, so that's no problem. Tomorrow, I was going to go next door to check on things and wondered if you and the kids would like to walk over, too."

"I know they'd love to run through an empty place, so yeah, we'll go next door with you." She rolled her shoulders, then let out a sigh. "It's all overwhelming, but the crazy thing is that I must have already been thinking about some kind of change. While I was surprised you mentioned us moving here, I'm not nearly as shocked as I could've been. Let me sleep on it, and we'll talk some more tomorrow. I hate to involve the kids in an idea that's too soon, but I have to know their thoughts, too."

He squeezed her hand again, then tucked a strand of hair behind her ear. "I agree. Whenever you think it's right, we'll figure out a way to bring up the possibility, just to get their thoughts." He felt as though a weight had been lifted just by their conversation. Nothing was changed, yet it felt as though everything was different. No decision had been made, yet his heart felt lighter. Not wanting her to overthink things too much right now, he grinned. "Now, how about we settle in for a grown-up movie?"

Smiling in return, she nodded. "I'm going to check on the kids and get another glass of wine. Do you want another beer?"

"Wouldn't turn it down. I'll find something for us to watch." His gaze stayed on her as she walked away, thinking that having her in his house was the best thing he could've seen. Shaking his head, he grabbed the remote and started flipping through channels, settling on an old classic he knew she liked. And as much as he told himself not to start planning, he couldn't help but imagine what it would be like to have her and the kids next door.

Hayley ascended the staircase and tiptoed into the room where Eddie and Hope slept. The first time she saw this room with bunk beds in one corner, her heart had swelled. It was just perfect for Eddie and Hope. *What single man does that?* Deep within her heart, she knew the truth. He had wanted her and the kids to feel comfortable when they came to visit.

Moving closer, she leaned down and smiled at the sight of Hope, curled on her side with her well-worn and loved purple teddy bear in her arms. She had more stuffed animals than she could count, but this one was her favorite. Hayley sucked in a breath as she remembered the first time she'd seen it. The plush bear sat on the changing table when she and Sam brought Hope home from the hospital. Sam grinned and shrugged his broad shoulders when she asked where it came from. "Eddie and I went shopping so he could get something for his little sister." Hayley knew Eddie was too young at that time to think of a gift for his sister, much less ask for it. No... the gift, like so many gifts, came from Sam.

Climbing up the bottom two rungs of the ladder, she stifled a laugh, seeing Eddie sprawled out on his stomach. He no longer took a stuffed animal to bed but hugged his pillow instead.

Memories flooded her senses, ghostly imprints of how Edward used to sleep. They would always go to bed cuddled together, but sometime during the night, he would roll over and hold his pillow as he splayed on the bed. She used to complain that she had no room with him positioned like a starfish. But once she determined that when he slept in that position, he didn't snore, she stopped nagging.

Now, in the echoing silence that followed his passing, she hated that she'd complained about snoring or the way he took up so much room in the bed. When he died, she learned that the little things that seemed to bother her were trivial when faced with utter and absolute loss.

Stepping back down to the floor, she whispered into the dark night. *Oh, Edward, what would you think? What would you tell me to do? Would you be furious that I have feelings for your best friend? Would you tell me to think of the kids? Would you help me to think of myself?*

Silence was her answer. A quiet so deep it felt like both a balm and a wound. That was another truth she'd learned. Life wasn't always about the writing on the wall, the voice in the night, or the signs that we looked for and attributed to the great unknown telling us what to do. No... life was more about the simple moments that wove together to create a pattern so distinct that we could only view it in fullness when we stepped back and looked at the whole.

Sucking in a ragged breath, she realized the pattern was right in front of her. In bunk beds—both who put them there and who filled them now.

Worrying her bottom lip, she retraced her steps and walked into the kitchen. She knew Sam would have a movie for them to watch, and the heavy conversation would be over. He wouldn't require answers. He wouldn't demand to know her thoughts. He'd give her space to figure the situation out on her own. The idea of moving from their Newport News home was not new. The first time the idea struck, she'd been startled by her views and pushed them away, determined to banish them to the secret place of unbidden thoughts. Now that Sam's suggestion was spoken aloud, they had come flying back to the forefront of her mind. *How do I make a decision of this magnitude?*

She walked into the living room, and her gaze landed on the man who sat on the sofa, a TV remote in his hand and a heartwarming smile on his face when his eyes met hers. He jumped to his feet to take the glasses from her. They sat closely, comfortably ensconced in a house on the Shore, with the kids safely tucked into beds just for them, and watched a movie he'd picked, knowing she would enjoy it.

And once again, she saw the pattern woven right before her.

11

The following day, they walked out of Sam's front door and across the fifteen feet to the door of the other side of the duplex. Eddie and Hope burst through the entrance, their squeals of delight bouncing off the walls of the empty rooms, amazed to discover it was a mirror image of his house.

Hayley felt a mingling of relief and wonderment as her gaze swept the rooms. Relief because the interior only needed cleaning, painting, and a few repairs before it could welcome new tenants.

But it was the wonderment that took her by surprise. As she moved through the unoccupied rooms, she felt her imagination stir in a way it hadn't since Edward's passing. The empty spaces seemed to whisper possibilities. The rooms seemed to invite her to fill them with new memories. Was it because Sam was right next door? Was it because her children radiated joy? Or was it that she could already imagine her furniture fitting naturally into this house?

She braced, expecting to feel a sudden pull to return to her familiar Newport News surroundings. But that sensation never came. While the kids raced upstairs, their footsteps echoing new adventures to be discovered, Sam muttered while dictating into his phone.

"New hinges on upstairs closet door. Paint rooms. Hire cleaners. Need new light fixture in main bedroom. Check plumbing in kitchen..." He lifted his head and captured her expression. "Sweetheart, what's wrong?"

Her heart pounded as she simply nodded. "Yes."

He blinked and tilted his head to the side. "Yes?"

"Yes. I want to stay another day with the kids."

His slight gasp exposed his surprise. She stared, terrified at the chasm between them. Then he shoved his phone into his pocket and crossed the space until he was inches from her, dipping until his face was in front of hers. "Really? Christ, Hayley. Really?"

The hope on his face obliterated any doubt that his offer hadn't been sincere. "I can check out the school." She pressed her lips together and said, "I'm not sure about the kids, though."

"I have a friend with a goat and alpaca farm. I know Lizzie would love to have the kids visit."

Nodding her head in short jerks, she let out a long-held breath. "Okay. Let me talk to her, and we'll take it from there."

The rest of the day flew by, and instead of being filled with self-doubt and second thoughts, she found herself drawn to the Eastern Shore... and to Sam.

Normally, she would hesitate before imposing her children on a near stranger, but after talking to Lizzie on the phone, she agreed. The kids were overjoyed about visiting the farm, shouting their excitement as they drove down the long lane, seeing goats in a fenced field and the large white farmhouse with the barn in the distance. The moment she met Lizzie, she felt an immediate friendship with the warm and welcoming young farmer.

While the kids were at the Weston farm, she dropped in at the elementary school, and as though the fates were aligned, the principal agreed to see her without an appointment. As she sat across from Mrs. Rodriguiz, explaining her tentative plans and sharing her story, she was met with politeness and genuine understanding.

"Whatever your decision is, Mrs. Brooks, I will let you know that I understand. I was also widowed when my two boys were young. One was in middle school, and the other was finishing elementary school. So I understand much of what you've been through and how important this decision is."

The principal escorted her around the school and discussed how they handled everything, from standardized testing to student placement in classrooms, their gifted and talented program, and the schoolwide commitment to anti-bullying.

By the time she'd made it back to the farm to pick up the kids, her heart was full, but so was her mind. Leaving Weston farm with a bag full of goat milk lotion, a hug from Lizzie, and two excited children, they'd had time to meet Sam for lunch at the diner again.

"Did you catch any bad guys this morning?" Eddie

asked, excitement and interest burning in his hero-worshipping gaze at Sam.

Sam laughed and nodded. "Yeah. My partner and I were investigating stolen kayaks. I can't say that our excellent detective work solved the case. This morning, one of the deputies stopped to assist a motorist pulling a U-Haul trailer with a flat tire. The motorist opened the trailer's back door to get to the extra tire, and inside was a stash of kayaks. My partner and I were called to the scene and identified the stolen kayaks and canoes."

Eddie blinked, then shook his head. "You mean, the robber opened the trailer with the deputy right there? Wasn't that kind of dumb?"

Sam had laughed and nodded. "Yep. Sometimes we get lucky like that. Can't say that those cases make me feel like I've done much, but I'm always glad when cases get solved quickly, no matter how."

Eddie's nose scrunched.

"What's wrong?" Hayley asked.

Eddie's little shoulders lifted to his ears in a shrug. "I just thought it would be a more exciting story, that's all."

She held back her chuckle as she cast her eyes toward Sam, his gaze meeting hers with a twinkle in his eyes.

"Well, Eddie," Sam continued. "There are enough cases that don't get solved quickly, so I'm always glad when we get lucky. And never discount luck."

"I wish upon a star when I see the first one at night. That's supposed to bring luck," Hope chirped, holding her cup with both hands and bringing the straw gently to her lips.

"What was your last wish, sweetie?" Hayley asked.

Hope placed her cup carefully onto the table. "I wished we could stay here forever. I like Sam's house."

"I like the beach here," Eddie piped up with a smile on his face.

The air rushed from her lungs as she stared at Sam. His gaze rested on Hope before moving to Eddie, a gentle smile on his lips. She wasn't sure if he'd ever looked more handsome.

As the kids ate, excitedly recounting their morning activities at the farm with the goats and alpacas, she managed to let Sam know about her visit to the school quietly.

As they got ready to drive back to Newport News, he pulled her to the side when the kids clambered into her vehicle. "You've got a lot to think about, Hayley, and one thing about our friendship is that we've always helped each other with decisions. On one hand, my offer was made very selfishly because while moving out here has been good for me, my career, and, therefore, my mental health, I have missed you and the kids. And it's extremely selfish of me to suggest that you uproot the kids and consider moving out here. I hope you know I would have never made the offer if you'd continue to be one hundred percent happy in Newport News. And if you decide you want to remain there, I understand and support you fully. And I vow to work harder to be a better friend."

She stood with tears prickling her eyes and hugged him tightly. "You were the best friend Edward could've ever wanted. And you're the best friend that I could've ever hoped for. I'll let you know as soon as I make a decision."

"I have a couple of weeks of work to do to get the house where I want it to be. Take your time. And even if you decide later, and I've already got renters in, then we can find something appropriate for you and the kids to move into."

After a flurry of hugs, kisses, and goodbyes from the kids to Sam, she left him standing in the parking lot, and they drove back over the bridge. The kids fell asleep almost immediately in the car. She was glad because she desperately needed time to think about what she wanted. The truth stared her in the face, but she also needed time to make sure.

As soon as she and the kids stepped over the threshold into the house they'd lived in since they were born, the house she shared with her husband, for the first time ever, she wasn't filled with a sense of it being the only place she could ever be happy. In fact, she wondered if she hadn't clung to the house as though clinging to Edward. Certainly, Hope, while having never lived anywhere else, had no memory of her father. And even Eddie only remembered what he'd seen of Edward in photographs.

After the kids had gone to bed, she wandered through each room and cried. She cried for the dream she'd had that no longer existed. She cried for the man she'd loved, who was no longer there. She cried for the changes in her life that she didn't think she'd have to face alone. Her wanderings ended in her bedroom as she sat on the bed and stared at her reflection in the mirror over the dresser.

But I'm not alone, am I? Edward was always with me in my heart, but not in these walls. And Sam had been the greatest friend Edward and I could've ever wanted. She knew her feelings for Sam had grown and realized that moving to the Eastern Shore and living right next door to him could end up causing heartbreak.

But I'd rather be close to him, even if he shares his life with someone else, than not have him in my life at all. She'd already kept the kids out of school that day but decided one more day wouldn't hurt. Much to their excitement, they started the day with a big pancake breakfast and settled into the living room. Hope was delighted that she had another day to play with her dolls, already planning her no-school day. But Eddie held her gaze with utmost seriousness.

Oh yes. The child so like myself. The one who ponders everything with such care. She asked them what they liked about the trip to Sam's house. They both talked excitedly about visiting the beach. They also enjoyed eating out and spending time with Sam. But then both kids said that a favorite thing they'd done was to go around the house next to his.

Using their delight, she approached the subject weighing heavily on her heart. "What would you think about moving to Sam's place? Not his house, but moving our furniture into the empty one next door to him?"

Immediately, Hope threw her arms into the air and

shouted, "Yay!" not seeming concerned that they wouldn't have this house anymore.

But Eddie considered her carefully. "If we move, our things wouldn't be in this house anymore, would they?"

Hayley shook her head. "No. Everything would be packed up. Furniture, toys, clothes... everything. And movers would take it and put it in the empty house next to Sam's. And it's important that you understand that someone else would come live in this house. This wouldn't be our house anymore."

Again, Hope only paused for a second, then began bouncing in excitement, talking about what she would put in her room. Hayley watched Eddie carefully as he pondered the new information.

Finally, he nodded his head very slowly. "This has been the only house I've ever lived in, Mom."

"I know, sweetheart. And if you don't like the idea, then you need to let me know."

"Would we have to drive all the way over the bridge to get to our school each day?" he asked, then pressed his lips together as though dreading the answer.

"No. You and Hope would go to a new school." At that, both kids continued to study her, Hope now a little quieter.

Hayley continued, wanting to make sure the children had all the information so they'd have no surprises. "You would have a new teacher, a new classroom, and a new school. You would make new friends. The friends you have here won't be there. But we can come back to visit them."

She bent closer, holding their gazes. "I know this is a

lot to think about, and you don't have to let me know right away. Please ask any questions you can think of."

Hope shrugged. "I like my friends here but can make new friends!"

Hayley smiled at her bright and resilient daughter. If there was ever a child who found joy in each situation, it was Hope. For the millionth time, Hayley knew she'd chosen the right name for her. Turning her attention to Eddie, she waited, giving him time to think.

"I have some friends here, but I know I can make new friends there, too. I don't mind going to a new school, Mom." He shrugged and looked so much like his sister at that moment. "I don't really like school here very much anymore." He still seemed a little quiet, then looked up, a new intensity in his gaze. "I'd like to try something different. This is the only house I've ever been in, but I don't really remember Daddy. But I remember Sam always being here after Daddy went to heaven. And I really miss Sam. So if we could be close to him, I'd really like that, Mom."

Hayley was sure that her heart might burst with the mixture of emotions seeming to explode inside. "Okay, then I'll check into what we need to do."

While the kids played and got online to ensure they caught up with the two days of school they missed, Hayley called her neighbor and asked if she would sit with them for an hour. As soon as Martha arrived, Hayley darted to her vehicle and drove to the cemetery.

Walking the familiar path to Edward's headstone, she knelt for several long moments on the towel she always kept in her car. She sat quietly, then finally said,

"I think it's time for a change, Edward. I used to come out here and talk to you almost every day. And slowly, over the years, I would talk to you wherever I was. You were my first love. The father of my children. The keeper of my heart. The light at the end of every dark tunnel. And the person I was going to grow old with. But I know now it's time to make a change. For me and for the kids. And Sam will help us, just like he always has. I might lose my heart, or my heart might get broken. But it won't be the first time, will it?"

A fall breeze kicked up, swirling the leaves in little whirlwinds between the headstones. There were no words boomed from the heavens. No butterflies or birds to land on her shoulder, letting her know she was doing the right thing. She'd long since stopped looking for those kinds of signs. But what she knew was to listen to the voice deep inside her that told her she was making the right decision. Moving on didn't mean forgetting. Making a change didn't mean the past was forgotten. But life was to be lived. And that was exactly what Edward would want her to do.

Arriving home, she thanked Martha and checked on the kids. Finally, she picked up the phone and called an acquaintance of hers who was a real estate agent. After setting up a meeting, she felt excitement flowing through her veins. The next call she made was to Sam.

12

ONE MONTH LATER

"Man, I am fucking sorry that you got called in on your day off."

Sam looked over at Aaron and held back the growl that threatened to erupt, knowing it wasn't his partner's fault. "You and me both."

"Colt wasn't the one who called you in because he knows what you had planned today. Chuck made the call before he realized what you had going on."

Sam had no problem with Chuck, one of the detectives in charge of scheduling, but he also knew Chuck rarely gave thought to anything other than his scheduling of assignments.

"What the hell was so important about a new robbery case?" He was once again in the passenger seat with Aaron as they drove south of Baytown.

"Rental house, broken into. Some televisions were stolen."

Sam's head swung to the side, certain his incredulity

was written on his face. "I get called in on a vacation day for fucking televisions?"

"I don't think it's so much what was taken as who owns the house."

His mind was so firmly on helping Hayley and the kids move today that it took a second for Aaron's statement to sink in. Flopping his head back against the car's headrest, he growled. "Please tell me we're not going back out to interview Harry Malroney again?" The silence that greeted him from his partner let him know he'd hit the nail on the head. "Fucking hell."

"You got it. And if I know Malroney, he'll have already made calls to the mayor of Baytown, who can't do anything because the houses aren't in the town's jurisdiction. So then he'll start calling the board of supervisors for North Heron County. Christ, the man will probably call the governor if we don't find who stole his televisions."

"Was it just one of his houses this time that was hit or more than one?"

"Right now, just the one. There were no renters in it, and, of course, he doesn't live there."

"He's got a security system with alarms. Didn't they go off?"

"Nothing came into the station. I assume the alarms must not have sounded because he wasn't notified. He went over this morning to check on things and found the back door broken. Of course, instead of waiting for the police to come and secure the area and make sure no one is still inside, he goes in to see if anything was missing."

"Great. I'll bet the deputies were real happy with that, weren't they? He fucks up a robbery scene and then will be on our asses if we don't get all the evidence we need."

"As soon as I heard you were being called in, I made sure the deputies there attempted to keep him outside."

The partners were silent for just a few seconds before laughing and shaking their heads. "I bet Malroney didn't like that very much," Sam surmised.

"I know the deputies can handle themselves, and I've seen a lot worse than Malroney. But if they can actually contain him until we get there, I might owe them a beer."

They pulled off the lane and onto the driveway leading to the large house. Much to their surprise, the two deputies were outside the front door with Harry between them. The man's mouth was moving, and Sam could only imagine the weight of Harry's self-importance was pushing on the deputies' nerves. As they parked and climbed from Aaron's SUV, Sam offered a chin lift to the deputies, hiding the grin that threatened to escape when they shot him looks of gratitude.

"Deputy Johnson. Deputy Carter," Sam greeted.

"Detective Shackley," Deputy Johnson acknowledged in return. "Forensics just came, and they're in the back. As soon as you give the word, Deputy Carter and I will start looking at the perimeter."

He nodded, and the two deputies started around the corner of the house, leaving him and Aaron to face the once again blustering homeowner. Sam understood Harry Malroney's frustration. Being robbed again was not good. While his kayaks and canoes had been returned, Harry was now faced with having to deal with insurance companies again and getting bids for repairs to whatever damage had occurred during the break-in.

"Mr. Malroney, I'm sorry we have to meet again under the circumstances."

"I don't understand why there is no patrolling of the streets around here!"

Neither he nor Aaron would attempt to explain to the irate man that the county was large, filled with winding backroads, many houses away from the roads, and no streetlights. Right now, Harry only wanted someone to take the heat for his anger.

"Mr. Malroney, I'd like to ask about your security system and why no alarm was sounded with the break-in."

"I'd like to know that, too! I paid top dollar to have motion detection lights and security alarms set on the doors and windows. And I got nothing! It wasn't until I showed up this morning that I discovered what happened."

"And you have no renters at this time?"

"No. That's why I was going to take today and walk-through to make sure the cleaners had done the job they needed to do because I have people coming in on Monday. Now, I'll have to shift them to one of my other houses—one that would normally go at a higher cost, but I'll have to give them the lower rate."

"Were your cleaners here yesterday?"

"No, they came in on Wednesday. But today was the first day I had a chance to get in and check on things."

"Do they have their own key?"

"Yes, I've used them for years. But I hardly think they gave the key to somebody, considering the back door is smashed in!" Harry rolled his eyes and huffed as though Sam's question was ridiculous.

"So when you got here this morning, walk us through exactly what you did."

"I told the deputies that I came in the front door, and as I went into the kitchen, I saw the mess! It was then that I turned and realized that there was broken glass on the floor and the TV had been stolen! There are six smart TVs in this house, and every one of them was taken!"

"Okay, Mr. Malroney. Let's go to the front door, and you can show us exactly what you found. And since I know you have pictures of everything, we want you to send photographs of the TVs to my tablet, just like last time."

For the next hour, Sam accompanied Harry through the house after the forensic team allowed them to move freely. They'd taken fingerprints from around the kitchen door, knowing there'd be too many fingerprints in the house for them to check each room. Between the cleaners, the Malroneys, and all the renters, the house would be a cornucopia of fingerprints. But Sam was hopeful that if the thieves didn't wear gloves, the kitchen door would be the most likely place to get a hit.

After Aaron recorded Harry's official statement, they moved away from the fuming owner, who was now on his phone, threatening anyone and everyone he could get ahold of. Sam actually felt sorry for the insurance agent who would be coming to the house soon.

Sam looked at the security system, noting it was average and not top-of-the-line. He found it interesting that a man with Harry's money and bluster about his properties wouldn't have installed a better system. But, nonetheless, the system didn't alarm.

He and Aaron shared a few looks, but neither spoke, not wanting any of their thoughts to be overheard until they had a chance to process the scene completely.

Several hours passed before they were ready to leave the house. They found Harry standing in the living room with the insurance agent. Sam interrupted Harry's harangue. "Mr. Malroney, I have one last question for right now. Is there anyone you can think of who would want to target you for these robberies specifically?"

"What are you insinuating?" Harry yelled, lifting his hand and shaking his fist.

"Sir, I'm not insinuating anything. I'm concerned that you have had more than one property as the site of thefts. And now, this house has been hit twice. We're not getting reports from anyone else in the area having break-ins. So I just want to rule out that someone you know might have a personal vendetta against you, or they're targeting your properties for some reason."

Harry narrowed his eyes but, for once, kept his mouth shut. He appeared to think, then slowly shook his head. "I may have had a few arguments with people over the years, but I can't imagine anyone targeting me. I get along with my neighbors. My renters leave excellent reviews on their experiences renting my houses. I just can't imagine that someone is specifically targeting me."

"Okay, sir. Then we'll be in touch."

Once they were back inside the vehicle, Aaron looked over. "Thoughts?"

"The person who took the kayaks and canoes knew exactly where they were and what they were looking for. Most of the houses in the area have outdoor equipment, and nothing was taken from anyone else. And this? Busting in the back door and then the security system not working? It doesn't line up."

"Do you suspect Harry?"

Sam rubbed his chin. "Not necessarily. Only because I can't come up with a good reason he'd do this himself, but it's too easy. Something doesn't add up."

Glancing at the time, he said, "When we get back, I'll write up my part of the report and make sure I log in the evidence I have. Then I'm heading home."

Aaron grinned. "Do you think the movers are still there?"

"They're probably gone, and that's why I want to get home. Hayley will run herself ragged with the house and the kids right now."

"I'm glad she's here," Aaron said. "While I don't completely understand your relationship with her, it's obviously a good one." His sincere voice cut through Harry's grating tone still in Sam's head.

"Right now, we're just good friends. The same good friends we've been for the past ten years. If that's all we'll ever be, then I'll always watch over her and the kids."

He turned his head slightly and looked out the window as they pulled into the station. His heart hoped there would be something more one day between him and Hayley. But he held on to that thought tightly in silence.

"Mom!"

"Mom!"

The dual shouts from Eddie and Hope resounded throughout the house, halting Hayley in her tracks. These shouts from her children did not set off alarm bells in her head. Nor did they cause her heart to pound in fear. Years of motherhood had honed her ear to the subtle nuances of her children's vocal tones. She could easily discern between screams for "Somebody's bleeding or throwing up" from "My brother/sister is irritating me" or the shouts of "Please come, I found something really cool for you to look at!"

She smiled, recognizing the latter.

The kids were opening boxes they'd packed, unearthing treasures they'd forgotten, even though the items had only been in boxes for a couple of days. Hope was a whirlwind of activity, racing into Eddie's room, and Hayley knew her son was at his wit's end with his sister. He liked to arrange items meticulously in place, while Hope's idea of unpacking was tossing things everywhere. Hayley wondered if she could ever get Hope's room straight.

Before she had a chance to referee, Eddie called out, "Sam's home!"

It was a Friday, and the local schools were out for a teacher workday. She'd chosen this day to move, wanting to have a full weekend to put her house to right before the kids needed to be back in school. They'd finished one grading period in Newport News, and the two school systems were so similar in their calendars that Monday would be perfect for a fresh start for Eddie and Hope. Sam had planned on being home on moving day and grumbled mightily when he was called into the station on a case. She assured him there was no reason for him to be present while the movers went back and forth from the truck to the house.

Eddie and Hope kept themselves entertained while staying out of the movers' way, and she was able to focus on where the major pieces of furniture needed to be placed and then directed the labeled boxes to the various rooms. The movers had left a couple of hours ago, and looking around, she rolled her eyes at Sam, thinking he had missed all the action. There were boxes labeled kitchen placed in the living room and a box labeled for Eddie in the dining room.

She followed Hope's scampering footsteps as her daughter raced down the stairs after her brother. Eddie threw open the front door just as Sam's hand hovered in midair, preparing to knock.

"Hi, Sam! Welcome!" Eddie shouted with more enthusiasm than she'd heard from her son in a while. "You don't have to knock. You can just come on in." His small hand reached out, and Sam enveloped it in an affirming grip.

Sam stepped over the threshold, ruffled Eddie's hair, and then looked up as she and Hope arrived at the bottom of the stairs. Hayley stopped on the bottom step, and her fingers curled around the railing, her grip holding her upright. Seeing Sam standing there, she fought to breathe. The fragmented pieces of her life slid together—the smiles on her children's faces and the peaceful expression on Sam's face—and she knew moving to the Eastern Shore was the right decision. Living here didn't have to mean forever. But for now, she had the best neighbor, landlord, and friend she could ever hope for.

Hope darted forward, grabbed Sam's hand, and dragged him farther into the room.

"We put the sofa over here," she stated unnecessarily, considering the sofa was in plain sight. "And Mom had the movers put the chair over there. And when the TV gets set up, it will be on this table right here. And in my room—"

"Hope, honey. Give Sam a chance to come in and rest without pouncing on him."

Hope whirled around, planted her hands on her tiny hips, and huffed. "I'm just giving him a tour. He needs to know where everything is!"

Eddie stepped in and said, "Hope! He can see where the couch is. He's not blind."

Hope blinked back tears that threatened to spill

forth. "You be quiet, Eddie! Everybody is ruining my chance to show Sam around!"

Hayley recognized her tired, overwrought, excitable daughter was a few seconds away from a meltdown, but before she had a chance to do anything, Sam scooped Hope up in his arms, gave her a big hug, and said, "I absolutely love where you've put everything in the room and having you next door is icing on the cake."

Hope giggled, and Hayley and Eddie shared a grin, knowing that an emotional catastrophe had just been avoided.

"Icing on the cake? Did you bring cake?" Hope asked, her eyes even wider and brighter if that was possible.

Hayley was about to explain that it was just a saying when Sam nodded.

"Some of my friends wanted to make sure that you all had a great welcome to your new home, but I begged them not to come today because I knew you'd be tired. We've got friends coming tomorrow, and we'll do a cookout in the backyard. You're going to meet some new playmates, your mom will meet some new friends, and we'll have a party."

Hayley's eyes widened at his pronouncement, and the air rushed from her lungs. Her gaze darted around at the complete mess in the house.

Sam shook his head at her. "Don't even think about it, Hayley," he warned. "That's what this party is for. If any furniture still needs to be put together or moved, I have some men who will help. And I have some friends who are experts at going through clothes and toys and will be perfect at helping to break down a few boxes.

Nobody will get in your business and bother you, but it'll be a great help."

She had to admit she was intrigued by the idea and simply nodded. "Thanks, Sam. Actually, that sounds really nice."

Still being held by Sam, Hope grabbed his face and turned him toward her. "I want to know about the icing and the cake!"

"That will be tomorrow," Hayley began.

"We don't have to wait for tomorrow to enjoy that," Sam added, rubbing noses with Hope. "One of the women brought by a *Welcome to the Eastern Shore* cake, and I have it, plus some pizza out in the car." He looked down at Eddie and said, "How about you go get it?"

Hope squirmed, but he held her a little longer, giving Eddie a chance to run out first to bring the cake inside.

This subtle action didn't escape Hayley's attention. Sam always knew exactly what to do to help both her children.

He finally set a wiggly Hope on the ground but held her hand. "Go help your brother, but no squabbling, okay?"

Hope hopped from foot to foot, almost quivering with excitement. "I promise!" As soon as he released her, she darted out the door screaming, "I'm coming, Eddie! I'll help you!"

Sam chuckled, then stepped over to Hayley, bending slightly to hold her gaze. "How are you holding up?"

She was lost in his blue-gray eyes for a few seconds, wanting nothing more than to continue gazing at him. Suddenly, she blinked out of her Sam-induced trance.

Clearing her throat, she glanced around at the chaos and smiled. "There's a lot to do, but you know what? I'm okay. The kids are excited. They're ready for a change. And I am, too. We're glad to be here, Sam."

He smiled in return, and she could swear she felt it in the deepest part of her heart. Warmth flooded her, and she turned, blinking to hold back the tears of joy springing to her eyes.

13

As Sam navigated the last curve on the road leading to his house, seeing Hayley's vehicle parked in front of the garage on her side of the duplex struck him like a lightning bolt of emotion. He'd found solace in the Eastern Shore's briny winds and sun-drenched waters, but his residence was still just a place to crash. Happier once the neighbors had moved out, he felt his entire body ease at the thought of home, knowing Hayley and the children were there.

He'd spent the previous night alone in their empty living room, sitting in a folding chair with a tumbler of whiskey in his hands. The sun glistened through the back windows, and he sat in silence, imagining what the next day would bring when the house was full of the people he loved. He leaned back in the chair and lifted his whiskey in the air.

"Edward, I still can't believe you're fucking gone. But I've done everything I could do to make sure your family was taken care of, and your memory was honored. And maybe I'm a selfish bastard, but I know in my heart you'd never want Hayley to spend the rest of her life alone. If something grows between us, I'd like to think I have your blessing. But if the only thing Hayley and I will ever be is close friends, then my vow to watch out for your wife and children is unbreakable."

With a flick of his wrist, he tossed back the last of the whiskey, its liquid fire tracing a path down his throat and into his soul. Inhaling deeply, he released the breath slowly, willing his hopes and fears out into the universe. Finally standing, he folded the chair and set it out of the way. With his empty tumbler in his hand, he moved to the door, turning and looking back into the room. A smile curved his lips. Hayley, Eddie, and Hope would soon arrive, filling the empty space with their belongings and giving the house a spark of life. Sleep came easily that night as his heart filled with anticipation.

Now, he put all thoughts of his cases away as he stepped from his SUV. He heard the shout of "Sam's home!" and hearing Eddie use the word *home* to describe where they all lived filled his heart.

A tornado of activity engulfed him the second he entered the door. Eddie's smile beamed as he greeted Sam man to man, offering his small hand outward. A flash of how Eddie was growing into the man of the house hit him, and he returned the shake, his breath hitching as he watched the pride shine in the small boy's eyes. Hope, quivering with excitement, was hell-bent on showing him everything. And Hayley looked radiant even in her bone-tired exhaustion. Their eyes met, and at that moment, everything clicked into place. *Jesus, it feels just like coming into a real home.* His pulse quickened. This wasn't just coming home. This was the divine sensation of recognizing he was part of a home for the first time.

Humbled, he swallowed back the emotion and entered the fray, soothing Hope's impending tirade. He gave Eddie a task and greeted Hayley with the news that dinner was taken care of.

Once the kids raced to his SUV to get the pizza and cake, he reached over to hold Hayley's hand. "Let's go to my place to eat. Then we'll come back, and I'll get to work."

She placed her palm over her forehead and droned dramatically. "Oh, it takes *so* long to get to your place."

Laughing, he tugged on her hand. "Come on, sweetheart." They walked onto the front porch and over the few steps it took to get to his front door. "Kids, bring it this way."

The kids were so excited, but Hayley made sure they washed their hands first. They could barely sit still while shoving in the pizza slices, anxious to get to the cake. Their tales of the movers dominated the conversation, and Sam loved each story.

Looking at Hayley, he asked, "Do you have everything settled at your old house?"

She laughed and nodded. "Since you came to help us get everything packed up and moved around last weekend, it was really easy. Once the movers got the large pieces of furniture into their truck, I quickly went behind them and vacuumed. I had already wiped down the baseboards and cleaned out all the closets. The bathrooms and kitchen had also been cleaned just before the movers came. Then, as the movers loaded the boxes out of each room, I quickly vacuumed those rooms, too. The real estate agent hired a company to come in in the next couple of days and do a professional cleaning, but she's already got two potential buyers."

Sam was thrilled with her news. Getting her house sold so quickly would go a long way to taking some of the stress of her decision away.

She and the kids exclaimed over the cake when they opened the top of the container. Fancy scrolled icing on top and said, "Welcome Hayley, Eddie, and Hope!"

"Whoa!" Eddie called out, eyes wide.

"There's my name!" Hope shouted, throwing her hands into the air.

Hayley beamed as she cut slices, and Sam made a mental note to thank Belle.

"You'll meet the woman who made the cake tomorrow. She's the head nurse at the nursing home and is married to one of my detective friends."

"Kids, you'll have to be sure to thank her when we meet her," Hayley said.

Eddie and Hope nodded, too polite to talk with their mouths full, but both could barely chew with the huge bites they'd taken. Hayley rolled her eyes at them, and Sam just laughed. In the months since he'd moved to the shore, the kids and Hayley had sat at his table numerous times when they visited. But he was finally struck with rightness, knowing they would be there almost constantly this time.

As the last forkfuls of cake were devoured by the kids and savored by the adults, and the leftovers put in the refrigerator, they trooped back to Hayley's side. Deciding to start in the kids' rooms first, Sam checked the mattresses on the floor. "I'll get my tool chest and get the beds together—"

"Don't worry about it, Sam," Eddie said, grinning. "Mom said we can sleep with the mattresses on the floor tonight."

Sam turned to see Hayley standing in the doorway.

"He's right. The kids will be fine tonight with the added *adventure* of mattresses on the floor."

Sam ruffled Eddie's hair. "Sounds good. Tomorrow, I'll have some friends over, and we'll make sure all the furniture is put together."

"Can I help?"

"Absolutely."

Hayley walked back into the room. "I found the box labeled linens and dug out the children's sheets. I considered buying new comforters but decided it was best to give them as much continuity and familiarity as possible at first."

"We can make a trip to purchase new ones if either of them decides they want something different," he replied. While she made the beds, Sam moved into her bedroom.

With their houses being mirror images of each other, his bedroom shared a wall with hers. He was sure Hayley hadn't done this consciously, but her bed was placed against the shared wall, where his bed was placed just on the other side. He placed his hand on the wall, contemplating the scant inches of wall separating their worlds. Pushing away the idea of how close they'd be when in bed yet so far apart, he busied himself with the task of checking her bed and mattress since it appeared the movers had put her bed frame together.

Hayley walked into her room, her arms full of pale lilac linens, and placed them on the mattress. "I'll make my bed later."

"I'll help you now. Easier with two people," he said.

She hesitated for only a second, then smiled and nodded. They each grabbed a corner and had the queen-sized bed covered in soft cotton sheets and a thick, geometric comforter in blues, lilacs, and greens in a few minutes.

"You were right." She laughed. "This was so much easier with help. I usually run to each corner, hoping the last one I did won't pop off before I get it all together."

"Mom! What about the TV?" Eddie called from downstairs.

"I'll get it set up," Sam offered.

"Are you sure you don't mind?"

"Eddie and I can handle it," he said, winking.

She laughed and nodded. "That's true. He's been your little helper with a lot of projects, hasn't he?"

"Best helper I could ask for." Turning, he headed out of the room, calling down the stairs, "On my way, buddy."

"Yay! Me and Sam get to do the TV!" Eddie called back.

As Sam descended the stairs, he grinned at Eddie's

enthusiasm, once more loving the chaotic sounds of a real home now so close to him.

He and Eddie situated the TV cabinet correctly against the wall, then unearthed the television. As Sam manipulated the cables and sockets, Eddie bombarded him with a rapid-fire series of questions.

"How does the electricity make the TV work? And how does the Wi-Fi get the internet onto the screen?" Like most kids, Eddie was adept with the remote but now wanted to understand the workings of the appliance.

"You want to get the washer and dryer installed?" Sam knew the answer before he asked the question, and Eddie nodded, his grin wide. It didn't take long, and again, Sam patiently answered Eddie's questions.

Sam was increasingly impressed by Eddie's intuitive intelligence and insatiable thirst for knowledge. He thought about the boy who'd bullied Eddie for a moment, and his anger renewed. He hated that Eddie had to go through that but vowed he would not let something like that happen again.

"Catch any bad guys today?" Eddie asked.

Sam chuckled, remembering Eddie's disappointment when he last asked that question and wasn't impressed with how the bad guys got caught. "Well, I didn't catch any bad guys today, but I did get an interesting case."

Eddie's eyes were wide as he waited to hear what Sam had to say.

"A house was broken into, and a whole bunch of TVs were taken."

A crinkle formed between Eddie's brow. "How many TVs were in the house?"

"Well, it was a big house, and they had one in almost every room. Six TVs were stolen."

At that, Eddie's eyes went wide. "How could somebody carry out that many TVs?"

"That's a very good question. Either more than one person was the thief or they made a bunch of trips back and forth from the house to their vehicle."

He watched as the wheels began turning behind Eddie's eyes as he thought through possibilities. "And the weird thing is that it was one of the houses where those kayaks were stolen a month ago."

Now, Eddie's brow furrowed again. "That sounds fishy!"

Sam laughed and nodded. "I agree! It certainly sounds fishy. That's one of the cases my partner and I will work on."

The children's earlier exuberance finally waned, evidenced by the telltale signs of eyes struggling to stay open. Hayley corralled them into the upstairs bathroom, where she had laid out their shampoo, toothbrushes, and Hope's bubble bath. She began the dance of bedtime routines, overseeing Hope's bath. Once finished and in her pajamas, Hayley ushered her yawning little girl out into the hall, passing Sam as he herded Eddie into the bathroom.

He checked the temperature of the water before stepping out of the bathroom to give Eddie his privacy. Soon, Eddie emerged, his wet hair slicked back and dressed in his pajamas, yawning as widely as his sister had. Sam had planned on reading them a story, but Hope was fast asleep by the time Eddie finished.

Sam and Hayley tiptoed inside the room, their movements almost synchronized as they bent to kiss Hope's head. Her shampoo's sweet, familiar smell was once again a reminder that she was here to stay. Hayley's gaze met his, and in the few seconds of silent exchange, an epiphany seemed to pass between them. They were not just setting up a house to live in but creating a home that went beyond mere proximity to each other.

Heading into Eddie's room, Sam hugged the boy and promised, "I'll start getting your room decorated the way you like tomorrow. Deal?"

Eddie grinned. "Deal!"

With a chin lift, he walked out as Hayley walked in to say good night to her son. Hayley then headed into her room, and he followed. She emptied another box, filling her bathroom with items, and Sam broke down a few empty cardboard boxes. Neither spoke, but the silence was comfortable. By the time they finished, she cast her gaze around the room and sighed.

He walked over and wrapped his hand around hers, gently tugging her from the room. "Come on, sweetheart." They made their way to the bottom of the stairs, where the mess was just as bad.

Turning, he let go of her hand and placed his on her shoulders. "Don't worry about this. Moving is always crazy."

"You know me so well, don't you?"

"Had years of practice to get to know you," he said,

his gaze never leaving hers. "Just remember that tomorrow, lots of people will come to help. And you'll get a chance to meet some people who will be some of the best friends you could ever hope to have in your life."

Her lips curved as she nodded. "I'm really looking forward to that."

"Normally, sweetheart, I'd ask if you want to settle in and watch some TV. But right now, I think you need to sleep. So lock up after I leave, and I'll see you in the morning." He pulled her gently forward, wrapping his arms around her, and she eased into his embrace against his chest, the top of her head tucked underneath his chin.

They'd hugged often over the years, but somehow, right now, in this place and at this time, the hug felt even more special. Something was growing. Changing. Evolving. He hoped she felt it as much as he did. Kissing the top of her head, he released her and stepped back.

"Sleep tight, Hayley."

Her beautiful smile in the house next door made his world a hell of a lot brighter.

14

The next day, Hayley gazed out her living room window in sheer disbelief at the spectacle unfolding before her eyes. The drive was filled with vehicles, and she watched as a swarm of men, women, and children filled their yard.

Hope ran outside, immediately in her element as princess of the castle, excited to meet other little girls, but Eddie held back slightly. Sam placed his hand on Eddie's shoulder, gave him a reassuring smile, and walked him over to where a few of the other boys were already kicking soccer balls back and forth. Her heart melted for the millionth time at the sight of Sam stepping in to nurture her sensitive son. She pressed her hand to her chest, battling the urge to cry... or maybe just cheer. Instead, she walked outside to begin rounds of introductions.

Sam had assured her that she wouldn't need to lift a finger, and it seemed he hadn't exaggerated. When he said the food would all be brought by the others, it exceeded her wildest imaginings and gave her a glimpse of the Eastern Shore hospitality.

Tables were already being set up in the backyard to hold the items that didn't need refrigeration. Meat to grill, buns, condiments, bowls of side dishes, bags of chips, beer, soda, water, and desserts galore. She knew she'd have to keep an eye on Hope or her sneaky daughter would taste everything with sugar and then bounce for the rest of the day and end up with a tummy ache by nighttime.

A cadre of men shifted some furniture around and then broke down the cardboard boxes with a speed that left Hayley reeling. Others set up the kids' beds, checking the bolts and screws. Then, they loaded the trash into a few pickup trucks to be hauled to the local recycling center. Hayley was stunned at the open arms welcoming her and the kids. And when the women discovered she worked in web design and marketing, she was inundated with requests to set up appointments for work.

A beautiful woman with a cheerleader smile approached. "I'm Jillian, as you can see," she said, pointing at her lapel, then rolling her eyes. "Oh my God! Get that out of your mouth!" She laughed as she pulled the partially ripped name tag sticker from the toddler in her arms. Looking back at Hayley, she grinned. "Sorry about that. I hope you don't think it's weird that the women are wearing name tags. I know that might seem strange, but it can be hard for those who come from other places to put a name with a face. Now me? I was born and raised in Baytown, only leaving for college. But many of the women came from all over. So we decided whenever we had one of these get-togethers to welcome someone new, we'd slap name tags on so that it helps."

"I love it!" Hayley enthused, grinning at the smiling woman and the adorable toddler in her arms. "And thank you because it will help me start putting a name to a face." She cocked her head to the side and asked, "You run Jillian's Coffee Shop and Galleria downtown on the main street, right?"

Jillian beamed and nodded. "I know you're going to get lots of people today who want to talk to you about updating their websites, starting websites, or just how to do marketing. In fact, we've been desperate to have somebody out here who could do that."

"That sounds wonderful," she said. "I work for a marketing firm, but they handle large companies. So it wouldn't be a violation for me to work on websites and marketing on the side for smaller businesses."

Jillian set her toddler on the ground, and they watched as he waddled to one of the men, who swooped him up and cuddled him close. Jillian looped her arm through Hayley's as they walked toward the back door. "Well, I'm going to snag you now since Grant will keep an eye on our son. The woman who's been doing my website for about six years has retired. I'm desperate for somebody to look it over, update it, and give me some fresh ideas. We have many vacationers to Baytown during the summer, but I am more interested in a website that will draw people's attention all year even when they can't come to the town."

"That sounds perfect. We can get together anytime."

Another woman with long, dark hair tied back with a ribbon approached her. Speaking softly, she said, "It's nice to meet you, Hayley. I'm Belle. My husband works as a detective with Sam."

"Oh, I want to thank you for that amazing cake yesterday!"

Belle beamed her appreciation. "I work for the local nursing home, and our website, while efficient, lacks a personal touch that people want to see when looking at a nursing home. When Hunter told me what you did, I've already spoken to our director, and he's interested."

Over the course of the afternoon, not only did the kids' rooms, her kitchen, dining room, and living room get organized, but pictures were hung on the walls, and everything was placed where she asked it to be. Throughout it all, Sam moved beside her continually, a steadfast anchor in the whirlwind of activity. Even when he wasn't with her, their eyes would meet across a room or the lawn, and each time, it was as if the cacophony of the world quieted for a heartbeat, focusing all her energy into that unspoken exchange.

During one of these moments, standing amid the picnic and dizzying swirl of people moving about, Hayley realized she was not just a newcomer but was rapidly becoming part of the community, thanks to the man whose eyes seemed to reflect her hope of a shared tomorrow.

By the time the house was set to move-in ready, she

had also talked to Lizzie about the Weston Farms website. Also a woman named Lia, an accountant in town, and Samantha, the local veterinarian. Katelyn Harrison worked as a private investigator with her husband, and they also wanted updated websites and marketing information. Tori Evans and Shiloh Newman approached her about the Sea Glass Inn, which Tori owned and Shiloh managed.

Most of the women had toddlers, preschoolers, or kids a little older running around with them. Hayley easily caught sight of Hope dashing among them all. Looking at the other side of the yard, she spied Eddie with a few boys, his face glowing with a wide smile.

Her attention was snagged as Rose Boswell bounded over, her eyes twinkling as she laughed. "Well, I know you remember me from my ice cream shop."

"Of course!" Hayley said, glad to see a familiar face from her previous visits with Sam.

"Well, I feel like I need to get in line because, of course, the same woman doing Jillian's website was doing mine." Rose leaned closer and said, "Actually, I think Mrs. Dawson was doing a lot of people in town. Don't get me wrong, she brought most of us into the age of how to market digitally, but with her leaving, it's hard to accept work from just anybody you don't know."

"I know what you mean. Your website is so important to your business. It's often the first thing people see about you, so making it easy to maneuver, colorful, and inviting while keeping it up-to-date is important."

"My husband, Jason, runs the garage across the

street from my ice cream shop. I know he's interested but doesn't even have a website!" Rose laughed. "You can drag him into this century!"

Looking around, Hayley realized she had a group of almost twenty women crowding around, nodding, and then vying for her attention. As much as she loved it, she was glad when someone called out, "Food is ready!"

She turned to corral her kids, finding Eddie surrounded by new friends and Hope being dangled upside down by Sam who'd rescued her from the dessert table. The adults assisted the kids through the line, then the men insisted the women go next. She had met many more women than men, but it was easy to see both the camaraderie they had with each other and the respect they had for their wives or girlfriends.

After turning over the grilling duties to one of his friends, Sam found her easily in the crowd. Leaning closer, he whispered, "How are you doing?"

"Good," she said, smiling. "Really good. I can't believe how many friends you have, and everyone is being so nice."

"I've met some of them from work and most all of them from the American Legion."

Everyone settled into lawn chairs sprinkled across the yard. Despite the diversity in age and backgrounds, the group coalesced naturally. The position of their chairs pulled close together spoke volumes about the bonds of their friendship. Laughter, the clinking of glasses, and the crackling of the firepit filled the air.

"You should attend one of the American Legion

Auxiliary meetings, Hayley. You don't have to be a family member of someone in the military."

Lifting her eyes from her plate, she smiled at the woman speaking. "My husband was in the service."

A hush fell over the people sitting nearby, and she realized that not everyone knew her story. Over the years, she'd developed a keen intuition for how much to reveal about her widowhood, depending on the situation. She felt no urge to hold back now, considering these people would be her friends and neighbors. Hoping to dispel anyone's uncomfortableness, she opened her mouth to explain when Eddie spoke up.

"My daddy was in the Army. Then he was a policeman, and he died when he was working."

Hayley's heart pounded—not out of embarrassment or social awkwardness but because she was terrified someone might say something that would upset Eddie.

"Then I think your daddy was a really brave man, and I know he'd be proud of you."

Her gaze landed on Eddie's smile, and she pressed her lips together, her heart warm. She glanced at the man who'd said those kind words and realized they came from Colt, the sheriff. She offered him a smile and a slight nod, hoping it conveyed her thanks. He replied with a barely-there nod of his own. As everyone continued to eat, talk, and laugh, the moment passed. Turning to the women, she said, "I'd love to come to an Auxiliary meeting."

After the meal was over, Sam navigated his way around the gathering to thank everyone with Hayley right next to him. The temptation to reach down and intertwine his fingers with hers was strong. It was a simple act between them, but he didn't want to overstep any boundaries in case she felt that the physical connection was too intimate in front of others.

Finally, everyone left, and as he and Hayley walked back toward the front of the duplex, she turned and reached over, taking his hand. His heart leaped at her initiation. She looked up at him, a gentle smile on her face. "I can't believe what all was done today." They walked inside her house, and both looked around. She was still shaking her head when she marveled, "Look at this place, Sam! Everything is exactly where it should be!" Her breath hitched. "It's beautiful."

He squeezed her hand and agreed, but he wasn't thinking about the furniture placement, the pictures on the wall, or even the way she'd transformed the duplex into a home anyone would love. All he could think about was her words in a different context. She, Eddie, and Hope were exactly where they should be, and it was beautiful.

Choking back the words he wanted to say, he looked over to see a droopy Hope stumbling into the room, dragging her favorite stuffy. She wore a smile on her face but could barely keep her eyes open. Eddie was behind his sister, and his youthful expression was equally a mixture of exhilaration and exhaustion.

"I'll help Eddie if you want to take care of Hope," he offered easily. Hayley didn't answer for a few seconds, and he turned to see her teeth worrying her bottom lip.

"Sam, you've done so much the past couple of days." She shrugged and dropped her gaze before taking a deep breath and lifting her head to stare into his face. "I mean… it is Saturday evening. Are you sure we're not cramping your style?"

He barked out a laugh and shook his head. "First of all, Hayley, I don't have a style. My Saturday nights are usually lounging in my living room, watching some TV, maybe alone or with a friend, catching a game. If the neighbors were partying or too loud, I might go into town and go to the pub just to chat with whoever was there. But a lot of times, I didn't do that in case the party next door got out of hand, and I needed to break it up."

Her brows lowered, and she shook her head. "That doesn't sound like a lot of fun. More responsibility than enjoyment."

He heaved his shoulders and nodded. "Maybe. But in all the years you've known me, was I ever a partier? Someone who went out all the time? Someone always looking for the next place to be?"

She threw her head back and laughed. "No, you're right. I've known you for a long time, and you were never that kind of man."

He leaned down to hold her gaze again and asked, "What's really on your mind?"

Her gaze jerked upward, and she scrunched her nose. "Honestly? I'm just so glad to be here. At first, I worried that I was acting in haste about Eddie's situation at school, but in reality, I needed this change as much as he did. And let's face it... Hope is a *bloom where she's planted* kind of girl."

Sam agreed. "I think that is one of the best descriptions of Hope I've heard."

"I know that Eddie doesn't really remember Edward, but he's seen pictures of the first couple of years of his life with Edward in them. So there's a connection. But Hope? She doesn't really miss what she's never had. And the only man holding her in her baby pictures is you. So I know she feels things deeply, but her feelings are a little different than her brother's."

Realizing the conversation was getting heavy, and not that Sam ever shied away from important conversations with Hayley before, he wanted tonight to be about the peaceful change.

Hayley stepped closer and wrapped her arms around Sam, giving him a hug. "I didn't mean for the conversation to get so deep. Tonight should be about celebrating."

As he wrapped his arms around her, he was once again struck by how in sync the two of them were. "I couldn't agree more. So since it's now established that my Saturday nights are not out partying, and I'd much rather stay here and celebrate with you, let's get the kids in bed so they can get a good night's sleep."

She squeezed his waist, then let go and stepped back, her face more relaxed and her smile wide. "You got it. You handle Eddie, and I'll take care of Hope."

And much to Sam's utter joy, that was exactly what they did. The kids fell straight into bed for the second night in a row without a story. Sam couldn't think of a better Saturday than to spend it with Hayley and the kids, a bunch of friends, and now settling on the couch to watch TV. *This won't be every weekend. And I may have to face her going out sometime. But for now, I'll enjoy every moment of this that I have.*

15

Sam had accompanied Hayley that Monday to register the kids for school. She hated for him to be late for work, but he was resolute, looking at her with a seriousness that sent warmth throughout, calming her nerves.

"Sweetheart, I'm right where I want to be, doing exactly what I want to do." His tone was so definite that she didn't argue further.

She spent the day on pins and needles, walking a tightrope of anticipation. Attempting to find the same calm she'd felt earlier with Sam, she immersed herself in her work. The kids had grown used to seeing her working at the dining room table when they lived in Newport News. Now, she wanted to carve out a place of her own even though she didn't have a separate office space.

The main bedroom in the rental house was larger than what she had in her previous home. Anticipating her need, Sam spent part of the previous day setting up a desk, a small filing cabinet, and a bookcase in the corner of her bedroom near a window overlooking the backyard. It wasn't a large space, but then she didn't need one. Sitting at her desk, she enjoyed the natural light coming through the window, the space fitting her laptop, and organizing materials perfectly.

By the time the kids were expected to get off the school bus, she anxiously paced the living room. Her emotions teetered between eagerness to hear how their first day went and apprehension to find out that they might hate being the new kids. When she was afraid of wearing a path on the rug, she walked out onto the porch so they would see her when they stepped off the bus... and she would see them.

Unexpectedly, Sam's SUV pulled into the driveway. When he climbed down, she watched him walk toward her. His gait was purposeful while still appearing loose-limbed in a way that only a man secure in his skin could be. For a few seconds, as her gaze centered on him, the world's worries fell away. And then he joined her on the porch and smiled down at her. "Hey, sweetheart."

She jolted back to the reality at hand. "Hey, what's up?"

"You think I was going to miss the kids' first day of school getting off the bus?"

His words caught her off guard. "Well, you did go with me this morning to register them."

"That was this morning. Now, I want to see how things went for them."

Her heart filled with joy as her eyes filled with tears, and she reached over to take his hand. So many words rested on the tip of her tongue. *You've always been there for us. You've been there for me. And my feelings have grown deeper—*

The rumble of the oncoming bus halted her thoughts, keeping the words from erupting. Their fingers naturally moved toward each other, linked, and then squeezed tightly. Their expressions held both nerves and dreams. She didn't realize she was holding her breath until Sam whispered, "Breathe," and the air rushed out.

With her eyes trained on the bus, she nearly cried out in joy when Eddie and Hope jumped off the bus steps and raced toward them with huge smiles. And if she wasn't mistaken, she could have sworn she heard a sigh of relief leave Sam's lips.

"Mom! Sam!" both kids called.

The four met in the middle of the walk. Hayley bent to scoop Hope into her arms as her daughter began talking a mile a minute.

"I have a pretty teacher. She said she loved my name. And I got to sit next to a girl whose name is Jessica who was here at our party. And we played outside, and I knew my numbers, and I love this school!"

As much as Hayley wanted to hear all about Hope's day, she glanced over her daughter's shoulder to see Eddie. He lifted his hand and high-fived Sam, his little boy's face smiling widely.

"It was a really good day, Sam. My teacher is nice, and I have Jeremy Perdue in my class. I met him here the other day!"

"Oh, that's Luke and Allie's son," Sam said, nodding.

"You met them the other day. He'll be a good friend. And if Hope is talking about the Jessica she met here, then that's Luke's daughter."

Like a balloon lifting into the air, Hayley's heart felt lighter than it had in months. Eddie looked over toward her, and she offered a reassuring smile in return. "Let's go in, and you can tell me all about your day over a snack."

Sam stood with his hand still on Eddie's shoulder. "I have to head back to the station, but I didn't want to miss your first day of school. Glad it was as good as it was."

"Okay, kids, head inside. I'll be right there." As soon as Eddie and Hope chased each other inside the front door, their laughter filling the air, she moved closer to Sam. Staring up into the face that was so familiar... more familiar than...

She sucked in a hasty breath to halt the direction her thoughts were going. Instead, she placed her hands on his arms and peered deeply into his eyes. "Thank you, Sam. You being here today meant the world to them. And to me, too."

His eyes stayed locked on hers as he leaned forward and kissed her forehead. "See you tonight."

She watched as he retreated to his SUV, then waved as he pulled out of the driveway. Blowing out a long, releasing breath, she hurried inside to hear all about their wonderful first day in the new school.

Hayley couldn't believe she'd already spent a week on the Eastern Shore. She kept waiting for moving remorse to hit. The *"Oh my God, what have I done? I've made a terrible mistake! Ruined everything for my children"* feeling that she half-expected and even feared was oncoming. But surprisingly, it never arrived. Instead, the only emotion she felt was a serenity that seemed to fill the empty cells in her body the way the sunshine flooded through the windows.

Initially, she assumed her relocation would involve seeing Sam often since he lived next door. She glanced toward the wall against her headboard and thought of the scant distance that separated her bedroom from his. *He's not just next door but just on the other side of the wall dividing the duplex.*

But Sam had become a daily presence in their lives, much like when they lost Edward. Back then, she'd barely functioned, so Sam's visits were what held her together as they moved through the early months of their grief journey.

Now, they'd had dinner together every night except for one evening when he was stuck on a case and couldn't get home early enough. Even then, he'd texted to tell her he'd be late and to make sure to tell the kids good night for him if he wasn't there to tuck them in. Their times together were filled with fun, conversation, the kids, and their work.

Wondering about the following weekend in the new house, she had no idea if he planned to spend part, none, or all of it with her and the kids—and found the uncertainty unbalancing. The changing of their situation entwined itself around her heart, adding a layer of complexity to her emotions. And to Eddie's and Hope's emotions. They were quickly becoming used to having Sam intertwined in their lives.

Pushing the tangled thoughts to the background, she was determined to stay busy until the kids got home from school. And what better way than to meet with some of the women who wanted her marketing and web design expertise?

She drove into town and parked outside Jillian's Coffee Shop. Walking inside, Jillian raced forward and hugged her before giving her a tour of the small gallery of local artists in the back and the upstairs loft of the shop. Sitting at one of the tables with a steaming cup of coffee in front of her, she pulled up Jillian's website on her laptop and showed her where improvements could be made. Jillian's smile widened with each suggestion.

Sam had mentioned that Jillian was married to Grant, one of the Baytown Police officers. She'd also learned that Tori was married to Mitch, the police chief of Baytown, and Shiloh's husband was an officer for the Virginia Marine Police. Hope's sweet teacher, Jade Greene, was also married to a police officer. She was beginning to realize how close-knit the community and law enforcement community were. She had felt a sense of belonging when Edward was on the force, and certainly, when he was killed, they rallied. But it was nothing like how she was being enveloped in friendships here.

Jillian looked over Hayley's shoulder and grinned. "It looks like your next customer is arriving."

Just as Hayley turned to see who was approaching, Lia McFarlane, the accountant she met at the party, reached their table, her warm smile beaming her greeting. "It's so nice to see you again, Hayley. I hope you don't think I've hijacked your day, but Jillian thought you and I should meet again soon. I definitely want to hear more about how you can help my business, but... well, we have things in common."

Jillian thanked Hayley and then walked back behind the counter, giving her seat up for Lia. Hayley waited to see what Lia wanted to say.

"I know you're busy, so I'll get straight to the point. I was going to let you know I'm also a widow."

Not expecting those words, Hayley was surprised. "Oh! Lia, I'm so sorry."

"My situation was not a particularly happy one, to begin with. My husband was in the military, and we had a daughter with a hearing impairment. I'm afraid he could never quite understand what needed to be done for a child who had exceptional needs. Emily is bright and so delightful. Her situation was hard for my husband to deal with. He was killed in the service, and while it was so difficult to get used to, I moved out here, looking for a different way of life." She smiled warmly. "I actually met the man of my dreams here, and he's become the best father to Emily I could ever have hoped for."

"I'm so glad you shared, Lia," Hayley gushed, her heart aching for the young mother who had been alone in marriage yet even more alone in widowhood. She now remembered seeing the beautiful little girl, who appeared to be close in age to Eddie, with a hearing aid as well as signing with a few of the other children. "Being a widow so young is something none of us expect. My husband had been in the military but was out and working as a police officer. It was always in the back of my mind that he could be injured or killed on the job. But I never dwelled on it because Edward used to tell me that no good would come from me worrying. But I still remember the day I opened the door and saw Sam, Edward's best friend, and the station chaplain beside him. And behind them was the sergeant and the captain walking toward the house."

Lia reached out and held onto her hand, nodding. "I'm also so sorry that you had to experience that."

For a moment, the two women simply sat and held hands, understanding and shared grief moving between them. The moment was broken when the server brought over more coffee. Moving to a lighter topic, Hayley pulled up the website for the small accounting firm and agreed that it needed updating and possibly reinventing.

Lia stood to return to work and said, "My husband is Aiden. He and his brother Brogan and their sister, Katelyn, own Finn's Pub."

"I've been there with Sam and the kids when we visited before."

Lia held her gaze and said, "Look, it's none of my business." She stopped herself and laughed, shaking her head. "Actually, it's none of our business, but it was pretty obvious to us that Sam has very deep feelings for you."

A rush of heat moved through Hayley's body, and she felt her cheeks burning. "We were good friends before Edward was killed. And he's been my rock since then. I was pregnant with Hope when Edward died."

At that, Lia winced, her face plainly showing her sadness. "I'm so sorry, Hayley. You'll meet Amy Sullivan at an Auxiliary meeting. She's now married to the sheriff of Accawmacke County. She was a single mother who was pregnant when she became a widow." Lia pressed her lips together for a few seconds, then blurted, "All I was going to say earlier is that I don't know if your feelings for Sam are deeper than friendship. But if you have had those thoughts, my advice would be to go for it. Women like us who've suffered great loss know that sometimes you simply have to grab all the happiness you can, when you can." With another warm smile and a wave goodbye, Lia headed out of the coffee shop.

Feeling overwhelmed, she said goodbye to Jillian, then walked along the sunlit sidewalk to visit Tori and Shiloh at the Sea Glass Inn. The beautiful historic bed-and-breakfast was right on the beach road. Hayley was immediately taken with the inn and lost herself in excitement over how they could update their website and reservations.

Finishing with them, she had just enough time for one more stop, ending her afternoon at Sweet Rose Ice Cream Shoppe. They talked about marketing, and she enjoyed a delicious rose-flavored ice cream. Promising to bring the kids back soon, she hurried home, her thoughts filled with new friends and customers, but mostly Lia's words.

Women like us who've suffered great loss know that sometimes you simply have to grab all the happiness you can, when you can. Hayley knew precisely what would make her happy, which would be for Sam to be part of their lives permanently. But she had no idea what his definition of happy would be.

Sam and Aaron met the Virginia Marine Police at the dock behind an old crumbling barn. A reported stolen boat had been sighted by some kids kayaking in one of the inlets. They were surprised when they saw the new speedboat tied to the dock with nothing else around but farmland and the old barn. The VMP would haul it back to the harbor, but since it had been stolen from the owner's dry dock, it had been under the sheriff's jurisdiction.

Once there, they approached the VMP vessel, seeing Aaron's brother, Andy, and Callan Ward. Another officer was inside the wheelhouse, and nearing, they recognized and waved at Joseph Newman.

"Is this the one we've been looking for?" Sam called out.

The old dock was falling apart and too dangerous for anyone to step onto it. Sam and Aaron stayed on the land, and Andy climbed onto the vessel while Callan handled the ropes tethering the two boats together.

Aaron looked at the identification on the boat, then

turned toward Sam and nodded. "I thought it was a match, but I wanted to be sure. Yep, this is Nelson's boat."

"Because it has to be checked out, we'll tow it back to the Baytown Harbor," Callan said.

"We can call Mr. Nelson and let him know where he can go to claim it," Aaron said.

"Make sure you let him know that we'll give him a call when he can come. We need to process it first."

"Do you want us to send forensics to the harbor?" Sam asked.

Callan looked around and nodded. "Because of the state of the dock, there's no way that a thief could have hauled the boat here by land and then lowered it into the water. It would have to have been brought here by way of the bay and inlets. Normally, I would look for more evidence here and have your guys come out, but this had to have been an all-water job once they got the boat away from the Nelson's place."

"Our people have scoured that area, and it appears that whoever took it, lowered it from the dry dock straight into the water," Sam surmised.

Aaron and Andy chatted as Andy hooked the stolen boat to the VMP vessel, Callan called out to Sam.

"Tell Hayley that if she calls Sophia my wife has a line on a man who needs a website set up for some kind of alumni event. Sophia helped him with his interior decorating, and she thought of Hayley after the picnic."

"Sounds good. Text me Sophie's number, and I'll give it to Hayley. I'm sure she'll be excited about another possible new customer."

Goodbyes were called out, and Sam watched as the VMPs pulled away from the old dock, the stolen vessel trailing behind. Walking back to Sam's SUV, Aaron looked over and asked, "How is Hayley settling in?"

"Really good. She's already getting so many work requests out here on the shore to keep her busy. She enjoys this work much better than just working for her firm."

"Why doesn't she just start her own business here? Or, if her firm would agree, they could move her down to part-time."

"I asked her that, but she reminded me that their health insurance is through her job. They lose her health insurance if she goes down to part-time or quits and works for herself."

"Damn, I never even thought about that."

Sam nodded as he pulled out onto the road and headed toward the Nelson house. He felt Aaron's stare on the side of his head and glanced over to see a pinched, contemplative expression on his partner's face. "What?"

Aaron shrugged. "I was just thinking that if the two of you get married, then she and the kids would fall under your health insurance plan with the county."

Sam's body jerked slightly, and he lifted a brow but remained silent. Aaron's hands jumped up as he quickly added, "Not trying to freak you out. I'm just throwing that out there."

Sam sighed heavily. "Yeah, I hear you."

"Do you really, Sam? I mean, it was obvious to everybody that you and Hayley have a long-standing, close friendship. Lots of history and emotions are shared between the two of you. But I'd catch her looking at you sometimes, and I would swear it was more than friendship. And hell, you can barely contain the way you really feel about her when you look her way."

Sam wanted to argue, but the words halted in his throat.

Aaron continued. "I might not have found it yet, but I've been around a helluva lot of people who've fallen in love. Think about Andy—it wasn't until Ivy reappeared in his life that he realized what he felt all along. I don't know Hayley well enough to know if she'll ever want to get married again. You know her better than anybody."

Sam thought about what Aaron said. As close as they were, he did know her better than anyone else. But as to whether or not she'd ever want to move forward with him, he had no idea.

"Just don't let the idea of trying something and then it going south keep you from grasping at real happiness."

Sam barked out laughter. "What the hell happened to my partner? Are you getting advice from the Dr. Phil show?"

"Shut up, fucker," Aaron quipped. "And stop deflecting. The bottom line is, you have a chance to take what's already a great relationship with Hayley and those kids and turn it into something more permanent."

"What if it all gets fucked up?" Sam mumbled under his breath.

"That kind of fear will keep you from ever having

real happiness," Aaron said. Then grinning, he added, "And yeah, I think that did come from Dr. Phil."

Snorting, Sam couldn't hold back his laughter. But as they continued down the road in silence, he wondered if Aaron was right.

16

Hayley drove north of Baytown, noting that the houses on the bay couldn't be seen because they were set back from the road, and large trees and natural shrubs lined the road, obscuring the view. Her phone rang, and she pressed the hands-free answering on her car.

"Hello?"

"Hayley, it's Sophie. I just talked to Mr. Young, and he's excited to meet with you."

"Good! I'm almost to the turnoff to his house."

"You're going to love it. I think his family has been on the Eastern Shore for several generations. At least, that was what he told me when I was decorating his home. I'm pretty sure his family owned a farm at one time."

"I really appreciate you getting me in contact with him. I swear, I'm going to have so much business on the Eastern Shore, I might have to start turning people away."

"You should do this full-time," Sophie encouraged.

"Yes, but there's something called job security when you have kids. Also, my retirement savings and health insurance."

Sophie sighed. "Ugh. I know what you mean. It was hard when I first opened my own interior design business here. It wasn't until I got the contract at the Dunes Resort to work on some of the houses that were going to be in *Southern Living Magazine* that I could finally take the plunge. Of course, it helped that Callan and I were getting together at the time, so when we got married, I went on his health insurance."

"It's too bad we have to think about these things, isn't it? You know, being a grown-up." Laughing, she said, "Well, I'm at his house. I'll talk to you later."

Disconnecting the call, she turned off the road, threading her way between towering pine trees. The tires crunched over the white driveway created from crushed oyster shells. Finally, the trees gave way to expose a large house perched atop a dune overlooking the Chesapeake Bay.

"Wow," she enthused as she stared at the beautiful home. By the time she parked in the front of the house and fetched her laptop case from the passenger seat, the front door was thrown open. A large man stood in the doorway and smiled widely. His barrel-chested body was smartly adorned in khaki pants and a long-sleeved casual knit shirt. His steel-gray hair was shot with white, trimmed close on the sides. As she approached, his mature features gave evidence of a youthful handsomeness that had aged to attractive and distinguished.

"Hello! You must be Mrs. Brooks," he boomed as his

eyes met hers, and the corners crinkled slightly as he smiled.

She returned his smile. "I am, and you're Mr. Young?"

"Please, call me Malcolm. Doesn't matter how old I am, Mr. Young always makes me think of my father." He stepped to the side, ushering her into the entry foyer. From there, she had a straight view of the large family room at the back of the house, with full windows facing the bay. He walked in that direction, and she followed, awestruck with what was obviously Sophie's beautiful decor and a magnificent home. Stepping into the family room, she gasped at the floor-to-ceiling windows that rose two stories to the vaulted ceiling. Glancing over her shoulder, she could see the upstairs had an overlooking loft and a perfect view of the bay.

"Your home is stunning," she said, turning from side to side, trying to take it all in.

"Thank you! We like it. My wife and I had it built several years ago but recently had Mrs. Ward do all the interior design for us."

An attractive middle-aged woman walked in carrying two iced teas.

"Here's my beautiful wife, Anne," Malcolm said, walking over to take the glasses from her.

"It's lovely to meet you, Mrs. Brooks. Please don't think I'm being rude, but I know Malcolm will tell you all about his fraternity, and I assure you, I've heard it all before." Anne spoke with a twinkle in her eyes and no malevolence in her voice. "I'll leave you two to talk about DEPA." She waved her hand casually to the side, and her gaze rested warmly on her husband. "Forgive me if I don't listen to the virtues of the fraternity for the millionth time."

After she left, Hayley sat on one of the sofas and gave her attention to him. "Why don't you tell me what you're looking for? I understand you'd like a website for your fraternity alumni, not a business. Is that correct?"

Malcolm nodded with enthusiasm. "That's absolutely right. I attended the University of Richmond, class of 1980, and was inducted into the Delta Epsilon Phi Alpha fraternity."

"Oh, that's the DEPA your wife referred to."

Malcolm chuckled. "Yes, exactly. It's a much easier way to refer to our beloved fraternity. We were very active on campus, but as alumni, we've begun to lose touch with some of the members over the years. Other than some of the past alumni officers continuing to go to the national conference, the fraternity alumni have mostly kept up with each other through letters and phone calls originally and then eventually using social media. I'm now the president of the fraternity's alumni. I want us to have a website that will post announcements, the new members from the university, and a directory of all the alumni. I'd even like to have a section for fallen members so that those of us reaching a certain age can know when someone passes."

"I think this is a wonderful idea and could easily help design one for you."

"I will be paying for this myself, preferring to keep the alumni money for our charitable organizations."

Lifting her brow, she said, "Let me caution you that

when you are no longer the alumni association president, or in the eventuality of your death, if no one else has access to the back end of the website, then it wouldn't continue."

Blustering, he shook his head quickly. "Oh, I didn't mean that it would be my website. I just didn't know how much it would cost for the design and upkeep and was willing to put in the money to make it happen."

"Since it's for a nonprofit organization, you wouldn't have to worry about a lot of things that a business would. The design could be fairly simple to set up, and as long as each new president or the officers... or however you wanted to do it, had access, they could handle any updates and changes. Does this sound like what you're hoping to do?"

"Absolutely!" Malcolm agreed, his smile wide as he enthusiastically nodded his head. "In fact, I wouldn't want to be the sole person who had access. I understand there's a danger in just one person being responsible for anything. And being in a fraternity taught us how to work together to solve problems."

"Excellent. Then let me show you a mock-up I created." She opened her laptop and then cautioned, "Now, keep in mind this is a very basic mock-up for you to get an idea of the types of things that might go onto the site and for you to let me know of changes you'd like to make."

They spent the next half hour going through what she'd designed as a preliminary site, and he proclaimed that he loved how she organized it.

"Can there be a section of photographs? Sort of a down-through-the-years type of section?"

"Absolutely. And since that would constantly be changing, you could put out a call to the alumni members. I assume they're considered alumni as soon as they graduate from college, correct?"

"Yes, that's right. Although they do pay annual dues, I'm sure a few choose not to. Why they wouldn't is beyond me!" he huffed, shaking his head.

She suppressed a grin. Clearing her throat, she added, "You could have a section going back to the earliest days where someone can provide photographs, right through the days that you were there in the late seventies, and then continue it on. Depending on how many photographs you get, you might want to organize it in terms of decades, or it could be classes."

Malcolm's grin continued to widen as she talked. Standing quickly, he motioned for her to follow. "Let me show you something."

She followed him into a nearby room that was obviously a study, with built-in bookcases and a large desk over to one side and a matching credenza behind. He began pulling down several photo albums, flipping through them until he came to what he was looking for. "Are these the kind of photographs that you're thinking of?"

In front of her were pictures of college students from years ago. Her gaze landed on one with clear light blue eyes, just like those staring at her now.

"Is this you?" she asked, pointing at the laughing young man, surrounded by others.

"Yes! I tell you, those were some of the best years of my life. We studied hard, but we played hard. We felt like being part of the fraternity was just as important as our college choice. It wasn't all partying, you understand. We were active in many community service projects. In fact, I feel certain that most of us are still involved in our communities, using the skills we learned. Being in DEPA was much more than just being a frat boy."

Her gaze scanned several more photographs, and it seemed like most of them centered on him and three other young men. "I take it these were your closest friends?"

His gaze was on the photograph, and he nodded. "Right, again, Mrs. Brooks." His voice was now softer, tinged with what sounded like pride as he pointed at the individual men. "That was Ted Redford, Michael Salzberg, and Brian Harcourt. We're still friends today, I'm pleased to say. But then, I'm sure that each DEPA class has the same relationships with some of their brothers who went through the initiations together."

She looked up and smiled. "I've heard about some of those initiations. Were they as wild and harrowing as the news and movies make them out to be?"

He belted out his laughter and shook his head. "Oh my, no. They were certainly character building, but not hazing."

"These pictures are certainly the type you could ask other classes to send you. I would have them make sure they identify the people in the photographs. Once the website is built, it will be something easy for you to maintain." She glanced back at the pictures again, thinking of the men in front of her as young eighteen-year-old college freshmen with their whole lives in front of them. "You're still close with them?"

He chuckled and said, "All three are coming to my house soon. We get together several times a year, and since I have the most gorgeous view, they often come here."

Laughing, she looked out the window again and couldn't argue that his joking boast was probably true. As their meeting drew to a close, she promised to bring a revised mock-up for their next encounter. He escorted her to the door, thanking her profusely for her work. As she drove home, her mind began to weave through the personalities and new friends she'd met since her arrival.

Her freelance projects offered a sense of fulfillment that was lacking in her mundane full-time marketing job for the large company. She exhaled heavily, pondering the dilemma of accomplishing all the work for the people in her life now and keeping her full-time job.

Shaking off her work-induced worries, she focused on something much more uplifting and hurried home in plenty of time to meet the school bus. Seeing Eddie's and Hope's radiant faces with huge smiles each day when they alighted from the bus affirmed the rightness of their move to the Eastern Shore.

That evening, as they sat around the dinner table, Eddie once again plied Sam with questions about his day. "Did you figure out who stole the TVs?"

"Well, I have to tell you that I had my suspicions about the owner of the house," Sam said.

Eddie's eyes widened as he gasped. "The owner! Why would he want to steal his own things?"

"Well, technically, he couldn't steal his own things because they belong to him. But I thought maybe he was allowing someone else to steal his things so that he could get the insurance money."

Hayley knew the concept of insurance was over Eddie's head, but she also knew Sam would patiently explain.

"What that means is that when we have valuable things, we pay some money to insure them so that if they are stolen or damaged, then the insurance company will pay us money to replace them."

Sam waited, and Hayley glanced toward Eddie, seeing him give careful consideration to Sam's words. Eddie turned toward Hayley and asked, "Do we have insurance, Mom?"

"Yes, we do. I have insurance on the things in our house. And I have insurance on my car. And we have insurance in case one of us gets sick."

"If someone stole our car, you'd get some money?"

"Yes. I have to pay for the insurance, so it's not free. But if someone stole our car, or if a storm damaged it, then I would contact the insurance company and work with them to get some money to buy another car." The explanation was simplistic, but for an nine-year-old, it was all he needed.

Eddie turned his attention back to Sam. "But it wasn't the owner who had someone steal his things?"

"No, it wasn't. The next people I suspected were his house cleaners. They would know what was in each house and have keys to get in since they came often. As it turns out, it was neither of the housekeepers but it was a cousin of one of them. When we questioned her, she admitted that her cousin came along with her one day because he was on his way somewhere else, and she was giving him a lift. He stole the key and made a copy. He also returned with her to one of the houses to see what kind of security was on the house."

Eddie's eyes grew round, and he bounced in his chair slightly. "So you *did* catch the bad guys!"

Sam laughed and leaned over to ruffle Eddie's hair. "Yes, we did. It's not always the first suspect we have or the first idea we think of. But if we slowly review the facts and look at everything carefully, we usually come up with the answer."

Hope, no longer willing to be left out of a conversation, piped up, "Did you arrest him? Did you put handcuffs on him?"

Sam's chest moved as his deep laughter rumbled out. Leaning toward Hope, he tapped her on the nose and nodded. "Yes, we did."

Suddenly, Hope's smile faded. "Is jail a really scary place?"

Sam looked toward Hayley, both of them sending wide-eyed, *"What the hell do we say?"* looks to each other. Deciding to handle the question, Hayley said, "Do you remember when you have time-out, and I won't let you watch TV or play games?"

Hope nodded. "I don't like time-out."

"Well, jail is kind of like that for grown-ups. It's not a fun place to be. It's a punishment. But you don't need to worry about anything else right now. Just think of it as a grown-up time-out where they can't do any of the things they really like to do."

Hope thought for a second, then shrugged, digging back into her mac and cheese. Hayley shared another look with Sam, this time both hiding their grins. It was obvious that Sam wanted to move the conversation away from his work, so he began asking about school.

Hope and Eddie reported that they loved school and had run into many of the kids they met at the welcome picnic in classes, the halls, lunch, or recess. It gave her children a sense of belonging, and once again, Hayley knew she was in the right place.

And looking across the table at the man who held her heart, she knew she was also with the right person. And maybe... just maybe, now was the time to see if he felt the same way.

17

Sam stayed until the kids were in bed, as had become his habit. He was almost afraid that Hayley would ask him to give them some space one day. He hoped she wouldn't but would understand if she did.

While Hayley was saying her last good night, he walked downstairs and into the living room. Restless, he didn't immediately move to the sofa. Instead, he walked over to the mantel and studied the photographs filling the frames. There were a few with Edward—him sitting on the hospital bed with Hayley, holding newborn Eddie, and another one taken at Christmastime when Eddie was almost two. But Sam was also prominently displayed. A photograph of him, Hayley, Eddie, and newborn Hope, as well as others throughout the past seven years.

In all the years since Edward died, Sam had often looked at the pictures, missing his close friend, hoping he was doing the right thing for Edward's family. His gaze moved across the photographs again, and he was struck with one that was now missing. Hayley had always kept a framed picture of her and Edward's wedding day. But now, it was no longer displayed on the living room mantel.

He lifted his hand and rubbed his chin, pondering the change. Perhaps she just needed more room on the mantel. Or maybe—

"Hey, looking at the pictures?"

He was startled, having not heard Hayley come down the stairs. He turned to watch as she walked toward him, a gentle sway to her hips and a barely-there smile on her lips. Her gaze followed where his was now, moving over the photographs.

"Yeah, I was taking a look. It's amazing to see the kids so little then and how much they've grown, isn't it?"

"I know! I love each stage they go through and what they're learning to do. Yet, I find myself wanting to hold on tight, afraid the years will pass so quickly before I even realize it."

She turned toward him, her gaze now roaming over his face, searching, and then a little crinkle formed between her brows. "What are you thinking about? You looked very contemplative when I came downstairs."

Swallowing deeply, he gathered his courage, no longer willing to be silent. Yet fear like he'd never known in his life moved through his veins. Everything could change, and not knowing which way the change would go sent him straight to standing on the precipice of a cliff, stepping off into the chasm. Would he crash on the rocks below, or would a hidden bridge arise to hold him up?

"Your wedding picture isn't here."

Refusing to look away, he held Hayley's gaze with an intensity that conveyed the gravity of their conversation. She swallowed deeply. He could swear her lips quivered slightly if his eyes were not playing tricks on him.

"Yeah. I... um... placed it in my bedroom." She spoke so softly, her voice barely rising above a whisper. The soft echo drifted across the space between them.

Nodding slowly, he hesitated before prodding for more. "Why?"

Her lips parted, and he feared a hollow answer would be given when all he wanted was her honesty. She swallowed again, her lips visibly quivering this time. "It was time."

"Time for what?" He continued to nudge softly.

Her fingers grabbed the hem of her sweater, mindlessly fiddling and tugging on the material. "My wedding to Edward will always be a special memory, but it was a decade ago." Her gaze cut to the side, her eyes once again moving over the framed photographs. "I thought it was more important to maintain his place of honor with Eddie in the pictures."

Her answer was rational. Respectful. And wholly logical. Yet a pang of disappointment gnawed at him. Pushing away the emotion, he nodded, ready to offer a gracious response. But before he could say anything else, she continued.

"And ... I'm ready to move forward."

The pace of his heartbeat changed. Or maybe it was just that the sound was now audible, and he was surprised she didn't hear it. "Move forward?"

She nodded, her eyes filled with vulnerability. "See if there's something out there for me. Well, me and the kids. I came out here for a new start for all of us, and I'm ready to put my heart back out on the line. But I'm scared."

He turned his body to fully face her. They were still several feet apart, and he battled the urge to move closer. She was trying to tell him something but seemed so afraid with her carefully chosen words that he wasn't sure what she wanted to convey. "What are you scared of, sweetheart?"

Her answer was so soft he almost missed it. "You."

His eyes widened, not expecting that answer, and his chin jerked back. "Me? Why on earth would you be scared of me?"

"Because I'm scared of losing you."

Now convinced her fear was of losing his friendship if she started dating someone, he sucked in a breath that burned as it moved into his lungs. "You're never going to lose me, Hayley."

"Promise?"

He closed the distance between them and reached down to pull her fingers away from her sweater, calming her actions as he wrapped his hand around her. "I promise."

Her gaze never strayed from his face. He hoped sincerity was conveyed in his eyes, offering empowerment.

She spoke again, her voice filled with fragile courage. "Even if I told you that I want to move forward with you?"

With those words, his heart seemed to stop and then restarted, slamming against his rib cage, pounding thunderously. "Move forward with me?"

She nodded slowly as both hope and fear filled her eyes.

"I know whatever you're trying to tell me, Hayley, it's probably the most significant conversation we've ever had. But too much is at risk, and I don't want to misunderstand you. So I need you to tell me plainly what you're thinking, and I promise you that I will always be here for you."

Her tongue slowly dragged over her bottom lip. She inhaled deeply, and then the air whooshed out on her exhalation. "What I feel for you… you are my best friend in the world. At one time, that title belonged to Edward. But that was many years ago. And in the years since, you've moved from just being a good friend to being my best friend. And somewhere along the line, the love I feel for you has only deepened. I don't want to lose that friendship, Sam. But if there's any chance that you could love me, not as a friend, but as a woman, a potential partner, a lover… um… because that's what I'm feeling—"

Her words dissolved into silence as his lips found hers, unable to hold back his desire to kiss her. A jolt of energy surged through him, setting every nerve ending ablaze. The electricity of the kiss was more potent than anything he'd ever felt in his life. His first marriage was a long time ago, but he still knew, without a doubt, that he'd never felt such a pull as he did with Hayley. Beyond that thought, all rational musings fled his mind. His cock reacted, swelling in his jeans, but he leaned his hips back, not about to make their first kiss anything other than just a kiss. He let go of her hand only to lift his hands to cup her cheeks. Her hands slipped around his waist, holding tight.

Resolved to take everything slow, he shifted the angle of his head so that his mouth sealed more firmly over hers. Every molecule in his body felt alive and completely tuned to her. Her breath hitched just before a little moan slipped out, quickly swallowed by him.

His tongue slid into her mouth, gliding over hers, the velvety softness sending tingles along his spine. Her breath was fresh and minty like she'd just brushed her teeth before coming downstairs. The taste was intoxicating, and as he continued to explore her mouth fully, her tongue pushed back, gliding into his mouth, too.

His senses were on overload, firing in every direction. He wanted to memorize every nuance, every touch, every scent, every taste.

Hayley never wore perfume, but he inhaled the delicate floral scent of her shampoo, and it fired his blood as much as it warmed his heart. He vowed to be a gentleman and not pull her closer, afraid she'd discover just how hard his cock was. But she moved forward, tightening her arms around his waist. Now, with his erection nestled against her soft belly, it took every ounce of self-control not to grind himself on her.

Discovering the heaven to be found in kissing

Hayley, he wasn't sure he'd ever be able to return to his lonely existence again. His life had changed as if the earth altered its path around the sun. Everything he knew fell away, leaving only his desire for this woman to stay where she was in his arms.

Finally, their kissing slowed to gentle nibbles before they barely separated.

Her lips were red and kissed-swollen, and her eyes blinked as though waking from a dream. Their breaths came out in raspy pants. His thumbs gently glided over her soft cheeks. Her fingers were on the sides of his waist, digging in slightly as she clutched his shirt tightly.

Fear struck him to the core for an instant, afraid she would backtrack, apologize, and say it wasn't right. But instead, her lips curved slowly while her eyes stayed glued on him.

He leaned so their foreheads touched and held her close until they finally eased backward ever so slowly.

"Wow." The one word uttered from her lips that he'd just kissed was said with such reverence that he wanted to kiss her again.

Instead, he nodded and agreed. "*Wow* is right, sweetheart."

"I was so afraid to say anything to you," she admitted. "I was willing to just stay friends for the rest of our lives than to risk saying or doing anything that would make you not want to be around me."

"I have to tell you, Hayley, that I felt the same way. But I was recently advised that it was time for me to move forward with you, and I was just trying to figure out when the right time was to do it. I'm so happy you had the guts to be honest with me."

Her teeth worried the corner of her bottom lip for a moment. "Do you know Lia McFarlane?"

"Not very well, but I'm friends with her husband, Aiden."

"I met her recently, and she told me that she was also a widow with a little girl."

"I don't think I realized that. I just thought she was Aiden's biological daughter."

She smiled. "Yes, that's what Lia said. She also told me that the sheriff of Acawmacke County... I think his name was Liam—"

"Yeah, that's right. He's married with a couple of little girls."

"Well, those girls were his wife's before she met him."

Sam's eyes widened as he nodded. "Didn't know that either." He tucked a strand of hair behind her ear. "Looks like families come in all ways, don't they?"

A soft smile graced her face. "Lia told me that I needed to take a chance, too. I've been thinking about it so much, maybe even before we moved out here. But especially since we've been here." The air rushed from her lungs. "Oh, Sam, I finally decided to take a chance."

His palm cupped her cheek. "I don't really remember when my feelings for you changed from friendship to more, sweetheart. I hated moving away, but I needed to for my work, and I had to admit that seeing you with Dave was hard. But I thought if I weren't there, you'd be able to build something with him if that's what you wanted."

"I think that's the most selfless gift I've ever heard of anybody giving. Certainly, it's the most selfless gift I've ever been offered. But, Sam, it was never going to work with anyone else. Because the truth is, it only made me realize that I was in love with you."

As soon as the word love left her mouth, her fingers twitched, and she jerked, her wide-eyed gaze shooting up to him. She opened her mouth as if to refute what she'd just said, but he jumped in.

"Don't you dare take that back."

"Is it too soon to mention love?" Her voice was once again barely a whisper.

"Is it true? Do you love me?" he gently demanded.

Her head slowly moved up and down. "Yes, it is true. I do love you."

Still cupping her face, he brought her close and kissed her lightly. Finding the kiss as sweet as the first, he leaned back and said, "No, it's not too soon. And just so there's no misunderstanding, I love you too."

"And the kids?"

He regarded her carefully. "I'm not sure exactly what you're asking, Hayley. If you're asking if I love Eddie and Hope, I think you know the answer. I've always loved the kids as though they were my own."

She grinned. "I know that. I guess I was wondering exactly how we'll handle the change in our relationship, not only with us but in relation to them."

"I say let's not make a big deal of it right now. I'm over here all the time, and the kids have certainly seen us hold hands, hug, and even sit closely together watching TV. I honestly don't think they'll think that much about it if we end up kissing in front of them. We'll ease into a little more displays of affection, and they won't be surprised to realize we're a couple."

Chewing on her bottom lip again, he pressed his thumb on the reddened flesh. "What are you thinking about?"

"I thought maybe this was a good time to let you know that Allie asked Eddie and Hope to spend the night with them tomorrow night since they're now friends with Jeremy and Jessica."

Sam's brain immediately jumped at what he and Hayley could do with an entire night with no kids around. His smile widened. "Are you thinking what I'm thinking?"

"I hope so," she said, laughing. "I thought maybe it would be a good time for you and me to have a sleepover, too."

He picked her up and twirled her gently, loving the sound of soft laughter falling from her lips. As he slowly lowered her to the floor, their mouths sealed once again. Laughter from her had now slid into second place, as he decided that kissing her was definitely at the top of his list.

18

Hayley's fingers nervously gripped the porcelain edge of the bathroom sink, her knuckles pale against the cool, smooth surface. Her eyes amped up with a swipe of mascara and a soft eye shadow, stared back at her from the mirror. Her hair fell about her shoulders in soft waves. The illumination of the room cast a glow on her face. The hint of blush on her cheeks matched the rose-hued dress. The fabric draped over her curves, a shirred bodice elevating her figure while a wide belt cinched her waist.

She closed her eyes, trying to steady her breathing in an effort to calm her racing heart. She accepted the fact that her body was no longer nineteen years old. She accepted the fact that she was going to have sex tonight with a man she'd known for years and had grown to love beyond friendship. She didn't fear awkwardness because she and Sam had already seen each other at their worst.

And she didn't fear having sex with another man

besides Edward. She'd loved her husband and would have given anything if he'd lived to enjoy the future they'd envisioned when they were first married. But there was no changing the past. No denying that widowhood had created a different person for herself.

What caused her stomach to tremble was that she hadn't had sex since Edward died. Almost eight years had passed since she'd last made love with anyone. She suddenly snorted, lifting her chin and staring at her reflection. *It's got to be just like riding a bike, right? You never forget how. I've seen sex in movies. Read them in romance novels. It's not like I don't know that part A goes into slot B.*

At that thought, she laughed aloud, then shook her head. "Oh God, I'm losing my mind."

A knock on the front door snapped her out of her reverie, and she cursed softly under her breath. She looked at the clock by her bedside as she hurried through the room, realizing she'd spent more time standing in the bathroom than she'd meant to. Halfway down the stairs, she realized she hadn't put on her shoes. Not stopping, she rushed to the door and threw it open, seeing Sam standing on the porch with a gorgeous smile on his face.

In fact, everything about him was gorgeous. His neatly trimmed hair was just starting to get a touch of early gray. He wore dark pants and a dark suit jacket with a white shirt open at the collar. *Jesus, he's more beautiful than I've ever thought, and I've always thought he was handsome.*

The smile on his face slowly morphed into an expression of concern. "Are you okay, sweetheart?"

"I don't have my shoes on."

His gaze dropped to her feet, then traveled slowly back up her body, sending tingles straight through her. When his gaze landed on her face again, he said, "I can see that. But I don't think that's an unsurmountable problem that would keep us from having dinner."

That was another reason she was dressed up. It wasn't just that the kids were out of the house, having a fun night with other friends. It was that Sam wanted to take her to dinner. Just the two of them. They'd eaten out many times before, but never as a *couple*. He said he wanted something special, but she knew it was because he didn't want her to think it was just about sex. *But it is... just about sex.* "I don't want to put my shoes on."

He blinked. Slowly. "I don't know of a restaurant that's gonna let us in without shoes, Hayley."

She realized she wasn't making any sense as confusion filled his eyes. She shook her head, trying to dislodge the crazy thoughts flying through her head and settle them all into place. "What I mean is that I don't want to go to dinner."

His expression fell. "I see. Well, can I at least come in, and we can talk about... your shoes?"

Instead of stepping back, she blurted, "I don't need dinner. I mean, it's not that I won't be hungry at some point tonight. But I don't need you to take me to dinner. We can go to dinner anytime. Alone or with the kids, it doesn't matter. But right now, all I want is you. You, me, us. I want us to do what we both want, which is to go to bed. Specifically, I mean sex. But I haven't had sex in a long time. I haven't had sex since Edward died." Her shoulders drooped as a heavy sigh left her lips. "Oh God, I'm messing this all up."

Now, Sam shook his head, his lips curving upward. "Sweetheart, you're not messing anything up. It took me a while, but I think I get what you're saying. Tonight is about us, not menus, fine china, and candlelight. Right now, you want to cut out being around other people and just focus on our intimacy."

His words, tinged with the raw sincerity that had first drawn her to him years ago, washed over her like a calming wave. She jerked her head up and down in agreement. "Yes, that's exactly it. I just want to have as much time as we can tonight for you and me."

"And that makes you nervous?"

"Terrified. I'm really nervous about the sex. Or rather, not us *having* sex, but what you're going to think since I'm not sure I even remember what to do." Her cheeks grew warm, and she was sure her face was red and blotchy. "Well, at least I'm sure I remember the basics." She dropped her chin and stared at her bare feet, noting that at least her toenails were painted the same rose color as her dress.

He placed his hand on her stomach and gently pushed her backward, stepping inside her living room. With his knuckle underneath her chin, he looked down and lifted her face so that her gaze was staring straight into his eyes. Her breath caught in her throat. She understood what it meant to want something so badly, be on the cusp of having it, and simultaneously be terrified of it.

"Stop overthinking," he ordered, his words teasing and gentle. "I'd love to take you out, but you're right. We can do that anytime. Tonight was just supposed to be about us. Being here at home and focusing on ourselves is probably the best thing we can do. So, darling, don't worry about how long it's been. Just focus on how much I want you and hopefully how much you want me."

"I do. More than I can say." She lifted on her toes, and they met in a sweet kiss. She wondered if he would take it deeper, but for right then, he kept it light.

"Tell me what you'd like to do," he encouraged.

Suddenly emboldened by all that was Sam, how much he meant to her, and how he truly knew her better than anyone else in her life, she smiled. "I want us to go upstairs. To my bedroom. To my bed. And I want you to take away all my insecurities and fears and just love me."

His drop-dead-gorgeous grin widened into a smile that warmed her heart and caused her womb to clench.

"Sweetheart, your wish is my command."

He slid his hand from her face to her fingers, where they linked tightly, and he led her upstairs to her bedroom. Once there, she pushed all nerves to the side, dropping his hand and sweeping her hair over her shoulder as she presented her back to him. "Unzip me?"

The zipper lowered slowly down her back, the sound easily heard in the quiet house. His hands slid underneath the material at each shoulder, and he gently pulled it down her arms. She let the dress pool on the floor, then turned around.

Wearing peach satin panties with lace around the top and a matching peach satin bra, she once again felt emboldened as his hot gaze roved over her body. She had originally spent money on new lingerie when she first went out with Dave. She didn't expect he'd ever see it, but somehow, it felt like a gift she wanted to give herself. Seeing Sam stare while offering a wolfish grin in obvious appreciation, she was glad she had spent the money on lingerie.

"My God, Hayley. You are more beautiful than anything I could've imagined, and I won't lie. Lately, I've imagined a lot. In fact," he said, inclining his head toward the wall behind her headboard. "I lay in bed just on the other side of that wall and think of you being so close."

"I have, too," she admitted. A tremulous smile curved her lips as she stepped closer. Her hands moved to his jacket. Sliding the material over his shoulders, she grabbed it before his jacket hit the floor. She folded it and neatly placed it over the bench at the end of the bed. When she turned around, he was undoing the buttons on his shirt, but she brushed his hands to the side, taking over the task. Once it was off, she folded his shirt and placed it next to the jacket. He was already toeing off his shoes and then sliding down his pants by the time she made it back over to him. He pulled his wallet out of the pants pocket and tossed it to her nightstand. His pants also went on the bench while he pulled off his socks.

Now, they stood, she in her matching satin lingerie and he in his boxer briefs that did little to hide his erection. His body was beautiful, and she was no longer self-conscious.

With trembling fingers, she reached behind her and unhooked her bra, dropping it to the floor. He moved closer and lifted his hands, his palms covering her breasts before he circled her nipples with his thumbs. She breathed out a hiss at the ache elicited by his simple touch. She squirmed slightly, rubbing her legs together, a need for friction building in her core. He backed her up until she was against the bed, and his hands left her breasts as they circled her waist. He lifted her onto the bed. She lay back, and his fingers hooked into her panties as he dragged them down her legs. Then he stood and simply stared.

The initial urge to close her legs or cover herself was almost overwhelming, but she was determined to lay herself bare in front of him emotionally and physically.

"At the risk of repeating myself, Hayley, you are so fucking gorgeous."

He crawled over her, then lowered himself on his forearms, taking her mouth in a searing kiss that went beyond friendship and straight into lovers. Their heads moved back and forth, and their tongues tangled. She lost herself in the sensations but, staring at him, found herself in his eyes.

She started to moan when his lips left hers, but then he kissed his way down her jaw to her neck, sucking slightly before moving to each breast, kissing, licking, and nipping before pulling a taut bud deeply into his mouth. Now, her core screamed for the friction to be eased, and all she wanted was for his cock to be in her.

"I don't want to wait," she moaned.

"I promise, babe, I just want to get you ready."

He left her breasts, and she groaned again as he kissed his way over her mound and spread her legs with his hands before latching his mouth over her sex. Her eyes nearly rolled back in her head as she forgot how to breathe. His talented mouth licked and teased before he added his fingers, and her orgasm hit, the pulsing sensation finally causing her to suck in much-needed oxygen.

She was relieved he was taking charge because she wasn't sure her body would be able to move when her release eased, and her muscles relaxed. She was barely aware that he had shifted away from her until the cool air moved over her body. She rolled her head to the side to watch him grab his wallet and pull out a condom.

"I haven't had sex in years," she reminded.

"It's been a while for me, too, and I get checked at work. I'm clean, and we'll talk about the idea of more kids later, but I want you completely comfortable."

"You're right, honey. I'm not on birth control, and it only makes sense to be careful."

She watched as he rolled the condom over his impressive erection. He crawled back over her body and smiled as he slowly lowered his lips to hers. He kissed her, then leaned up just enough to line his cock to her entrance. Easing himself in, she gasped at the fullness. Once he was fully seated, her hands kneaded his ass as she urged him to move.

He started slow, but she wanted more. She began to

lift her hips, and it took several tries, but they finally moved in sync, thrusting and parrying in a dance as old as time. The friction she sought was everything she hoped it would be.

She couldn't imagine that she had it within her to have another orgasm, but she felt it building, and her fingers shifted up to his back, her nails digging in slightly. Suddenly, the coils that had twisted inside sprang free, and she cried out as her body shook underneath his.

As she was coming down off the high, she felt him quicken the pace of his thrusts. His face flushed as the corded muscles in his neck tightened just before he cried out his own release.

He stayed planted in her as deeply as possible, with her legs wrapped around his waist, holding him tight. Finally, her body relaxed, and she loosened her grip. He slowly pulled from her and rolled to the side, his arms encircling her body. They lay facing each other, hearts laid bare. There were no secrets with this man. Nothing about her was hidden. She knew everything about him and loved him fiercely. "Thank you. Thank you for this."

"You don't ever have to thank me for loving you."

"But you need to know, Sam, that I do truly love you."

They moved together, their lips meeting in a long, slow kiss. A kiss that told of hearts broken that now were mended. Of battles fought and now won. Of having come from the depths of despair to the soaring heights of mountain tops.

They slowly separated, ending the kiss, and he left

her side to move to the bathroom. She heard the toilet flush and the water in the sink run. When he came back, she was still in the same place, a smile on her face. "I thought nothing was as gorgeous as seeing you naked walking toward me. But I have to tell you that the back side of you is a pretty good sight, as well."

He threw his head back and laughed. Looking down, he said, "How about I go downstairs and fix a sandwich? I don't mind skipping dinner at a restaurant, but I'll need some strength to keep going tonight. And sweetheart? I plan for us to keep going."

"How about we go downstairs together? After all, I certainly want us both to have enough energy to continue."

She crawled off the bed as he pulled on his boxers. She moved to her robe hanging on the back of the bathroom door and tied it around her waist. Then, linking fingers together again, they walked downstairs.

19

Sam lay in bed hours later, his mind racing as Hayley slept. After they'd made love the first time, they went to the kitchen. While she made ham and cheese sandwiches, he cut up an apple and grabbed the potato chips. Leaning with their backs against the counter, they shared a plate, munching while laughing and talking. The conversation was easy, just like it always was with her. No stilted, uncomfortable, trying to think of what to say after sex.

First and foremost, they were friends. Friends who simply became lovers because they were *in* love. After returning to the bedroom, they made love again, this time slower, exploring each other and learning each other's bodies. He discovered what made her breath hitch and what he needed to do to elicit the sweet smile she graced him with.

Afterward, they showered together, and his soapy hands glided over her body. And when she lowered herself to her knees and took his cock in her mouth, he had to lock his own knees to keep from dropping straight down with her. He didn't think there was any way he could come again, but she brought him right to the brink and had him sliding over the edge into heaven.

When they climbed back into bed and pulled the covers over their naked bodies, they lay facing each other, whispering in the dark, sweet words between old friends and new lovers. Her eyelids slowly drooped, and he kissed her forehead, feeling the moment her body grew heavy against his.

But for him, sleep was much slower to come. Not because he was worried, filled with regrets, or doubted what they were doing was right. He was simply awed that he'd been given such a gift. He vowed to continue to do everything in his power to protect and take care of her, Eddie, and Hope, but love them with everything he had. An idea struck him, but he wasn't ready to bring it up to Hayley yet. One day, when they married, he wanted to be able to adopt Eddie and Hope. Never to take away Edward but to give them his name as much as his love. His gaze drifted back to her as she snuggled in her sleep, burrowing in tightly against his body.

Finally letting go of his thoughts, he fell asleep as the woman he loved slept, tucked in his embrace.

The following morning, he'd run back over to his side of the duplex, hanging up his suit and pulling on jeans and a long-sleeved T-shirt. He was only gone a few minutes, then headed right back over to Hayley's side. They cooked breakfast together, something they'd done many times over the years, but now, as he watched her move about the kitchen, he was entranced with how their new intimacy made him even more aware of everything about her. He loved the way her hair glistened in the sunlight streaming in the window. He noticed how delicate her fingers were as she plated the breakfast they'd prepared together. She was fully clothed, yet he now knew the little freckle she had on the side of one breast. He'd certainly kissed it enough last night.

And as her eyes lingered on him, he had a feeling she shared the same thoughts—intimacy only made them stronger.

Finally, the sound of a vehicle in the driveway had them walk out onto the porch, seeing Luke driving Allie's minivan. The adults climbed out, and as the side doors slid open, Eddie and Hope, followed by Jeremy and Jessica, tumbled out. Eddie and Hope raced to offer hugs to Sam and Hayley.

Hayley thanked Luke, Allie, and their kids for letting Eddie and Hope spend the night. "I hope everything went okay."

"Oh my gosh, they were wonderful," Allie exuded. "They played outside. We had pizza for dinner. And then, honestly, the kids went to bed without too many giggles."

Luke added, "I'll warn you that the boys are now determined to search for dinosaur bones." He shrugged. "That was in the book I read to them last night."

Sam grinned at Luke. "Glad to see you survived."

"It was all good, man. Our kids loved having

someone over, and I figured it was a nice break for you, too."

After saying goodbyes, Eddie and Hope raced into the house with their overnight bags, and Sam and Hayley followed with their fingers linked. The kids shared lots of stories about what they'd done, what they ate, and what they watched on TV.

"Jeremy had a really good book on dinosaurs," Eddie said. "We had quiet time before we had to go to sleep, so I was reading it. And there was another book about archaeology digs where they can find bones by digging in the ground. I thought that sounded like a really cool job."

"You were really interested in dinosaurs when you were about four years old," Hayley said. "We should get more books on the subject from the library."

Eddie nodded, then turned to Sam. "Sam, can I dig in the yard for dinosaur bones?"

"Oh, honey, I don't think there were any dinosaurs here," Hayley interjected.

"Well, can I dig somewhere in the backyard just to see?"

"Absolutely," Sam agreed. "The backyard goes all the way to those trees. If you want to take a shovel or something to dig close to the back to see what you find, that's fine with me." Seeing Hayley about to protest, he added, "Honey, I was going to put in some shrubs back there anyway. It's no problem for them to dig some in the dirt."

She hefted her shoulders. "Okay, if you're sure."

"Can I start today?" Eddie asked.

"Me too!" Hope said, bouncing in her seat.

"Sure. Let me get you a couple of small shovels, and as long as you stay in our yard, you're fine."

He went over to his garage and found two garden spades. Walking around to the backyard, he met Hayley and the kids on the back patio. He gave each one a spade and then walked with them toward the back. Waving his hand, he said, "You can dig anywhere that you'd like. Just be careful, and no fighting between yourselves, okay?"

The kids promised, then eagerly began digging. He watched them for a few minutes, offering advice and a little help when needed. Once they had the hang of what they were doing, he walked back to the patio, pulling Hayley into his arms.

He couldn't define his feelings, but *domestic bliss* was probably as close a phrase as he could come up with. It might sound ridiculous, but just being at home on a Saturday with Hayley in his arms and the kids playing in the backyard—an event so similar to other weekends he had with them, yet earth-shatteringly different now that he and Hayley had gotten past their fears of rejection and embraced the love they both felt.

A week later, Hayley could not imagine that her life could possibly be any better. She pulled into Malcolm Young's driveway, having been invited back on a Sunday morning to meet the other three DEPA fraternity brothers.

Sam was home with the kids, although Eddie and Hope were still entranced with digging for dinosaur bones in the backyard. In fact, Jeremy and Jessica were over there with them while Luke hung out with Sam. She'd learned that Luke was the medic at the county jail, and that was how he and Sam had met.

Once again greeted at the door by Malcolm and Anne, she walked into the beautiful home and was met by three other men. Their easygoing smiles put her at ease as Malcolm introduced Ben Abbot and Ted Miller.

"And, of course, Reggie needs no introduction, I'm sure," Malcolm said, beaming at the third man.

Hayley offered her hand, immediately feeling her face heat as she had no idea who Reggie was. Gratefully, Anne came to the rescue.

"Reggie goes by Reginald now. Reginald Olson, State Senator."

"Oh," Hayley breathed, offering silent thanks to her hostess for stepping in to rescue Hayley from a possible social faux pas. "It's nice to meet all of you."

Malcolm offered to show them the mock-up for the fraternity alumni website, and once they viewed it, they expressed their excitement with what she'd created. Even Anne had stayed and commented on how excited they were finally to be working toward a website that would truly showcase the fraternity through the years.

Ben brought out a photo album and said, "My wife and I met in college, just like Anne and Malcolm did. She was always taking pictures, and I'd forgotten she had made this album. When she knew I was coming this weekend, and Malcolm had made a callout for photographs, she suggested that I bring it. There may even be some pictures in here that would be good to go on the website."

She flipped through the album, finding the year they were freshmen pledging the fraternity.

Tom set his old college yearbooks on the table. As she looked through the photographs and listened to the men's comments, it was easy to see that the idealistic young men who had been so excited to pledge into the fraternity were just as excited in their reminiscence forty years later. Besides the four men, there was another man in a number of the pictures, his smile just as wide and his arms linked to theirs.

"I see this man in several of the pictures, but not later on. He was also in your freshman yearbook. Did he decide not to join the fraternity?"

There was only a few seconds pause as Ted looked over her shoulder to see who she was pointing at.

"Oh, him. I don't even remember his name. He hung out with us a little bit, but I don't think fraternity life was for him. He never even pledged."

Ben commented, "Oh, I sort of remember him. He was always trying to hang around, but he never seemed very serious about the fraternity. To be honest, I don't remember us being with him much once we pledged."

Malcolm cleared his throat. "I don't even remember seeing him after the first year." He shrugged and looked over at Hayley. "When I said that there was an initiation but no hazing, that was true. Some people have the idea that they really want to pledge into a fraternity, but they just don't have the heart for it. Like the others, I don't remember him after the beginning of our freshman year."

She nodded, then closed the yearbooks and photo albums. "It was so nice of you to take time out of your weekend get-together to meet with me. If Malcolm has your approval, I'll keep working on the mock-up. It'll take me a little while because I am doing this on the side and have several clients. But because this isn't a business and we're not trying to integrate a sales page, this should go pretty quickly."

The gentlemen stood and shook her hand, and then Malcolm and Anne walked her to the door. "Thank you so much," she said again. Waving, she climbed back in her car, anxious to get home. Not that home was much different than it had always been with Eddie and Hope, and often Sam there as well. But now, it all felt different. After only one spectacular night, she felt a warmth in her heart that had been missing for a long time.

With a smile on her face, she hurried home.

"Why the fuck did you show her all those yearbooks?" Malcolm asked, his face red with anger.

"How the hell was I supposed to know what all was in there?" Ted argued, his face just as flushed.

"It doesn't matter," Ben interjected. "It's nothing. We'll just make sure that the only photographs she gets are ones of us. No one else will have anything with him in it."

Reggie gave each man a hard stare. "I have too much

to fucking lose if this little project goes sideways. My campaign does not need anything from the past to rear up. Do I make myself clear?"

"Sure, sure," Malcolm agreed as Ben and Ted nodded. "No problem. Mrs. Brooks will set up the website, and I'll take care of the photographs."

"Make sure you do. We can't afford anything to come back to bite us in the ass," Reggie growled.

The four men shared a look, nodded, and then each let out a long-held breath. As Malcolm put away the albums, he felt his heart pound. "It'll be fine. We took care of things a long time ago."

"And I expect you to take care of them again if needed."

With those last words from Reggie, Malcolm nodded, hoping his sweaty palms were not noticed.

20

"I told my teacher that I wanted to be an archaeologist."

Hayley looked across the table at Eddie and smiled. "And what did she say?"

He'd just taken a big bite of a cookie, and she waited patiently while he chewed and swallowed.

"I'm digging, too!" Hope said, taking advantage of the moment while Eddie was still chewing. "That means I'm an ark-oly-isty, too."

Eddie looked at his sister and rolled his eyes before turning his attention back to his mom. "She said she was bringing a book in for me to read tomorrow. It was one she had at her house that talked about dinosaur bones." He laughed and added, "Jeremy made sure to let her know that he was part of my famous dig, too!"

"Well, just remember that when you're digging in the yard, you don't want to go outside the boundaries of where Sam told you."

"We won't, but he said he was going to dig there in the spring, so we're just making things easy for him."

"It's true that in the space that he marked out as where he wants to put in some shrubs. If you dig all over the place, then it just messes up his yard."

Hope's nose crinkled. "It's our yard, too."

Hayley shook her head. "No, the whole house and the yard belong to Sam. Because the house is divided into two sections, he's letting us stay on this side, and I pay him some money so that we can do so."

"Will you have to keep paying that money when you get married?" Eddie asked, shoving in the last bite of cookie.

She blinked, her heart stuttering in her chest. "When I... uh... get *married?*"

"Yeah. When you and Sam get married, will we keep living on this side even then?"

Hayley could feel her cheeks warm, and her heartbeat raced even faster. "Honey, what makes you say that Sam and I are getting married?"

Setting down her glass of milk carefully, Hope turned a milk-mustache smile directly toward her mom and answered for her. "Because he's your boyfriend, and after you have a boyfriend, then you get married."

Hayley blinked, uncertain what to say to that. She didn't want to lie to the children and say that Sam was not her boyfriend. But they'd been so casual about their hugs and kisses that she wasn't even sure the kids had noticed. On the other hand, she didn't want the kids running around telling everyone she was getting married. Rubbing her forehead, she thought of what to say. "Right now, Sam and I are dating, which is still being friends, but we're even closer friends."

"Like he's your boyfriend, right?" Eddie asked.

She nodded, wishing Sam was here to help her navigate the awkward conversation. "Yes, you could say he's my boyfriend. But there's no rushing anything. So everything stays the same as it is, and you just remember not to dig outside of where he pointed out. Okay?"

Eddie and Hope both shrugged at the same time, and she almost laughed at how similar their mannerisms were.

"Sure, Mom," Eddie agreed.

With their snack now finished, the kids grabbed their jackets and raced to the backyard. She watched for a moment as they each took their spade and began digging a little more.

She wondered what would happen when they didn't find a dinosaur bone, but surely they would get tired of playing at being an archaeologist before that.

Since the kids would be outside playing for a while, and Sam was still at work, she headed upstairs to her bedroom office. She had spent the morning getting all the work needed for her job and managed to make a trip into town to talk to Katelyn Harrison. She and her brothers shared ownership of the pub, but she worked with her husband, Gareth, and their private investigation business in town.

Katelyn had explained that they had plenty of jobs by word-of-mouth, working with local law enforcement and being hired by several attorneys on the Eastern Shore or the Virginia Beach area.

But the Harrisons wanted a website that might draw

in more private clients. The two women chatted, discovering similarities as they discussed family, kids, the school system, and their jobs. Katelyn gave her the date of the next auxiliary meeting, and Hayley assured her she was looking forward to attending.

She was working on a basic mock-up to show Katelyn next week. She glanced up from her computer, another smile gracing her lips as she watched Eddie and Hope work together. Like most siblings, they had their share of squabbles, but she was pleased that they often got along. And right now, she could tell that Eddie had patiently shown his sister what to do with her spade, and while he seemed to be directing the *archaeology dig for dinosaur bones*, he certainly let his sister play a prominent role. They were both kneeling on the ground, digging in the dirt together, their heads almost touching as they worked.

Shifting her gaze to the top of her dresser, she spied her wedding photograph now sitting among other framed pictures of the family.

"You'd be so proud of them, Edward. And I hope you'd be proud of me, too. You knew Sam was a good man before you and I ever met. And you've been gone so long that it doesn't seem weird for me to date him. But I really hope that you would be pleased for us."

She turned her attention back to her computer screen, her fingers flying across the keys as she immersed herself in work. After a while, she leaned back and stretched the kinks out of her back while glancing at the time on her laptop. Sam would be arriving home from work soon, and her thoughts drifted to dinner. She started to shut down the program when her hand halted on the mouse by the electrifying cacophony of screams.

"Mom!"

"Mom!"

The urgency in those screams caused her to leap from her seat, knocking her chair over. While it clattered heedlessly on the floor, adrenaline propelled her through the bedroom and down the stairs. Rounding the bottom railing, she made it to the kitchen just as the kids had burst into the kitchen, not bothering to close the sliding glass door. Their eyes were wide and wild, but no obvious blood was flowing. She gasped, "What's wrong? Are you hurt? What happened?"

"We found it!" Eddie screamed as Hope jumped around, waving her hands in the air. "We found it! It's real!" Eddie swung his hand from behind his back, revealing what he held tightly in his grip. A large bone.

A scream of surprise catapulted from Hayley's mouth as she jumped back. "Drop that thing! Drop it!"

Startled, Eddie's body jerked. His fingers immediately opened, and the bone clattered onto the kitchen floor. "What's wrong, Mom?"

The bone could've come from any animal, yet cold dread slithered down her spine. It looked like an exact image of every human forearm she'd ever seen. She couldn't remember the scientific name, but at that moment, she couldn't even remember her own name.

Lifting her gaze to Eddie's and Hope's wide-eyed faces staring up at her, she found surprise written in their expressions. Swallowing deeply, she blurted, "It's fine, I'm sure it's fine. It's probably from an animal that... un... yeah..."

"Can we keep it? Can I take it to school to show them I found a real bone?" Eddie asked, his face shining with excitement as he bounced on his toes.

"Just leave it where it is right now. I'm going to call Sam, and we'll see what he thinks we should do with it. You can go wash your hands upstairs and start your homework."

Her phone was still on the kitchen counter, and she grabbed it, her hands shaking so badly she was glad she had Sam on speed dial.

"Hey, sweetheart. I was just getting ready to—"

"Sam, the kids found a bone."

"I'm sorry, the kids found a what?"

"A bone. In your yard. They were digging after school, and they came running up to the patio, and Eddie was holding a bone."

"Okay, Hayley. Take a breath. It's probably just from an animal—"

"Sam, no. I mean, it could be. I don't know. But I swear it looks like a human bone. Jesus, I don't even know why I'm saying that. I wouldn't know a human bone from a dog bone from a cow bone—"

"Sweetheart, calm down. Have the kids leave it on the patio, and when I get home, I'll take a look."

"It's on the kitchen floor. Hurry, please. I just don't have a good feeling about this."

"I'm leaving right now. I should be home in about fifteen minutes."

Disconnecting, she tried to settle her racing heart,

but her eyes kept returning to the floor and the bone that took center stage.

Sam stared at the bone on the kitchen floor. He knew it was a human bone, but he had to hold on to his cool with the kids jumping around and Hayley shaking.

As soon as he got home, he looked at the bone and then asked Eddie to show him where he found it. The excited little boy raced outside, and Hope quickly followed. Sam wished he'd asked Hayley to keep Hope inside, but he hadn't thought quickly enough, and her little legs raced to keep up with her brother.

Once they were in the back of the yard, he knelt where Eddie pointed.

"What if there are more? The book says that archaeologists have to preserve the site. Can we keep digging?" Eddie rushed to say as though afraid the hole would close up, keeping its secrets hidden.

Placing his hand on Eddie's shoulder, he held the boy's gaze. "Eddie, you did a really good job. Both of you. You found something extraordinary. But now, I need you to go back inside and stay with your mom while I take a look around." Seeing them about to argue, he added, "I really need you to do this for me. I need you to go in and stay with your mom. She seems nervous, and she's going to feel better if you're there."

Hope eagerly raced back toward the house, but Eddie stayed and held Sam's gaze for a moment, indecision written on his face. Finally, he nodded and ran toward the back door. Sam didn't want to disturb the scene but had no idea what he was looking at. Finding a bone could be anything from an animal having dug in an old grave, then bringing it here and leaving it years ago. For all he knew, a family cemetery plot could be nearby from a century ago. Taking the spade that one of the kids had left behind, he gently scraped away more top dirt in the same area where the bone was found. And it only took a moment for more white bone to be seen. "Fuck," he growled. Stalking back to the house, he stopped halfway and pulled out his phone.

He knew Aaron had already left for the day but thought Hunter might still be there. Dialing directly, he hoped he would answer.

"Detective Hunter Simmons."

"Hunter, it's Sam. I'm at my house, and you're not gonna believe this. Hayley's kids were digging in the backyard, and they found a bone. From what it looks like, it's a fucking human bone. Hayley freaked and called me, and I came straight here. I've sent the kids inside, and I looked a little bit more. Sure enough, there are more bones. I'll call it in officially, but I wanted to give you a heads-up. We'll need to call in a team from our department and the state police. And once our team meets, we'll probably need to call in the state forensics."

"Fucking hell, man. Sorry as fuck that's in your backyard, and the kids found it!"

"The kids were digging for dinosaur bones, so right now, they're excited. It's Hayley who is shaking like a leaf."

"If you've got any tape, you might want to go ahead

and cordon off the area. Definitely tell the kids to stay away. You call in the official alert, and I'll get things started here. See you soon."

With that, Sam disconnected and called the dispatcher, reporting the findings of human bones on private property. He let her know that he'd already talked to Detective Simmons, and she said she'd send the others out.

Once again disconnecting, he walked straight into the kitchen. "Okay, kids, I will need you to leave everything alone. Since we found a bone, we wanna make sure everything's reported the right way, so I've called in some of my buddies. They'll be here in a few minutes. You'll have to stay inside with your mom and let me handle everything."

Hayley didn't even give the kids a chance to answer before she nodded and said, "Absolutely yes!"

"But I found it—" Eddie began, his brow furrowing as his gaze darted between his mom and Sam.

"I understand, Eddie," Sam said, once again kneeling to be at his height. "But right now, I have to consider it a… um… an investigation site."

Eddie's eyes widened at this new information. "Whoa! That's so cool!"

Sam grinned. "You got that right. Now, I'm going to go out to my car and get a couple of things, and I'll be right back. In the meantime, don't touch the bone. Just leave it right here."

As he passed Hayley to go out the front door, he cupped the back of her head, kissed her lightly, and then whispered, "Keep them calm, and you stay calm yourself. I'll let you know more as soon as I find out what will happen."

She shifted away and looked at him, holding his gaze for a few seconds, then nodded. "No problem, honey. You do whatever you need to do, and I'll keep the kids in here."

Squeezing her hand, he jogged out to his car, where he gathered evidence bags and the yellow tape to start cordoning off the digging site. As he walked back to the kitchen, he held the bone by a paper towel and dropped it into the evidence bag. Sealing it, he wrote the identifying information on the bag.

The kids were staring, so he casually explained what he was doing. "This will preserve our bone so some scientists can study it."

Eddie was fascinated, watching every move Sam made. Heading back outside, he was already met with several deputies. "I have some tape, but I don't have any stakes to drive in the ground."

"No worries, Sam. If you show us what we're looking at, we'll take care of it until the team arrives."

Soon, a wide circle of yellow tape stretched around a perimeter, closing the entire area where the kids had been digging. Within half an hour, his entire yard was crawling with deputies, Hunter and Aaron, plus Hunter's partner, Brad. Colt arrived shortly after. While the county sheriff didn't turn up at every crime site, considering it was in one of his detectives' backyards, Sam wasn't surprised to see his boss and friend.

A few hours later, they were all still there, including the state police and the head of the forensic team. As the evening shadows descended, large spotlights were brought in to illuminate the area.

Sam scrubbed his hand over his face and sighed. "This is crazy. I told the kids they could dig for dinosaur bones back here because I plan to plant shrubs there this spring. Christ, I had no idea they would actually find bones. A dinosaur bone would've been much better than this."

"There's no way you could've known this was out here, Sam," Colt said. "It's just pure fuckin' dumb luck that the kids found it."

Aaron shook his head. "They don't look too traumatized."

The men's heads swung around in unison, all gazes landing on the sliding glass door leading off Hayley's side of the house. Two little faces were pressed against the window, their big eyes taking in the entire scene. Sam snorted at Eddie's keen interest in the backyard happenings. Standing behind the kids was Hayley, looking as though she wanted to pull her kids back, draw the curtains, and pretend nothing had happened.

The state police took charge of the remains. Hank Rosetti, the head of the closest state forensic team out of Norfolk, walked over to Sam and the others.

"I wanted to give you guys an update. Definitely human. Female. And that's all I can give you definitively. Once we get the remains to the lab, I'll put it on the fast track."

"We can't get anything else other than that right now?" Sam asked.

Hank shook his head. "To do so would be conjecture,

and I don't want to taint an ongoing investigation. But I promise I'll let you know as soon as I have more."

"Can you tell us if the whole remains were found?"

Nodding, Hank said, "Yeah, sorry. I should've led with that. I can say that her skeletal remains are intact and are all located in the same burial site. We have to take it back as a whole, so that's why my team is digging a bigger hole in your backyard. We'll take the remains and the surrounding dirt. Right now, I can say that we aren't finding any evidence of a burial container."

"Thanks, Hank," Colt said, shaking his hand.

Another hour passed before the forensic team finally had the remains and the surrounding dirt in a container they'd brought and loaded into the back of a state police truck.

The deputies kept the tape up to secure the area and then left, giving Sam their sympathy and well wishes. Only Colt, Hunter, Brad, and Aaron remained with Sam. The small group stood on the patio, and Sam noticed that Hayley had finally ushered Eddie and Hope out of the kitchen. Glancing at the time, he wasn't surprised.

It was almost eight o'clock on a school night, but with the spotlights now turned off, the group was surrounded by darkness and shadows. Only the kitchen light cast its illumination through the glass door to expose their tense faces.

Colt spoke first. "Okay, I say everybody needs to head home to get a good night's sleep, and we'll start working on this first thing in the morning. There's not a lot we can do until we get the forensic report."

"I really want to work this, Colt. Is there a reason I can't since the remains were found on my land?"

When Colt didn't answer right away, Sam had a feeling he knew what the answer would be. But Colt surprised him when he said, "I'm going to ask you to stay in the background on this and let Hunter and Brad take the lead. But you've only been the owner of this property for about six months. That skeleton has been in the ground a hell of a lot longer than that. As soon as we verify that she is as old as I think she might be, you'll be right back, front and center on the case."

Sam nodded, relief spearing through him. He didn't want to do anything to fuck up the investigation, but he also didn't want to give up control on finding out why the hell there was a female skeleton buried at the back of the property.

Shaking hands with everyone, he walked the others around to the driveway where they were parked, then waved them off. When the last taillights disappeared, he headed toward Hayley's front door. As his hand reached for the knob, the door swung open, and Hayley flew out, hitting him hard. She plastered her front to his with her arms wrapped around his waist and pulled in tight.

"Oh my God, can you believe this? I mean, Sam, this is nuts! I can't believe Eddie and Hope found that. Or saw that. Or, oh my God, even picked that bone up! It was in the kitchen! Jesus, I can't even imagine that—"

"Sweetheart—"

"And to top it off, I didn't even realize that my mom had called just to chat, and Eddie picked up the phone. He told my mom there was a skeleton in the backyard.

Then Hope gets on the phone, and she's jumping up and down, and my mom doesn't know what's going on until I finally realize what the kids have just told her. I had to get on the phone and calm my mom down, then talk to my dad and keep them from freaking out."

He wrapped his arms tightly around her and squeezed gently. Leaning back, he started again, "Hayley, sweetheart—"

"And that's not all!"

At that point, Sam's head jerked back as his brows lowered, wondering what else could have happened besides a skeleton being found in the yard by the kids. He should have known Hayley wasn't about to take a breath to slow down in her story.

"Before the kids found the skeleton, they were asking about us. They wanted to know if we were boyfriend and girlfriend. Hope even thought we were going to get married. I didn't know what to say. But I couldn't lie to them. So I told them that you and I had always been friends and now we were dating. Then they asked if you were my boyfriend, and I said yes. So, of course, Hope told my mom that you and I are now going to live together and get married, and one day, she wants to have a baby sister."

"Well, sweetheart, we have—"

"Then I had to get back on the phone with my mom and explain to her that you and I had just started dating. What a day! I couldn't make this kind of day up if I had to!"

He leaned forward to place his lips against her forehead instead and murmured soft words as he gently rubbed her back, grateful when she started relaxing, and he could feel the tension ease from her muscles. "Let's go inside and get the kids ready for bed. Everything will work out. I promise."

It seemed Hayley had talked herself out when she nodded against his chest, leaned back, and let out a long, cleansing breath. Then she allowed him to lead her inside their home.

21

Hayley felt ridiculous for blabbing as soon as Sam got into the house. But for hours, she'd tried to corral her excited children while not thinking too hard about the fact that there was a body... or rather a skeleton in the backyard. While Sam conferred with his fellow officers outside, she'd kept a continual pulse on the children but found they were handling the situation much better than she was. Of course, the lights hadn't gone out for bedtime yet, and that was when she wondered if the fears would erupt.

She fed them supper, shepherded them through bath time, and helped Eddie with his homework. Thankfully, Hope didn't have any schoolwork to complete, so she'd even allowed them both to watch TV. It was hard to keep them away from the back door, but since they were limited in what they could see now that it had grown dark, they eventually decided that television was a perfect treat.

She'd offered several times to take drinks or snacks

out to the various law-enforcement personnel who had swarmed over their yard, and while Sam had thanked her, he insisted it wasn't necessary. And now that everyone had left, her calm facade had shattered, and she'd fallen apart in his arms the first moment she saw him alone.

"We can go upstairs where the kids are," she said. Her voice was clear, and she felt she could breathe easier now that he was with her. She hoped he would have the same effect on the excited children.

They scarcely made it to the top of the stairs when Eddie barreled out of his room like a miniature tornado, fatigue mixed with excitement on his face. Hope raced out of her brother's room, but her expression was tinged with apprehension. Hayley's gaze softened as she noticed her daughter was trying to clutch three stuffed animals to her small chest instead of just the one she usually kept by her side.

Sam calmly gripped Eddie's shoulder. "Okay, kids, let's go pile up in Eddie's room, and we'll talk."

Once everyone was settled, Sam began. "First of all, I have to say you two were absolutely amazing today."

From the kids' wide eyes and grins, it was easy to see they weren't expecting that. Hayley could've kissed Sam right then for that simple statement that made her children feel so special.

"I'm going to be upfront with you all," Sam continued. "But that's a big responsibility, so I'm going to ask a lot from you, too. I have to know that what I tell you, for right now, stays here in this room. Later, you can talk about it with your friends if you want, but not until I tell you so. Do you promise?"

The kids both nodded without delay.

"I promise!"

"I promise!"

"Good," Sam acknowledged. "First of all, you found a human bone. And we did find more of it out there. So it's amazing that you brought what you found straight to your mom so she could call me, and we could get the police involved."

"Who is it?" Eddie asked. Hope's eyes cut to her brother, and she pulled her stuffed animals closer.

"We don't know. But what happens now is that scientists will study the bones and tell us everything they can about the person."

"Is that like an archaeologist?" Eddie asked.

"Sort of. But there are people called forensic scientists or biologists. They're trained to study all kinds of bones and find out things about them. They can tell a lot about someone just by looking at the bones."

"How do they do that?" Eddie continued to ask.

Hayley kept her gaze on Hope, knowing that Eddie was able to process the information in a way that would hopefully keep him from being scared. But she wasn't sure her daughter would be able to do that. She shifted over in the bed and opened her arms, not surprised when Hope climbed onto her lap, dragging her stuffed animals with her. Over Hope's head, Hayley shared a look with Sam, breathing easier when she could tell he understood what she was trying to convey.

"We can talk more about that tomorrow, Eddie. Remember that you can't go out there until I let you know it's okay. But for right now, let's just focus on the fact that you guys found something super interesting in the yard, and the special police scientists are going to do everything they can to find out more about it. There's nothing you need to worry about and nothing you need to be scared of."

"I don't want to go in my room and sleep by myself," Hope whispered.

Hayley looked toward Eddie, but she didn't have to say anything. On his own, he offered, "Hope, you can sleep in my bed tonight."

Hope smiled, her gratitude overflowing. Suddenly, Hope's head swung around toward Sam. "You can't leave us. You need to sleep here, too."

"Oh, sweet girl, I won't be afraid," Sam said.

"No! You have to stay here in this part of the house with us!" Hope screeched. "I'm sleeping with Eddie tonight, and you need to be across the hall in Mommy's room."

Hayley's eyes nearly bulged out of her head. Before she could say anything, Hope continued.

"You're mom's boyfriend, and you're a policeman. So you don't need to go back to the other side of the house. You need to stay in our side so nobody can get us."

Once again, Hayley shared a look over Hope's head toward Sam, but this time, she had no clue what she was trying to convey. The only thought in her head was, *What the hell else could happen today?*

"That's right, I am your mom's boyfriend," Sam agreed. "You know that your mom and dad and I were friends before either of you were born. So I've been friends with your family for a long time. Since your dad passed away, I've considered it an honor to be able to look out for you two and your mom. But recently, your mom and I decided that we liked each other more than just friends. So, you're right. She's my girlfriend, and I'm her boyfriend."

"I told Grandma that you're going to get married," Hope said, pride resounding in each of her words.

"I know your mom talked to your grandma. And your mom and I haven't discussed anything beyond right now. We just enjoy being together like a family."

The kids seemed perfectly fine with his explanation. Hayley and Sam soon tucked both Eddie and Hope into Eddie's full-size bed. Hope had a twin bed in her room. Eddie used to sleep in a twin bed, but when they moved, she'd bought a full size for the growing boy. Now, she was glad she had since it gave both kids ample room for the few times they felt the need to stay close. Leaving the night-light on and the door cracked with a night-light in the hall, Hayley and Sam tiptoed down the stairs and walked into the kitchen.

"I know you've got to be hungry, honey," she said. "I fixed something quick for the kids because I was having a hard time keeping their interest away from the back door."

"Don't worry about anything fancy. A sandwich will be fine."

She pulled out the makings for a ham sandwich, and Sam grabbed the applesauce and potato chips, then poured a glass of tea. Looking over at her, he asked, "Do you want anything to drink?"

"Vodka?" she quipped, laughing.

His deep chuckle wrapped around her as he walked over and kissed the side of her head. Reaching around her, he grabbed the plate with the sandwich.

"Let's sit at the table. You were on your feet outside that whole time, and honestly, my legs are still quivering."

He agreed, and they settled in at the kitchen table. She waited until he almost finished eating, then couldn't hold it in anymore. "Sock it to me, Sam. What can you tell me?"

He wiped his mouth and took a long sip of tea. "We had to call the state police, and they brought in their forensic team based out of Norfolk. The full remains were found. They took the bones and all the surrounding dirt for evidence to assist in their work. They got that all bagged up and loaded into the big van you saw. The police tape will stay up just to keep anybody out, but since it's on private land, I'm not expecting anybody to come." He stopped and released a sigh that was laced with irritation. "We need to keep the kids out of the backyard for now. When it hits the news, there could be gawkers out here. But I'll soon send them on their way."

"Oh my God. I didn't even think about something like that." Now, she sighed heavily, puffing out her cheeks. "Anything else?"

"The lead forensic biologist out here said the skeleton was female, but he wouldn't give much more. I was afraid Colt would take me off the case since this was on my land, but that body has been there a hell of a lot longer than six months, so I'm not a suspect in anything."

Her entire body jerked at those words. "Jesus, Sam, I didn't even think about something like that. A suspect? I mean… I guess… Oh hell, honey, I don't know what I was thinking. I guess I just thought it was somebody from a long time ago."

"Chances are, you're right. Again, just from the looks of the dirt staining the bones, I'd have to say she's been there a long time."

Hayley thought about what he said, and then the weight of the skeleton find landed on her shoulders. "She. It was a woman. Even if it was long ago, why was she buried there? Or died there. That seems so lonely." After a moment, she looked at him again. "What happens next?"

"There's not much we can do until we hear back from the forensic lab. A lot of times, they can determine the cause of death, but the main thing will be finding out how long she's been there. It makes a big difference in our investigation if it's ten, fifty, or a hundred years."

"So she could actually have been someone who was here a hundred years ago and maybe just died naturally."

He nodded. "Absolutely. She could've come from a poor family who had no money for a casket, and the family just buried her."

"I wonder who used to own this land. I don't mean the owners you bought it from. I guess I'm thinking about a long time ago. The first registered property owners."

"That's what I thought I'd look into. I'm going to do a little searching and just see how far back the land records go on this property. It might come in handy with the case, and even if not, it'd be interesting to have that information."

"Well, God knows, Eddie would want to know that!"

"He's inquisitive, that's for sure. But you know what I said to the kids tonight was true. They found something amazing, but they brought it straight to you. As much as you were freaked out, they did the right thing, and then you did the right thing by calling me. In fact, I need to make sure I give them some kind of reward."

"Just them?" She lifted a brow, trying to keep her lips from curving upward.

He leaned forward, stopping a whisper away from her lips. "Well, I think you deserve a reward too. Got anything in mind?"

Her tongue darted out and swiped across his bottom lip, eliciting a growl. "Yeah, I can think of a thing or two for my reward. But with the kids upstairs, there's not a whole lot we can do about it.".

"Well, maybe not the full reward, but we could certainly make out on the sofa."

She stood quickly and grabbed his hand, leaving his plate on the table as she pulled him into the living room. She pushed him down onto the couch. "I need to check on the kids. I'll be right back." Racing quietly up the stairs, she peeked into Eddie's room and saw both kids sound asleep.

Hurrying back downstairs, she plopped onto his lap and wrapped her arms around his neck. "Now, about this reward—"

Her words were cut off as his mouth sealed over hers, the kiss stealing any other thoughts. It might have been a hell of an afternoon, but making out with Sam on her sofa would make it a hell of an evening to remember.

22

Hayley had barely gotten the kids onto the bus the next morning when a knock on the front door surprised her. Opening the door, she found Belle and Carrie standing on the porch with covered plates in their hands. "There's nothing like chocolate to help take your mind off everything," Belle said with a sweet smile. "I brought brownies, and Carrie made the most scrumptious chocolate pecan pie."

She invited them in, but Belle needed to get back to the nursing home. "Hunter told me what was going on, and I can't imagine what you must have thought when you saw that bone!"

"I was freaked out, but the kids were excited."

"If that had been my Jack, he'd probably still be digging in the yard!" Carrie laughed.

Hayley remembered that her son was older than Eddie, but she had a feeling their personalities were similar. While the skeletal find had not hit the news stations, she was about to discover how closely the law enforcement wives in the area were banded together.

Carrie's smiling face took a serious turn. "If you see one person skulking around who shouldn't be here, you make sure to call into the station. Colt has strict instructions that the deputies will be doing drive-bys."

"Thank you, but honestly, Carrie, all of this is so crazy!"

Shaking her head, Carrie agreed. "While the Shore is filled with farmland and tiny towns, don't think that crime sleeps here. We're just a microcosm of the larger society. And believe me, lots of us have felt that sting."

Having heard a few of their stories, she simply nodded. The two friends handed her the plates and promised to visit again when they had more time.

"Just let me know when you want to see the work on the nursing home web design," she offered.

"Oh, Mr. Weldon, the administrator, will be so thrilled. We'll do that as soon as the excitement dies down for you," Belle replied.

Carrie rolled her eyes. "Honey, that'll take a while."

With that, the ladies offered hugs and were on their way. Hayley carried the plates to the kitchen and peeked underneath the foil to unearth decadent brownies and a pie that smelled divine. Grabbing a brownie, she savored the taste and knew she would have to ration them to the kids, or they would inhale them quickly.

Later, she opened the door to another new friend on her front porch. She welcomed Tori Evans and an older woman introduced as Tori's mother-in-law, Nancy. Tori's husband, Mitch, had taken over as police chief of Baytown after his father had a heart attack. And over coffee, she found out that Nancy's husband had become the police chief when his father retired. It seemed the Evans had a long history of police work on the Shore. While the visit didn't last long, both women cautioned Hayley that she could expect a lot more visits and phone calls, all wanting to ensure that she and her children were okay.

"Those of us who are with the people in law enforcement out here on the Shore are very close," Nancy said. "It's always been that way."

Tori placed her hand on Hayley's arm. "I know your husband was in law enforcement and was killed on the job. So, of course, you understand the worst of any of our fears. But Sam is well-liked and respected since he's been out here, and we know you and the kids are his family." Tori then offered a little smile and added, "Although, a little birdie has hinted that you and Sam are dating."

When Hope had come home from school yesterday, she'd confessed that she'd told her teacher that her mom and Sam were now dating. Considering Jade was married to a Baytown police officer, Hayley had a feeling her daughter was the little bird.

Laughing, she admitted, "It's true, but we've hardly had a minute to ourselves with everything going on." Soon after the Evans left, her phone and email notifications began to ping, with others checking on her.

Her phone rang again, and she was tempted to

ignore it when she recognized Sam's ringtone. Grabbing the phone, she answered. "Sam. Are you okay?"

"I am, but I was calling to see how you were doing."

Laughing, she said, "I guess you've heard about the support brigade showing up."

"Yeah, I've had a lot of people say that everyone was worried about how you and the kids were doing. I have assured them that we're all fine, but I wanted to check on you."

"I'm pretty sure Hope has already told Jade that we're together because that news seems to have made it around the rumor mill, too." Sam's chuckle sent a smile over her face.

"How do you feel about that, sweetheart?"

"It's all good. You and I are in love, we're a couple, and even though we've hardly had a moment to ourselves, at least we don't feel like we have to sneak around."

"The kids seemed okay with me spending the night. How are you with that?"

"Honestly, honey, I'm fine with it. In many ways, you and I have been together for a long time, even if the intimacy is new. I guess we'll just play it by ear."

"Sounds good, sweetheart. Well, I'm getting ready to go into a meeting about our mysterious woman from the backyard. When I get home, I'll let you know anything I can. Obviously, it's an ongoing case, but if it turns out to be as old as I think it might be, I'll be able to tell you pretty much everything."

Disconnecting, she leaned back and looked around her bedroom office. Her mind wandered to the wall behind her bed, knowing that's where Sam's bed was in his room. She thought about how the downstairs was connected. Their stairwells shared a wall, as well as the kitchens. She'd seen enough house makeover shows on TV to know that turning a duplex into one house would not be that difficult.

And for several minutes, she pictured how to turn the two-story duplex into one large home. A wide smile slipped over her face because she knew for a fact that if Sam proposed, she would accept.

The following morning, Sam called soon after he got to the station. "Hayley, don't be concerned if you see patrol cars in front of the house and deputies occasionally walking around the property."

"What's going on?"

"The Virginia Beach morning news broke the story about skeletal remains found on the Eastern Shore. They didn't give our address, but it won't be long before someone sniffs it out, and then we may get the unwanted visitors I told you about. Colt wants to have our place on the radar of our deputies. And have the kids play indoors again when they get home. I don't want them in the yard and have a newshound come around trying to ask them questions."

"Oh my God. I never even thought about that. I'm beginning to hate that Eddie ever heard the word archaeologist!"

"I plan on getting home on time today, and I'll bring Chinese."

"Ooh, that sounds marvelous! Just get what the kids always want and make sure to get me—"

"Extra crab rangoons and egg rolls," he finished, laughing. "Think I know your Chinese order after all these years, sweetheart."

After saying goodbye, she fielded a few more calls from Jillian, Sophie, and Judith, who she learned was a doctor in town and married to one of the police chiefs. After her call from Sophie, she was reminded about the fraternity website. Deciding to spend more time on it tomorrow, she first worked on Katelyn's website and marketing program. Glancing out the window in front of her desk, she was distracted by the yellow tape still in the yard. The bright strands flapped in the breeze, creating an ominous distraction.

Shaking her head, she turned back to her laptop.

23

That night, after their Chinese takeout dinner and everyone had joked over who had the worst fortune in their fortune cookie, Sam effortlessly steered the kids and Hayley into the living room to play a board game. Soon, they were all laughing and having fun, allowing Hope and Eddie a chance to forget all about what they'd discovered in the backyard.

Sam was attuned to the deputy patrols driving by, but his calm demeanor assured the rest of the family that normalcy had returned. When the kids were getting ready for bed, he supported Hayley as she encouraged Hope to sleep in her own room after sleeping in Eddie's bed the previous night.

"Your night-light is on, and so is the one in the hall. Your door will be open, and Sam and I'll be right across the hall. Plus, you've got the protection of all your stuffed animals."

Hope finally acquiesced, and while Sam got Eddie in

bed, Hayley spent extra time with Hope before they traded places.

He ensured Hope was tucked in, careful not to displace any of the motley crew of stuffed animals and dolls piled on her bed like a guard detail. Even though she had little room for herself, if they made her feel more secure, that was fine with him. Leaning over, he planted a soft kiss on the top of her head, and she reached up to wrap her little arms around his neck, clinging to him tightly.

"Sam?"

"Yes, sweet girl."

"Will you stay here again in our house?"

"Would that make you feel better?"

"Yes, because I know nothing bad will happen. You're a policeman, and you have a gun, and nobody can hurt us if you're here."

"I'll be right across the hall, Hope. Sleep tight."

Leaving Hope's room, he met Hayley walking out of Eddie's room. He reached down and linked fingers with her as he led her into her bedroom. "Looks like I might forget where I live if Hope has anything to do with it."

She laughed as she closed the door and moved over to the bed, crawling up on the mattress. She crossed her legs as she nodded. "She's not the only one who feels that way."

He rubbed his chin, knowing what he wanted to talk to her about, yet hesitating because of the stress of the past couple of days.

"Hey," she said softly. "You look like you have something on your mind." She patted the bed next to her. "Talk to me."

He slipped off his shoes and settled on the edge of the bed before pivoting to the side to face her. His gaze roamed over her face for a moment, taking in every nuance. She was so beautiful, his breath caught in his throat. The first time Edward introduced her to him over ten years ago, he thought she was a very pretty woman but never allowed his thoughts to linger any longer than just the appreciation for the beauty he would give to any attractive woman.

As he got to know her more, he appreciated her quick wit and sweet personality, thinking Edward was a very fortunate man. Now, she was even more beautiful. Life had not dulled her personality but instead had given her a maturity that added to her allure. He didn't dwell on thinking of Edward's death as the way that eventually led her to him—the past can't be changed, and trying to wonder about all the what-ifs was futile and would never bring happiness. The fact remained that she was his to care for and love.

Before he gave any thought to prefacing his words, he blurted, "I love you."

A soft giggle slipped out, the delicate sound moving through him.

"I love you, too, Sam. But I hardly think that's what gave you such a serious face."

It was his turn to chuckle. "You're right. I supposed that it's a good starting place."

She waited silently, so he continued. "Unlike a lot of couples who need to spend time dating, getting to know each other, deciding whether they're right together before they move in with each other, or even talk about something more permanent, that's not where you and I are at."

Her gaze never left his face, but she nodded slowly. "Yes, that's true."

"I was thinking about this house, Hayley. We could always sell it, although quite frankly until the mystery of the buried woman in the backyard is resolved, I don't think we'd have any buyers scrambling to take it off our hands."

Another giggle slipped out, and she repeated her earlier phrase. "Yes, that's also true."

"I was thinking that I really like this location and would like to stay if that's good with you."

She nodded but pressed her lips together, not saying anything this time.

"Bryce is a friend of mine who works for the Virginia Marine Police. He bought a single-story duplex and had it renovated, knocked down some walls, and turned the duplex into one larger house."

"Okay," she said, dragging out the word, her head tilted slightly.

"He's engaged now, and it's a house that will be perfect for the family they want to have." He reached behind his head and gripped the back of his neck, squeezing slightly to ease the nerves he felt racing through him. "Anyway, I started thinking that this place would be great for that, too. There are lots of old duplex homes in Baytown that have been converted into large family homes. We could knock down the walls between the two sides and—"

"Have one big house for all of us," she said, her eyes bright.

The air rushed from his lungs, and he chuckled. "Yeah."

"I've seen a lot of flipping houses shows on TV where they've done that. And, I swear, Sam, I was just thinking of this very thing today."

"Really?"

"Yes!" She pointed at the wall behind the bed. "Your bedroom is just over there. I used to lay here and think of you being on the other side."

"Damn, woman, I did the same thing."

She laughed, then leaned forward, wrapping her hand over his. "Please, go on with what you were saying."

"Well, I guess that was about it. I know it would be a mess while the contractors are working, but this place would make a big house for all of us and any future kids."

Her brows lifted as she sucked in a quick breath. "What are you really saying?"

"We don't need any more time to just date. The kids are ready for us to become the family we've been for all these years. We don't have to bounce between the two sides of this duplex. We can just make it into one large home for all of us. What I'm really getting to is, will you marry me, sweetheart?"

"Yes, yes, yes!" she cried, throwing her arms around his neck and pulling him down onto the mattress.

Their lips met, and the sweet kiss he'd planned turned wild as their tongues tangled, vying for dominance. He rolled on top, her thighs cradling his hips. He rocked forward, his cock nudging against her soft body, and he wished no clothes were acting as a barrier. He broke the kiss only to nuzzle her neck and lightly nip along her jawline. Her pulse fluttered wildly at the base of her neck, and he paid special attention, making sure to kiss where her life force flowed.

Giving control over to her, he rolled so that she was now on top. She grinned down at him, then slid off the bed. She padded quietly to the door. "Let me check on the kids."

He nodded and watched as she slipped out of the room. While she was out, he headed into the bathroom and brushed his teeth. When she came back into the bedroom and locked the door, he lifted his brow in silent question. Walking to her, he pulled her into his arms.

She held him close but leaned back so their gazes could lock onto each other.

"I want us to make love tonight, Sam. And it might seem weird with the kids across the hall, but if we're going to live together and marry, then we can't just have sex when the kids are gone."

He nodded his agreement. "I'm going to follow your lead on this, sweetheart. I consider your kids to be my kids, but I never want to do anything you're uncomfortable with."

"It might seem weird at first... or maybe longer than that." She chuckled. "But couples have been having sex with kids in the house for centuries. I guess we'll just have to learn how to be quiet."

He grinned. "I can if you can."

"Then let's prove it," she whispered in return.

He ensured the door was locked to give them a chance to throw on clothes if one of the kids needed them. She hurried to brush her teeth then met him in the bed. They stripped quickly, not taking the time for finesse. Their actions weren't a slow, discovering each other's bodies type of making love they'd experienced before, but more of a let's get right down to it. He had a feeling that this kind of sex with Hayley might be what was more in their future, but he was determined to make it as special for her as he could.

She lay back on the bed, and he knelt on the floor, his mouth at the juncture of her thighs. He'd already memorized her scent, and knowing she was as ready for him as he was for her sent him diving in, lapping her slick folds.

Her hands reached down to scratch along his scalp gently, the sensation adding more tingles down his spine. He licked and sucked, then slid a finger into her core, memorizing the spot that solicited little gasps from her.

He felt one of her hands leave his head and glanced up to see she'd clapped her palm over her mouth. He hated for her to stifle any of those delicious noises she made but was equally amused that she was so unrestrained she'd have to work to keep from crying out.

His teeth found the bundle of nerves, and he gently nipped before lapping circles around the sensitive bud.

Her thighs quivered, and with another curling of his fingers buried in her sex, her muffled cry gave evidence of her orgasm as much as her inner muscles pulsating. He licked and sucked until her legs flopped open, and she finished riding out her release.

He was already addicted to her taste and kissed his way up over her body to her lips. Their tongues tangled, and he knew she could taste her essence.

Twisting onto his back, he snagged the condom he'd placed on the mattress and rolled it over his erection. Wanting her on top, he wrapped his fingers around her waist and lifted slightly so that she could swing her leg over his hips.

With her straddling him, his gaze roved over her perfect breasts that now filled his palms. He tugged slightly on her nipples, and she leaned forward and rested her hands on his shoulders. Her breasts hung at just the right height for him to capture a hard nipple in his mouth. He sucked deeply, not wanting to elicit pain but wanting her to feel everything… the slight sting before the rush of pleasure.

Her fingers dug into his shoulders as she flung her head back, pressing her lips as she ground her sex against his erection. He knew she was trying to remain quiet but wished she didn't have to hold back.

She dropped her head and groaned. "I seriously need you to get inside me now."

With his hands around her waist again, he lifted her slightly so that she could center over the tip of his cock, and then kept his hands on her ass as she lowered herself. Once he was fully sheathed, she began to rock back and forth, groaning with the movements. After a moment, he needed to go faster and harder. "I'll take over from here, babe."

She lifted slightly, so he could begin to piston his hips up and down, plunging into her, the drag and pull on his cock sending his mind into oblivion.

He kept his eyes on her, not wanting to miss a moment, but she clapped her palm over her mouth again, stifling any noise she might make. He felt her release squeeze him and, with only a few more thrusts, flung himself into the abyss along with her. Now, it was his time to keep from roaring out his release. As he continued to pump slowly, emptying every drop out of his body, he watched as her face eased into a relaxed, satisfied expression, and she lowered her hand from her mouth.

He held her gaze and was filled with so much love for this woman that there was no doubt they should be together.

Not wanting to stay naked in case the kids needed them, they cleaned up in the bathroom, their smiles meeting in the mirror's reflection. She pulled on a nightgown, and he wore the pajama bottoms he'd brought from his house. Finally, they snuggled in bed together. For a moment, he allowed his mind to roam to the past, wondering if he'd ever felt this level of contentment with his first wife. He was sure he must have felt something at the beginning, but it was more the rush of lust from a man barely out of his teens. It had no staying power.

Without hesitation, he knew that he and Hayley

would have no problem going the distance. They'd been friends for a very long time before falling in love.

They whispered loving words to each other before she finally fell asleep. He spent a few minutes thinking of ways they could reconfigure the house and decided not to delay the call for a contractor to discuss the possibilities. But thinking about the house inevitably led him to ponder the macabre finding in the backyard. And he hated that the discovery overshadowed their early days together.

He fell asleep wondering, *"Who was the mysterious lady who was buried in a shallow grave so long ago?"*

24

With a sense of accomplishment, Hayley clicked the Save button on her latest work project. Now, she was free to check her planner to see which freelance project she could work on next. She'd promised Katelyn that she would have a mock-up for Harrison Private Investigation finished by tomorrow, but her fingers itched to delve back into the world of the DEPA fraternity alumni website.

Ever since she'd met Malcolm and his friends, their camaraderie after all these years intrigued her. She found herself admiring their striking friendship. Contemplating her own college years, she sighed wistfully. All these years later, she only had a couple of college friends who she occasionally kept up with on social media. Certainly nothing like the four Delta Epsilon Phi Alpha friends.

She wondered if joining a sorority would have made a difference. At the time, she had no desire to spend the energy, time, and money necessary to pledge to Greek life.

She wished she had taken a few snapshots of some of the pictures with her phone just to remember the youthful faces for inspiration for the website. Even though she hadn't, she could still recall the smiling faces, their arms around each other, all directing their attention toward the camera.

As she navigated through her design software, her thoughts roamed to the young man in the pictures that they couldn't remember well. A strange sense of sadness moved over her. It was obvious that when several of those pictures were taken, he was part of their group. A member of the team. Welcomed into the camaraderie. Yet it was strange that the men couldn't remember his name after all these years. It seemed that after those pictures were taken and they were inducted into the fraternity and he wasn't, they never saw him again.

Did they only hang out with other fraternity members? Did they not see him in classes or in the dorms? Or at a football game? It was as though he simply faded away after being so close.

Then she thought of her own college life again. She met Edward soon after graduating, and their lives revolved around their jobs and then Eddie. She had to admit that friends she'd once thought would be in her life forever had also faded into the background.

She spent the next hour designing a few pages of the mock-up, then stretched her arms over her head and arched her back. Staring out the window for a few minutes, she looked back at what she'd created, and new ideas began to form. To gain more background information, she went to the DEPA national chapter's website to include some of that information on the alumni site.

That led her to some interesting articles about community service, distinguished alumni members, and even a link to newspaper articles on fraternity hazing. Of course, the national chapter denounced the practice of hazing, but the newspaper articles gave evidence that even today, the rituals for being inducted into a fraternity could be brutal. Each year, some deaths occur from alcohol poisoning or a variety of other hazing incidents.

Looking at the time, she closed down that page and pulled up the mock-up for the nursing home she would present to Belle and the nursing home's director, Mr. Weldon. Soon, she was submerged in what should have seemed like a depressing subject but was fascinated with the many activities the nursing home participated in to enhance the lives of its clients.

By the time she finished, she was once again loving her ability to get to know so many local businesses and people. *If only I could do this full-time. Maybe, just maybe, I can find a way.*

Sam sat in the meeting, anxious for it to begin. Colt had called him, Aaron, Hunter, and Brad to one of the conference rooms, saying they had a preliminary report from forensics. Colt handed out copies of the initial findings as soon as everyone was seated.

Sam scanned the report quickly, startled at what he was reading.

Colt summarized the information. "The skeletal remains were confirmed to be female. Approximately thirty years old at death. She had given birth. What stands out from everything else is that she was buried approximately a hundred and twenty years ago. There was no evidence of a coffin."

"Fucking hell," Aaron muttered softly. "I guess that's not so strange, except there were churches in the area back then. You think she would've been buried in a cemetery, even if she was poor."

"All this makes me wonder how she died," Sam said. He was immediately struck with a similarity between the woman and Hayley. About the same age. Both mothers. Looking back down at the report, he continued, "Her right arm had been broken and not set well when it re-healed. She also suffered a broken collarbone."

The facts should have made Sam glad. Now, there was no need for more investigation since the woman died and was buried so long ago. But instead, he felt a heaviness in his heart just thinking of the young woman who died and whether loved ones buried her or was all alone until discovered by two children playing at being archaeologists.

"At this point, we can consider this not an active case. We'll keep all the information, and the forensic team out of Norfolk will continue to double-check their preliminary findings," Colt announced, ending the meeting.

Sam had his elbows propped on the table and rubbed his chin, turning the evidence over in his mind. Looking up, he realized the others were quietly observing him.

"You okay, man?" Hunter asked.

He leaned back in his chair and sighed. "Yeah. I mean, this is technically good news. It's not an active case, and I can take the police tape down out of my yard, and the kids can play again."

"But..." Colt prodded.

"I don't know, boss. Just something about it doesn't seem right. Or maybe it just seems sad. Or maybe the fact that she was a young woman and a mom about the same age as Hayley. Hell, I don't know."

"Because of her burial, it makes her death feel suspicious, doesn't it?" Brad asked.

Sam looked over and could have sworn he spied a dark flash move through Brad's eyes. "Yeah, it does." They all stood, and as they walked out of the room, he turned his attention to Colt. "Do you have a problem with me continuing to look into this?"

Colt held his gaze, and the others stopped to turn and look at him as well. "What are you looking for?"

"Honestly? I'm not sure. I thought I would check into the land records to see who owned the land a hundred years ago. Not for any active police investigation, and I'd do this on my own time. I guess I'd just like to have an idea of who she was. Maybe because I don't like the unanswered questions, or maybe it's just a bizarre sense of responsibility since she was found on the land that I now own."

"I don't have a problem with that at all. You're right... if it happened in my backyard, I'd be just as interested in discovering everything I could."

"It helps that the county administration building is on the other side of our parking lot," Aaron quipped. "Looks like you may have a new place to start spending your lunchtime."

He agreed, chuckling as he stood, and they all walked out of the room. Once he was back at his desk, he called Hayley and gave her the information.

"Oh, that's so sad, isn't it?"

"I thought the same thing, sweetheart."

"It's like she just died alone and was there for so long. I mean, I know when you die, you're not in pain anymore, but it just seems so sad." After a pause, she asked, "Is that it? There's nothing more you have to investigate?"

"Officially, that's right. But I'll go to the county courthouse and look into the records. I would at least like to know who owned this property a hundred years ago. Or as far back as I can go."

"I think that would be fascinating to know, but you do realize that she might not have lived on this land just because she was buried here."

"I know, but it just seems like a little more piece of the puzzle. I'd like to know about the history of the land I now own."

"How about if I do some internet searching, also? Would it be okay?"

"Absolutely! But only if you really want to."

"Well, *somebody* asked me to marry him, so if this

land is going to be mine also, I think I should know what I'm getting into, don't you think?"

He laughed, and her words made his heart feel lighter. "I think you should definitely find out what you're getting into."

They disconnected, and he headed out with Aaron to investigate another case. By the time they finished, he didn't have a chance to make a trip to the county administration building but decided he managed to get in a call to one of the women who worked there.

"Janelle? It's Sam Shackley. I guess you, like everyone else, heard about the skeletal remains found at my place."

"I heard about it on the news, and then some people around here were saying that it was your backyard. I couldn't believe it! I think if my grandkids came in carrying a bone, I would've had a heart attack!"

"I can tell you that it's not an active case because the state has determined that her remains were at least a hundred years old—"

"Lord have mercy! You don't say!"

"But I still want to do some checking into the history of my property. If I'm gonna be living there, I'd like to know how far back the records go on it."

"I'll do some looking for you, Detective, if you give me a little something in return."

"Now, Janelle, I know you're happily married, so I can't imagine what you'd want from me," he joked.

Her cackle of laughter sounded out. "You've got that right. No, what I want from you is a little early gossip. I had lunch yesterday with the dispatcher. And she said that the word going around is that your sweet lady friend will be a lot more than just a friend."

Rolling his eyes, he was still getting used to the small-town mentality of everyone in everybody's business. "I can tell you that Hayley Brooks and I are dating. And that's all I'm gonna say because I swear this isn't high school."

She cackled out in laughter again. "Well, I'll say I heard it from the horse's mouth. Anyway, I'll do a little looking, and there are some amateur historians around who like to study the history of the Eastern Shore. I'll check with someone I think might know something about that area. He used to know all the things that went on around here. If you stop by here before you head home, I'll at least have some preliminary information for you."

"Sounds good." Disconnecting, he and Aaron worked in the station until the end of their day. He ran by the administration building and found Janelle's office. She greeted him warmly and said, "I'll give you the basics and print off everything else for you to review. The plot of land that you own has no recorded burial ground, cemetery, or any other reason there should be a body there. It wasn't the site of a church either."

She beamed proudly as she continued. "North Heron County has the oldest continuous records in the US, dating back to 1632. But since you're looking at the turn of the last century, I went back to around 1900. It was a big farm and belonged to the Young family. In fact, there was another farm right next door that belonged to the Mansfields. Two longstanding families on the Shore. But your property fell under the Youngs."

He leaned forward in his chair, fascinated by what she had already discovered.

"It was passed down through the years, and a man named Ralph Young sold it in the 1980s to some developers who divided up the farmland into lots. They auctioned off the plots, hoping that people would build on them, and most of them did. The man who bought your lot bought about four others and had duplexes put in on each lot. If I had to guess, that was so he could sell each one separately and make even more money. Anyway, sugar, that's all I got for you right now."

"Janelle, you're a dream."

"Honey, my husband tells me that all the time!"

Laughing, he took the notes he scribbled while she was talking and headed home. Once there, he walked into the backyard with Hayley and the kids, and they all participated in taking down the yellow police tape. Hope ran around with a long string of it flowing behind her, while Eddie was interested in how much dirt the forensic police took away.

"Sam, you can't plant shrubs here. It's too deep," Eddie called out.

"You're right. We'll have to bring in some soil to fill in the hole before I can plant anything."

Eddie walked over, his expression solemn. "They took away so much, and you have to put some back. That seems dumb. Why did they take so much?"

"There can be evidence in the soil that gives some

clues as to what was happening at the time the person was buried."

He loved Eddie's inquisitive mind and wanted to encourage his curiosity. He also knew how Eddie was like a sponge, soaking up information. Sam had no idea which direction his studies would go when he got older, but he had no doubt Eddie would memorize everything he could on a topic.

"How about we look online this weekend and see if we can find a good book that you could read about... well, I guess a children's book on forensic science. I think we could find one that you'd enjoy."

Eddie's eyes grew large and round, and a smile spread across his face. "Thanks, Sam!" He grabbed a piece of yellow tape and raced around the yard, chasing Hope.

Sam turned from the dug-out pit and saw Hayley walking toward him. Her smile warmed his face. When they met in the middle of the yard, he wrapped his arms around her waist and kissed her lightly.

"I think we have the only nine-year-old boy excited about learning about forensic science."

She leaned back and laughed while nodding. "You're probably right!"

After dinner, homework, and bath time were over, and the kids were in bed, he filled Hayley in about the land.

"I don't know if there's much more I can learn, but I was going to go back to the administration building tomorrow. After Ralph Young sold it in the 1980s, I'll be able to see who had the house before me, but no more on the land."

"I wonder if there's any family still around who might remember before then," she asked.

"Maybe. Janelle was going to see if she could find someone I could check with. She says a few amateur historians in the area might know more."

"What about one of the ancestry websites? I signed up for an account just to learn a little bit more about my family, and I can get on it right now and see if we can find anything about Ralph Young."

"Not gonna turn down any free research, sweetheart."

After peeking into each of the kids' bedrooms, she headed upstairs to retrieve her laptop. When she came down, he asked, "How are the kids?"

"They're asleep. They feel much better and don't have any nightmares. I think partially because you're here with us."

She sat on the sofa beside him, and he pulled her close. "It's because *we* are here together."

She smiled and graced him with a gentle kiss before turning back to her laptop. A few minutes later, and after a few failed password attempts, she finally logged into one of the more popular ancestry programs.

She typed in Ralph Young, but it was such a common name she narrowed her focus down to Virginia and then had to narrow it even more to North Heron County. Once she did that, the information started filling her page.

"Oh my gosh!" she cried out.

Sam's gaze shot over to her. "What? What is it?"

"Ralph Young is no longer living, but his son is living and still lives on the Eastern Shore. And you're not gonna believe it, Sam, but I know him."

"You know him? Who is he?"

"Ralph Young's son is Malcolm Young. He's the man I've been talking to who has that big beach house and is the president of his fraternity's alumni association. He's commissioning me to do a website for the fraternity alumni. In fact, I've met with him twice. The last time, he had three fraternity brothers with him. They still get together forty years later."

"I think I'll give him a call and see if I can find out anything."

"He doesn't live anywhere around here, so he definitely doesn't live on part of what had been the Young farmland. I wonder if it bothered him that his dad sold the farm. But then, if he didn't want to farm…"

"Lots of family farms are too big for people who don't want to farm anymore. Believe me, Ralph selling it to a developer meant he probably got good money from that. I guess that could have been his son's inheritance."

She slowly nodded, her top teeth nibbling on her bottom lip as she thought. "That makes sense. I mean, Malcolm has money. You should see his house on the bay!"

"I'll give him a call. Maybe he knew something about his grandfather or perhaps his great-grandfather. At least, he would remember this land if he grew up here."

Putting away her laptop, she leaned over and whispered, "How about a diversion?"

Lifting a brow, he grinned wolfishly. "What kind of diversion?"

"Want to try to see how quietly we can have sex again?"

He laughed and pulled her over onto his lap. "Loud sex, quiet sex, long sex, fast sex… any way you want to do it works for me, sweetheart."

Another giggle rang out, and he kissed her hard and fast. "Head on up, and I'll secure the house for the night."

As he made sure the sliding glass door was locked, he spied a small strand of yellow police tape that Hope had been running with that hadn't made it into the trash. Smiling, he was just glad there was no more need for that tape in his yard.

Flipping off the lights, he hurried upstairs to give Hayley all his attention… his favorite way to end the day.

25

Saturday morning, Sam navigated his SUV through the winding roads that led to Malcolm Young's home. Hayley offered to go with him, but after careful consideration, he explained that it was important to him to maintain a separation between her professional work and what he was doing on his own. She'd smiled her agreement and immediately began planning a fun morning with the kids. Now, he found himself at the end of the lane, staring at the beautiful beachfront property that Malcolm Young owned.

He'd called earlier, and Malcolm's wife, Anne, had answered. When he explained that he had a few questions about the old Young farm, she'd invited him to stop by to talk to her husband, who was out on a beach walk but would be back within the hour.

The front door opened, and an attractive woman with pale silver hair welcomed him inside. "It's so nice to make your acquaintance, Mr. Shackley. Or should I call you Detective?"

"Sam is fine. This is just a personal visit, Mrs. Young."

"Lovely," she said, her smile as warm as her welcome. "And please call me Anne. I just noticed Malcolm walking up the back dune from the beach. I haven't had a chance to tell him you were coming, but he'll be thrilled. Malcolm's a real people person. Oh my, he loves to talk."

Anne moved to her husband as he came through the back door from the deck. He had kicked off his shoes and left them outside but carefully dusted off the remaining grains of sand.

"Malcolm, honey, we have a guest. And stop worrying about the sand. That's why we live at the beach... to enjoy the sand!"

Malcolm smiled at his wife, then turned his welcoming face to where Sam stood.

Anne made the introductions and explained who Sam was and why he was there. Malcolm's mouth momentarily twisted, and Sam wondered if he wasn't the *people person* that his wife described him to be. But as quickly as the grimace crossed Malcolm's face, he quickly recovered.

Sam spoke first. "Mr. Young, I'm so sorry to drop in on you, but your wife had said it would be okay."

"Yes, yes, absolutely." Malcolm marched forward and thrust out his hand. "It's nice to meet you. Please have a seat."

"Your home is really something. The view is—"

"Spectacular, isn't it?" Malcolm said, his smile wide, although Sam thought it appeared forced.

"I'll leave you two to talk and will bring some iced tea in in a few minutes."

"Mr. Young," Sam began, "it's of utmost importance that you understand that I'm not here as a detective for the North Heron Sheriff's Department. I'm here simply as a homeowner in the county."

Malcolm's eyes widened, and his head tilted to the side. "Well, um... yes. So what can I help you with?"

"I'm trying to find out more about the land on which my house is built. I recently came to understand that it was part of the Young farm many years ago. It's my understanding that it belonged to Ralph Young, and I believe that's your father?"

Malcolm swallowed audibly, then his gaze darted over, relief slashing across his face as Anne walked back in with two tall glasses. She handed them to the men, then excused herself again. Malcolm took a long drink, and Sam waited patiently.

Clearing his throat, Malcolm nodded. "Yes, Ralph was my father. He was the owner of a large farm in the county. It had been in my family for many years. Well, for generations, actually. Can I ask why you're interested?"

Sam chuckled, dropped his chin slightly, and shook his head. "I don't know if you've heard about the recent skeletal remains that were found in the county. Believe it or not, that was in my backyard."

Malcolm had just taken another sip, but it appeared to have gone down wrong as he began to cough and sputter. His face turned red for a long moment as he continued to cough. Finally gaining control of himself, he looked back at Sam. "Well, that must've been a real surprise."

"This hasn't hit the news yet, but the preliminary report has come through, and I hope I can depend on your discretion. The remains were of a woman, and the skeletal evidence places her as having been buried probably about one hundred to one hundred twenty years ago."

"Oh!" Malcolm's eyes widened as his entire body jerked. "Oh," he repeated, seeming stunned. "Well, that's... um... my goodness."

"There is no investigation on the remains due to the age, but I found myself curious about the property I own, and while I'm sure I won't ever know who the young woman was, I wondered who owned the land before I bought the house."

Malcolm's smile widened, and his body visibly relaxed as he leaned back in his chair. Suddenly verbose, he began, "I agree with you, Mr. Shackley. While I don't spend much time thinking about family history, I will tell you that I have a cousin who loves those new ancestry programs on the computer. She's much older than me and learned how to work those programs so she could delve into the family. Now me? I didn't have any siblings, and my father was always harping on how the family had been land owners since God created the Chesapeake Bay or some such nonsense, but I do know my cousin did some real digging. And Lord knows she dominated every family get-together, making sure we heard all about the latest she'd learned about the family."

Sam noticed Malcolm's demeanor had morphed into the extroverted people person Anne had declared he was. It struck Sam that perhaps Malcolm's beach walk might have exerted him more than normal, and he was just coming into his second wind.

"So," Sam prodded, "the Youngs had a large farm on the Eastern Shore for several generations."

"Yes. My father, Ralph Young, was born in 1926 on that farm. There wasn't a hospital out here at that time, so it was a home birth like most people had. Now, it's my understanding from my cousin that statewide birth and death registrations were required starting in the early 1900s, but I believe my father's birth record was entered in the local Methodist Church nearby. I suppose there was a state record, but back then, residents probably trusted the church record more than anything recorded far away in the state capital."

Sam quickly realized that the more verbose, convivial Malcolm would take a bit to keep him on track. "The woman found would've been about thirty years old around the turn of the century. I couldn't find any records of a cemetery or burial area there."

Malcolm shook his head and lowered his brow. "I used to run all over that farm when I was a boy, and I never saw a family burial plot, either." He leaned back and narrowed his eyes in thought. "Now let's see, that would've been about my grandfather's time. His name was Lloyd Young."

They were interrupted when Anne entered the room with a large old book. "Forgive me, Malcolm, dear. I couldn't help but overhear, even though I wasn't trying to be a snoop. But I remembered where your mother's family Bible was kept. I thought it was in a box in one of the upstairs bedrooms, and I found it."

She handed it to Malcolm, who smiled at his wife and patted her hand affectionately. "Goodness gracious, Anne. I wouldn't have had any idea where to look for this."

He flipped through pages, then finally settled on one. "Oh, here are the family records. Of course, these are self-recorded, but back then, people wanted to be accurate, trusting an old family Bible more than the state. If you're focused on the turn of the century, that would be when my grandfather, Lloyd Young, owned the Young farm. Let's see, he was born in 1898."

Malcolm looked up at Sam and said, "I was born in 1962, and I don't remember my grandfather at all." He looked back down at the old Bible, his forefinger moving across the page where the family recorded births, marriages, and death dates. "He died in 1965, and I guess that's when my father took over the farm."

Anne looked over Malcolm's shoulder and said, "I remember your father once mentioning his stepmother. I'm sure that's what he said—stepmother, not mother."

Malcolm looked back down and shook his head. "My cousin would've known all about this, but she passed a couple of years ago. She lived at the nursing home up the road. She probably drove them crazy with her tales of old. Let's see... Lloyd's wife is listed as Edna." He paused, then looked over at Anne. "Darling, can you bring me my—"

Anne handed him his glasses, and he chuckled.

Looking at Sam, he said, "Are you married, Mr. Shackley?"

"No, sir." By now, Sam wasn't sure where the conversational turns were going.

"Well, find you a peach like my Anne here. Someone who knows you so well, no words are hardly needed."

Sam remained quiet, but Malcom's words resonated. He'd found his *peach*... the one who knew him so well, no words were hardly needed. Dragging his mind back to the task at hand, he waited to see what other information would be forthcoming.

With Malcolm's glasses now perched on his nose, he perused the handwritten records again. "Hmm. This is odd. Lloyd married a woman named Helen in 1932. I guess Edna died, but I don't see that in here. Funny that her death date isn't recorded. My dad was raised by this woman named Helen, who would've been his stepmother."

Malcolm returned the Bible to Anne and smiled at his wife before returning to Sam. "I don't know if that's giving you much information, but I'm afraid that's all I know, Mr. Shackley."

Sam stood and nodded, reaching his hand out to shake Malcolm's. "Mr. and Mrs. Young, you've been very helpful. As I said, I became interested in the history of the property I own." He started for the door, then turned back and said, "I assume your father sold the farm to a developer when farming wasn't something you wanted to pursue?"

Malcolm chuckled. "My father and I had a bit of a contentious relationship by the time I was a young man.

Farming was all he knew, all his father knew, and the land had been in the Young family for a long time. But it was a new time. I wanted to leave the shore, go to college, and become an attorney. I think my father held on until I finally graduated from college and went to law school."

"So I guess you expected him to sell the land?"

Anger flashed across Malcolm's face so quickly that if Sam wasn't used to reading people, he wasn't sure he would have noticed. But the image struck him as telling.

"Honestly, I didn't think my father would ever sell the land. I thought it could be handed down to me, and I could decide what I wanted to do with it later in my life. In fact, I'll tell you that the old codger didn't even tell me he was going to sell it. One day, it was in the family, and then the next time I came home from law school, he announced that it had already been sold to a developer. He only kept the old farmhouse and an acre or two right around it. Everything else was sold to the developer to be divided into lots, one of which I'm sure is what your house is now on."

Sam nodded, glad for the information he'd been given but not wanting to tread on what appeared to be ill feelings from Malcolm over his father's decision to sell the land. "Well, again, I thank you for your time. It was enlightening for me to have a bit of the history. I've only been on the Eastern Shore for about six months, but I've put down roots and plan on staying. So knowing the history of where I'm living is fascinating."

Anne and Malcolm walked him to the door and shook hands with him again. Driving away, Sam thought about everything Malcolm had said. He wondered how angry Malcolm had been when he found out his dad had sold his inheritance. But then, with Malcolm's large beachfront house, surely Ralph must have left him money from the sale. Of course, Sam didn't know that was a fact, and their family travails were not his concern.

What it did make him realize was that whatever Hope and Eddie wanted to be in their life, he knew he and Hayley would support them. He wanted them to choose their own destiny. Their relationship would've been better if Ralph had let Malcolm do that.

After he arrived home, Sam felt a burst of inspiration. The kids wouldn't be able to get into the water at this time of year, but he wanted to show the kids the town pier and walk along the harbor to see some of the boats that were moored. "Let's hit the pub for lunch and then head to the beach in Baytown."

The air electrified at his suggestion. Hope twirled with her hands in the air. Eddie bounced on his toes. And Hayley lifted to whisper in his ear, "I hadn't decided on what to fix for lunch anyway, so I'll give you a little kiss now and a much bigger one when the kids go to bed."

Chuckling warmly, he slid his arm around her waist and accepted the sweet kiss she gave him. Herding the kids took a moment since they needed long pants and a light jacket. Hope couldn't find the shoes she wanted, then came out with mismatched sneakers on her feet. Eddie raced off to find his football. Hayley dashed upstairs to help Hope find matching shoes. Sam retrieved the kids' jackets from the coat closet. Pausing, he stood by the sliding glass door and cast his gaze over the backyard, trying to imagine what the original farm would've looked like. He had neighbors on the sides and across the street, but the large lots provided generous spaces between the homes. And it wasn't hard to imagine the entire neighborhood covered in fields or pastures.

He knew family farms all across America were sold when sons and daughters no longer wanted to become farmers. Malcolm had mentioned a contentious relationship with his father. Still, other than the fact that he didn't want to be a farmer, he hadn't given any indication as to why their relationship wasn't good. The hesitancy he felt coming from Malcolm when he was first introduced still tickled the back of Sam's mind, but he shrugged it off.

"Hey, Sam! Are you ready?" Eddie called out.

Turning, Sam grinned, his heart full. "You bet I am."

They ate at the pub, sitting at a table in the small area that had been a bank vault many years ago. Eddie was fascinated with the idea of turning an old bank into a restaurant. Hope was more entranced with the pictures on the wall of days gone by.

After eating their fill, they walked a few blocks to the town beach, where they found they weren't the only beachgoers on the pretty but chilly late fall day. Sam tossed the football with Eddie while Hayley searched for sea glass with Hope. Eventually, Eddie and Hope played with a few other kids who had arrived, and Sam sat on the beach blanket that Hayley had set out.

He hadn't had a chance to tell her about his visit with Malcolm, so he took the few minutes that the kids weren't with them to give her the gist of his interview.

"He mentioned not having siblings, so I suppose his dad sold it off when he didn't want the farm."

"You said that Malcolm didn't even know his dad was going to do that? That seems kind of cold, doesn't it?"

Nodding, Sam said, "You're right." After a moment of silence with their gazes following the kids playing, he glanced toward Hayley, but the words he wanted to say were held back. They were words from his heart, but he didn't know how to broach the subject with Hayley.

"If you keep staring at the side of my head, I'm going to get a complex," Hayley joked, turning to hold his gaze.

A deep chuckle rumbled from his chest as he nodded. "Well, I don't want to give you a complex."

She placed her hand on his arm. "Sam, you can talk to me about anything. I hope you know that." When he didn't respond right away, she added, "Remember who we are and who we've been to each other. What has you so tied up in knots?"

He sucked in his bottom lip with a slight hiss and trapped it with his teeth for a few seconds. Finally, he said, "I guess this seems like a dumb time to bring up something like this. But I'm staring out at the kids playing on the beach, and honest to God, my heart is so full of love for them."

He halted at the sight of tears gathering in Hayley's eyes. She pressed her lips tightly together as though to keep her emotions trapped inside.

Now that he'd started, he needed to finish his thoughts. "Sweetheart, on a day like today, I find myself thinking of Edward. Over the years, when I watched the kids, I would think about what he was missing. And I don't want you to think that I have stopped thinking about him. He was your husband. He was my best friend. And he's the father of your children. It's important for you to know that if we never have any other children but Eddie and Hope, I would be a satisfied man because I love them as if they were my own."

Hayley lost the ability to hold back her tears as one rolled down her cheek. He lifted his forefinger and gently wiped it away. "And if we do have children of our own, Eddie and Hope will not come in second place. If they want to keep Edward's last name when you and I get married, that will also be fine. But I want to offer, from the bottom of my heart, my name if either of them wants that."

"You're offering them your name?" Hayley sniffed and reached into her small backpack to grab a tissue. Wiping her nose, she then dabbed at her eyes.

"Absolutely. I would consider it an honor if either or both of them wanted me to adopt them legally. They don't have to call me Dad. Sam is fine. That's who I've been to them all their lives. And if they want to keep the last name of Brooks, that's fine, too. I just wanted to make sure that you knew where I stood with them. No matter the name, they'll always have my heart."

Her bottom lip quivered, and another tear rolled down her cheek to be captured by his finger again. She swallowed deeply, then offered a tremulous smile. "I didn't think it was possible to love you more, Sam. But my heart is overflowing for you."

He pulled her closer and kissed her long and deep, not caring who was around. Finally, he leaned back and said, "Let's get the kids and head to the house."

"To our home," Hayley corrected.

With his heart much lighter, he nodded. "Our home."

26

It was the kind of day that Hayley liked best. A few good friends were over, enjoying food while the kids played in the backyard. The weather was perfect. As long as everyone wore long pants and a jacket, the sun beat down on the gathering, keeping them warm.

Ryan and Judith Coates had come over with their kids. Trevor was a total teenage hottie, and Hayley thought he was one of the coolest sixteen-year-old boys she'd ever met. Handsome, nice, and smart. Ryan and Judith's daughter, Cindy, was fifteen and a soft-spoken, intelligent beauty who played in the backyard with Hope. Hayley's daughter was eating up the attention of the sweet teenager.

Colt and Carrie were also there with their teenage son, Jack. He was comfortable in his own skin while still idolizing Trevor. The two teen boys were tossing a football with Eddie, and like Hope, her son loved the chance to be with the older boys.

It dawned on Hayley that she'd usually entertained

people with kids about the same age as Eddie and Hope. But getting to know Ryan, the captain of the local Virginia Marine Police, and his wife, Judith, one of the local doctors, as well as Colt and Carrie, made for an enjoyable afternoon.

Trevor ambled over to the adults. "Mr. Shackley. Eddie told me that you were going to put plantings in the back of the yard. He'd like to dig for *more* dinosaur bones, so if you'd like me to help him, I will."

Sam sighed but nodded. "That's fine, Trevor. Eddie knows where the spades are. But only assist if you feel like it."

"It's all cool, Mr. Shackley."

"That's how everything got started, isn't it?" Judith asked. "Digging for dinosaur bones?"

Rolling her eyes, Hayley groaned, "Only my son could have the desire to be an archaeologist and find a skeleton in the backyard."

Carrie looked over at Sam. "Did you ever find anything else about this land or the possible identity of the woman?"

He shrugged and shook his head. "Just a little. This was all part of a farm that had been passed down through generations of the Young family. In the mid-80s, it was sold to a developer who put in these houses and duplexes. The last Mr. Young has come back to live on the Shore, but not around here. He gave me a little information about the farm but wasn't close to his dad, so I didn't get much. However, it seems his grandmother died early, and his grandfather remarried around that time. I'll do more checking with a local historian who might shed light onto the identity of the woman."

The conversation rolled casually from one topic to another, and as Hayley kept an eye on the kids and the backyard, she could tell that with Trevor's and Jack's strength, the new ditch they were digging on the other side of the yard was growing.

"Sam, I feel like we're going to have to pay the kids for the yard work. They've almost got a ditch big enough for all the shrubs you wanted to plant there in the spring."

Sam chuckled and reached over to clasp her hand. "I appreciate cheap labor!"

Everyone laughed, shaking their heads. "Well, I used to babysit. It was the only way for me to make money as a teenager," Judith said.

"I mowed grass and worked in a local store," Ryan added. "Now that Trevor is driving, he wants to get a part-time job over the holidays."

"It's a good way for him to earn some Christmas money," Carrie agreed.

Both Ryan and Judith rolled their eyes, and Judith explained, "I'm afraid Trevor wants to earn money so he can spend it on his girlfriend."

Hayley looked back at Eddie and Hope, knowing the years would fly by and they'd start talking about girlfriends and boyfriends. "Oh God, I don't even want to think about my kids being that age!" She glanced around and noted that several glasses were nearly empty. She stood and said, "I'm going inside to get some more tea. Would anyone like another beer—"

An ear-piercing scream that every parent knew was horrible met their ears, and Hayley whirled around, her gaze jerking to where the kids were in the backyard. Cindy snatched up Hope in her arms and started running toward the patio where the adults were.

Trevor yelled to Jack, "Get Eddie back! Get him away!" Jack immediately wrapped his arms around Eddie, stumbling as they moved backward. Trevor stayed where the shovels were dropped onto the ground, his gaze down and his chest heaving.

Hayley's body flew into action, and she raced toward Cindy, barely aware of the other adults running in the same direction. Reaching Cindy, she pulled Hope from the teenager's arms, crying, "What? What happened? Oh my God, are you hurt?"

Cindy's pale face and wide eyes were the only answer as her mouth opened and closed several times, but nothing came out. Judith grabbed Cindy, wrapping her arms around her daughter's trembling body.

Eddie screamed, "It happened again! It's there again! The body came back!"

Hayley's knees nearly buckled. She wanted to race to her son but didn't want to get Hope any closer to whatever terror was happening. She only caught her breath when she saw Sam skidding to a stop next to Jack, pulling Eddie into his arms.

Cindy, seeming to find her quivering voice, said, "There's... another... b... bone. There's another b... body."

Unsure she heard the young girl correctly, she

looked at Hope's wide-eyed expression and watched her daughter bob her head up and down in agreement.

"Oh God. Okay... um... Hope, go with Cindy... go to the patio... no, go inside."

Grateful that Hope didn't argue but instead grabbed Cindy's hand, and the two girls ran back to the house. Hayley turned and raced toward Sam and the others. Getting to Eddie, she pulled him into her arms, too, wanting him close.

Sam stalked toward Trevor, and Hayley noted the teen swallowed deeply, seeming to work to steady his breathing. She followed the others' gazes to where some earth had been overturned and spied the cause of the kids' terror. There, lying on the top of the freshly turned dirt, was a skeletal hand.

"Dammit! What the hell is going on around here?" Sam growled, standing on his patio. Two hours later, his yard was once again covered in yellow police tape and crawling with deputies, state police, and the state forensic team. He'd just stopped pacing back and forth, unable to be calmed by his friends, who were just as pissed as him. Although Colt was there, Aaron, Hunter, and Brad showed up to officially take charge of the site.

Sam was glad the others had arrived. The women kept Hayley company inside the house, and Cindy entertained Hope in her room facing the front yard. Eddie's face was plastered to the back sliding glass window again, but at least Jack kept him company.

Trevor was out with his dad and Sam and Colt on the patio.

Aaron interviewed Trevor with his dad present because the teen was digging when the bones were discovered. Trevor couldn't give them much information that they didn't already know. He, Jack, and Eddie were digging about ten yards from where the other body was found. Trevor had used a shovel and stepped on the tool to drive the shovel a little deeper into the ground. When he lifted it to dump the dirt off, the skeletal hand was among the dirt. He jolted and wasn't too embarrassed to tell the detectives that the sight scared the piss out of him. But unfortunately, all the other kids were right there. He wasn't sure Hope had seen it, but Cindy had. She screamed before grabbing Hope, trying to keep the younger girl from witnessing anything.

Sam was pissed, anger flooding his whole body. It was bad enough that the kids were the ones to discover the first skeletal remains in their own backyard but to have it happen a second time was a fuckin' nightmare... not to mention would probably *give* them fuckin' nightmares. He also hated that the teens had to witness the scene.

Once again, the forensic team arrived and began excavating and carefully discovering the full skeleton. Unlike the first one, this skeleton had remnants of some clothing. Just like before, the forensic team removed a large area of dirt from around the skeleton, wrapping it carefully as they prepared to load it on their truck.

Hank walked over, peeling the hood of his hazmat

suit off his head and removing the face mask. Holding Sam's gaze, he shook his head. "You've got quite the Halloween setup around here, don't you?"

Sam wasn't in the mood for jokes but assumed in Hank's profession, jokes might be how he got through each day. He nodded and said, "Had plenty of treats with Hayley and the kids here, but now, we're just getting the fuckin' tricks." Scrubbing his hand over his face, he asked, "Got anything you can tell us yet?"

"The skeleton has been here for years. Male. Young... late teens to early twenties. I won't know more until I get it in the lab. Like the first one, it was buried, and there doesn't seem to be any burial material, such as a coffin, around it. The bits of clothing will be a big assistance in our analysis."

"How did this back part of an old farm get to be where bodies were buried?" Ryan asked. "It doesn't make any sense."

Sam agreed but was relieved to hear that he would once again be able to investigate and not be off the case due to a conflict. The body was buried on this land long before he ever bought his lot. He once again scrubbed his hand over his face. "This is fuckin' unreal."

Colt turned toward him, his expression grim. "You got that right."

"There's no record of this being anything other than a farm, and the last owner has been dead for a while. The farmer's son hasn't had anything to do with this place since his dad sold it."

"What do we know about the old man?" Brad asked,

gathering everyone's attention. "Maybe the family was doing something."

"Couldn't have been with the first body. The female was too long ago."

"I'm talking about the Youngs who were here long ago." Brad shrugged. "Although, I don't guess there is anyone left from back that far who might remember."

Colt's brows lifted, and Sam turned his attention to his boss. Colt said, "Tomorrow, check with Janelle and see if she had a way to get in touch with the last Mansfield who lived here."

"I heard the Mansfields had the farm next to the Youngs, but my land is on the Youngs' farm."

"Yeah, but if I remember correctly, the last Mansfield who lived in these parts was a bit of a historian himself." Colt shrugged and added, "I don't know, Sam. But it's worth a shot. Like you, I'm getting tired of these remains turning up in the county, and I know you sure as hell are sick of having your backyard turned into a crime scene."

He nodded, ready to try anything to resolve the macabre findings in his backyard. As the evening shadows covered the yard, he said good night to Carrie, who was taking Jack home since it was a school night. Judith stayed to help Hope with her bath while Hayley kept track of Eddie getting ready for bed.

Then they said goodbye to Ryan, Judith, Trevor, and Cindy. Sam stepped up and shook Trevor's hand, man to man. "You did real good, Trevor. You helped Eddie and then ensured to get him out of the area when the discovery was made." Trevor nodded, but his face shone with pride as he cut his eyes toward his dad just before Ryan clapped his son on the shoulder, his own fatherly pride easily felt.

Sam then turned to Cindy. "I can't thank you enough for how quickly you grabbed Hope to keep her from seeing something I didn't want her to see." Cindy smiled shyly, then snuggled underneath Judith's arm.

Hayley said her goodbyes, then held Sam's gaze, offering her silent support before she headed upstairs to tuck Hope into Eddie's bed again.

Sam shook his head, planted his fists on his hips, and dropped his chin to his chest. The duplex he wanted to turn into a large home for his family was now beginning to seem like a horror dwelling. And he wanted to get to the fucking cause.

27

Hayley entered the front door of Harrison Private Investigations and smiled as Katelyn walked from the back. "I have your mock-up ready. I wanted to show it to you, and then you and Gareth can play around with it, and then let me know what changes you want me to make."

"Hayley, you are an absolute dream! And you definitely need to charge more than you are. It seems like everybody in town is using you for either marketing or a website. I don't see how you have any spare time at all!"

She shrugged, pleased by the praise. "Well, the kids are in school during the day, and I'm usually able to get my work done for my full-time job by about one o'clock." She crinkled her nose and added, "I talked to my boss and told them I noticed that the work they were sending me was less and less. I wondered if they were having a problem with what I was doing. She assured me they weren't but admitted that the company was having some financial *issues* and someone was coming from headquarters to make a few cuts." She made air quotes around the word "issues", having no real idea what her boss was talking about.

Katelyn's eyes widened. "Oh, no! Do you think you're going to be let go?"

Her shoulders hefted. "I don't know. But moving to the Eastern Shore, getting to know the people and the area, and working for myself has been enlightening. It's allowed me to be a lot more creative than I was in my job. Of course, I realize that I don't have job security, but then, I might not have job security anyway if they're making cuts."

"What about health insurance?" Katelyn asked. Before Hayley had a chance to answer, Katelyn rolled her eyes and threw her hands upward. "Isn't it ridiculous that we have to think about staying in a job that we don't like just because of health insurance?"

"Believe me, as a single mom, I've had to think about that a lot." She hesitated because while she and Sam had not made any formal announcements, she had a feeling that he would not want them to have a prolonged engagement, which was fine with her. But she also didn't want to speak out of turn. Looking at Katelyn, she said, "I know that you have to understand confidentiality in your work. So I'm going to ask you to please not say anything to anyone."

Katelyn's eyes widened, and she stepped closer, reaching forward to hold Hayley's hands. "I promise that I will guard what you tell me."

"Sam and I are not only seeing each other, but we've

been friends for a decade. And we're talking about getting married, but we haven't done anything specific." Now, it was her time to roll her eyes. "Especially if we don't stop finding bodies in our backyard."

"Oh, my gosh," Katelyn gushed. "I don't know if I should say congratulations on the first part of what you told me, or I'm so sorry about the second part!"

"There isn't much I can do about what's going on in the yard. But I do hope that once Sam and I have our plans made, I won't have to worry about health insurance and can just focus on building this business."

For the next half hour, she went through the website with Katelyn, made a few preliminary notes, and then gave Katelyn the login information so that she and Gareth would be able to spend time using it and coming up with more changes they'd like to have incorporated.

As she got ready to leave, she hesitated, then decided to go ahead and ask Katelyn the burning question that had been on her mind. "Would it be unethical for me to ask for some advice?"

"Not at all! What can I help you with," Katelyn asked, her eyes bright with interest.

She explained the fraternity website, not giving any details about which one or mentioning Malcolm's name, but told Katelyn about wanting to dig a little more into the fraternity. "I saw a photograph in an old yearbook and want to find out about one of the men. It's none of my business, yet I'm just…"

"Curious!"

She laughed at the word Katelyn had provided. "You're right, I am. I don't even know why I'm curious, but if I wanted to know more about the fraternity, how would I go about it?"

"You can easily find the yearbooks because many of them are scanned and online with the universities. Go back and look at some of the pictures. Take a look at some of the other people in the fraternity you might recognize from who you're working with. You can always call somebody just to say you were trying to identify some fraternity people. It might sound a little sketchy, but I assure you, it's not. Believe me, Garrett and I do that often when searching for information. There's nothing underhanded and certainly not illegal about doing some searching on your own. Who knows, it might give you more information to put onto the website for the fraternity that they'd all like."

"Thank you! That's a great suggestion!" After saying goodbye, Hayley glanced at the time when she climbed back into her car. She had thought about going to the coffee shop or the ice cream parlor, but now she left Baytown eagerly, wanting to get home to see what she could discover about DEPA's past.

Two hours later, Hayley glanced at the clock again, trying to decide whether she had enough time to make a phone call before the kids got off the school bus. Deciding that she did, she grabbed her phone from the desk next to her laptop.

"Hello?"

"Hello. My name is Hayley Brooks, and I'm trying to reach Martin Worthy. The Martin Worthy I'm looking for was a student at the University of Richmond in the early 1980s."

"This is Martin Worthy, and that description fits me, so I'd say you have the right person. What can I do for you?"

"I'm a web designer who has been commissioned to work on a DEPA alumni website. And I was just hoping to reach a few fraternity members from different decades. When I looked at the yearbook, you were listed as the fraternity president at one time. And I believe that was in 1979?"

"Why, yes! I was a freshman pledge and then served as the sergeant at arms, the secretary, and then, my senior year, I was the president." He chuckled, adding, "I can tell you some of those were my most fond college memories."

"I'm sure. I'm in the process of identifying some of the photographs that were in the yearbook. And I seem to have trouble identifying one young man."

"If you give me a moment, I'll take a look. I know where my college yearbooks are. Which year?"

"Absolutely, I'll wait. Please take your time. And it was the year you were a sophomore. 1976." Thrilled that she had found the right person and he was talking to her, she only had to wait a few minutes before he came back on the line.

"What page are you looking at, Ms. Brooks?"

"It's on page 132. A young man is standing in the middle of four others, and I believe they were freshman pledges the year that you were a sophomore. From what you said, you were the sergeant at arms, so you might remember some of the pledges."

After a few seconds of silence, he said, "Yes, yes. I

have that page in front of me. Let me see... hmm, it only identifies Malcolm Young, Ben Abbott, Reggie Olson, and Ted Miller. Reggie goes by Reginald and is now a state senator. In fact, we are proud that many of the DEPA alumni are prominent members of society."

"I'm sure you are," she said, adding a little extra sweetness to her voice. "And there is a fifth man in the center. He's not identified."

"Those other four were freshman pledges, and I was proud to be their fraternity brother for three years until I graduated. I heard that Malcolm was now the president of the alumni association. He would be an excellent person to get information from."

Not wanting to trip herself up with too many lies, she said, "Actually, Malcolm is the one who has contacted me about doing the website. The young man in question, the one in the middle of the group, he wasn't able to remember."

"That's odd because he was very good friends with those four others in the photograph. Let's see... now let me think. Oh, yes, his name is Will Rogers. I remember that because, of course, there was the actor and country singer named Will Rogers. Sadly, Will didn't finish out his pledge."

"Oh, do you remember why?"

"Oh, Ms. Brooks, I'm afraid that was too long ago for me to remember specifically why somebody didn't make the cut. Many people have a desire to pledge, but only the best make the selection."

"I understand. Would you mind giving me a little

idea about what makes someone a good fraternity pledge and why someone else doesn't make the cut?"

"Mostly, I would say it has to do with character. But at the university, we had many honor students and young men who we considered an asset to the community. Of course, only a limited number of people could pledge into this fraternity, so I'm sure we turned away some who would've been wonderful candidates."

She opened her mouth to ask another question when suddenly Martin blurted, "It's funny, but suddenly saying the name Will Rogers has brought back memories."

Excited, she said, "If you don't mind, Mr. Worthy, I'd be interested in hearing what you have to say. I assure you that none of this would end up on the website. I'm just trying to gain an understanding of the fraternity and the lifelong brotherhood you share."

"One thing I remember about Will is that he had a pronounced limp. No one made fun of him, you understand, but I know even a certain physical attribute can weigh against someone at times when others vote on whether they should be included in the fraternity. Nowadays, there are people of all abilities in the fraternity, which is how it should be. But back then, I'm ashamed to say that something as simple as a limp might have kept some people from voting him in."

"A limp? Had he had an accident?"

"Now that I think about it, he had shoes that were different sizes... or rather, one was taller than the other."

She realized that would make one of his legs longer

than the other, probably since birth. Pressing her lips together, she tried to scribble the notes she was gaining from Martin's remembrances. "But he was voted on? I thought you said he didn't finish his pledge."

Another slight hesitation was broken when Martin suddenly blurted, "You're right! I did say that. Yes, I remember that he didn't show up for the final pledge night activities."

"Was anyone surprised? Or see him later?"

"You know, I don't know. Now that I think about it, he hung out with Malcolm and the others in that photograph and then simply disappeared."

"Disappeared?"

"Yes," he said, his voice taking on a faraway tone. "It's rather astounding. I haven't thought about this in forty years, yet now I remember just from your questions. The mind is a funny thing, Ms. Brooks. I can hardly remember what I had for breakfast, yet I'm now remembering details from college life."

"You're right, Mr. Worthy. The little details we remember once our mind is prodded are amazing. I know that the University of Richmond is not a huge university. I would've thought people would have run into each other in cafeterias, libraries, sporting events, and dorms. But you're saying you don't remember ever seeing him again."

"That's right. He didn't even make it to the first initial voting. I don't remember thinking anything about it at the time because some people are not suited for fraternity. Many do drop out during the initial pledge process, and others drop out during the pledge process. But he never made it past the first couple of weeks of everybody getting to know each other. He never showed up for the first vote, and I honestly never saw him again after that."

"Did anyone come to ask about him? The police? Someone from the university? Parents? I just think that if he disappeared, someone would have looked for him."

"No... not to me, and I never heard anyone else speaking of it either." He sucked in an audible breath. "My God, now I remember even more. He was an orphan or had been in foster homes or something like that. He was very smart but at college on scholarship. I recall a conversation with one of the members who felt like he wouldn't be an asset to the fraternity, but our president at the time shut down that kind of talk. I suppose, when he dropped out of college to pursue other life plans, no one thought any more about it."

"Well, thank you for your assistance, Mr. Worthy. I'm sure Malcolm will be calling for photographs of those times, so if you have any you'd like to include on the website, please send them to me if you like. I'll make sure to get them uploaded."

They disconnected the call, and she stared at the faces in the yearbook photograph. Something about the young man... Will... that called to her. He looked so happy to be with the other four. So excited to be part of something bigger than himself. Thrilled to be included.

Suddenly, an image of Eddie hit her, and she gasped, her hand flying to her chest. He had smiled more since they'd moved to the Eastern Shore. He'd made friends and had been so excited to have Jack and Trevor hanging with him the other day... the older kids paying attention to him, treating him like an equal. And now, looking at Will's eyes in the decades-old photograph, she saw the same emotion.

And Will just disappeared... and no one cared? The part of her heart intricately tied up in being a mother ached for him.

28

Lying in bed, Sam wrapped his body around Hayley's. They'd made love and now talked about their day.

"I don't know why I kept trying to find out more, Sam. I just wanted a name and then to hear from someone who remembered him. It just seemed so sad. I looked at this amazing camaraderie that these four men had for the past forty years. And then I looked into the face of that other young man, whose smile just seemed to remind me of Eddie the other day when Trevor and Jack were hanging out with him." She pinched her lips, then sighed and continued. "And to think that Will left college and never kept up with any of those people who made him smile and not even remembered by them! I know it's been a ridiculous waste of my time and resources when I have so many other things to do." She sighed heavily again. "I guess, just finding out that he was an orphan or had been in foster homes, had a physical challenge with one leg being longer than the other, resulting in a limp which some people might have used as a way to shun him. Will had obviously worked hard and made it into a competitive college, found friends, and then poof... disappears, and it's like no one cared."

Sam heard her words but knew much of the emotion had nothing to do with Will but everything to do with being a mom worrying about her own children. He tucked a strand of hair behind her ear and held her gaze in the pale illumination of the night-light coming from the bathroom. "I think your emotions are running high right now, and that's understandable. You've uprooted your life when you moved, are looking at job changes, and are terrified whether all these decisions will turn out okay. But, sweetheart, the kids are great, and they're thriving. And you and me... we're better than ever. And as soon as we can, I want my ring on your finger and us to start working on this house. And if the company cuts your position, or you decide to resign to start your own business, we'll get married tomorrow if you need to go on my health insurance. Hell, we'll get married tomorrow anyway, just because we want to."

Her lips curved into the most beautiful smile, and he leaned in and kissed her softly. Kissing Hayley anytime was amazing, but kissing when her lips were spread into a wide smile was even better. If someone had asked him why, he wouldn't have been able to tell them. All he knew was that kissing her smile also made him smile.

"I don't think we have to get married tomorrow, but..." She paused as her top teeth nibbled on her bottom lip again.

"But what, baby?"

"I wouldn't mind if we got married soon. Sam, I don't want to keep you from having anything you want. But I had a wedding in a white dress, and my dad gave me away. The church was filled with flowers, and the reception had a huge wedding cake. If you want that, Sam, I'll love every minute of it again with you just as much, making new memories." She smiled again. "I was going to say that I don't care where we get married, but I don't think I want to get married in our backyard with the police tape all around—"

He snorted, nodding. "Yeah, I get that. Don't think our guests would be too thrilled about that."

She laughed, then grew serious again, her hand cupping his jaw. "If we want to pledge our love in front of a justice of the peace, that's fine. If we want a small church wedding with our friends and family, that's fine too."

"You know what I'd really like?"

She lifted both brows and shook her head. "I have no idea what you might come up with!"

He nuzzled her nose and kissed her lightly. "I'd like to get married in a church because I want to say in front of our friends, family, and God that I'm pledging myself to you forever. And I'd like the kids to be up there with us. Because I'm also pledging myself to them forever."

She nodded slowly, her gaze never leaving his. "I'd like that. But I don't want to wait too long. A simple dress for me and Hope. Just you and Eddie in suits. And then maybe a kick-ass reception in the church hall where the American Legion and Auxiliary meetings are."

Their hearts spoke in the silence that followed. When they closed the distance, their lips met, both knowing they'd found their soul mate and would soon be united in front of everyone.

Sam sat at his desk, working through one of his active cases, when his desk phone rang. He answered, "Detective Sam Shackley."

"Detective Shackley? This is Henry Mansfield. I received a call from my old friend Janelle. She said you were looking for information on my family in the area?"

Sitting up straight, he grabbed his pen and a pad of paper. "Yes, Mr. Mansfield. Thank you so much for calling me."

"I don't live in the area anymore, but my grandfather was Horace Mansfield, who owned the farm there on the Eastern Shore. I was born and raised there and lived there for many years until recently, retiring to North Carolina to be with my daughter's family. I was always interested in family history, and that led me to discover and write down some of the local lore of the area." He chuckled and added, "Not always the history that you read about in some of the tourist books, but the stories from the old timers that really let you know how things were."

"Mr. Mansfield, that is exactly what I'm looking for. I assume you've heard about the skeletal remains found here on the Shore? It wasn't on the old Mansfield's farmland but on what used to be the Young farmland. Actually, it was found in my backyard."

"Oh my Lord, Detective! I read something about that in the news, but to think that it was found on your property... well, that's astounding."

Sam chuckled, thinking that he'd had a lot of other ways to describe it besides *astounding*. Getting back to the task at hand, he said, "As it turns out, the skeletal remains were of a woman, about thirty years old, and she'd given birth based on forensic evidence of the bones. I just wondered if you had any idea why a woman would have been buried on the back of the Young farm around the 1920s?"

"A lot was going on between the Mansfields and the Youngs back then, Detective. Do you have a few minutes to hear it all?"

"Mr. Mansfield, I'll give you all the time you need. Do you mind if I put you on speaker so that my partner can also hear you?"

"Not at all! If there's one thing I love to do, it's talk about the Eastern Shore. And this story has a lot to do with Prohibition in the times you're referencing."

Sam's brows lifted, and he shot a glance toward Aaron, seeing a similar surprised expression on his face.

"Now, keep in mind that Prohibition in Virginia was from about 1915 to 1933. Interestingly enough, Norfolk, Virginia, and Washington, DC, managed to stay away from Prohibition. Many bootleggers were making whiskey, selling it illegally everywhere, and transferring it to Norfolk or DC. If you'll give me just a minute, I'll grab my notes from that time."

In the ensuing silence, Sam looked back at Aaron, seeing the keen interest on his face. Keeping his voice low, Sam said, "I keep hoping I can find out who this woman was. If I can, I'll ask the forensic office if I can bring her remains back to the Eastern Shore for a burial."

Aaron nodded, and then they heard Mr. Mansfield get back on the line.

"Lloyd Young and my grandfather, Horace Mansfield, were best friends back then. Along with the many crops they raised on their farms, one was corn. Most of the corn was harvested and sold as a cash crop, but some was kept back for them to make whiskey. In fact, both Lloyd's and Horace's dads had been doing that for years. There was a long-standing family tradition of farming and making whiskey on the Shore. And then, when Prohibition came in, they kept their stills going, making bootleg whiskey. My grandfather used to tell stories of them making the whiskey, loading it in barrels onto their boats, and then they'd carry at night either up to DC or over to Norfolk to sell."

The sound of shuffling papers met Sam's ears, and then Henry began talking again.

"Now, here is where the history comes from the storytellers. I used to sit with my grandfather when he was very old, and he would tell me stories of those days. I've written many of them down and even have a book about the bootleg days on the Eastern Shore. Oh dear, Detective... I digress. When my grandfather was on his deathbed, I was sitting with him, and he told me that he needed to confess something before meeting his maker. There wasn't anyone else in the room but me and him, so I told him that he could tell me whatever he wanted and die with a clear conscience. I'll tell you, Detective, I had no idea what my grandfather was going to say. For all I knew, it was going to be gibberish, but his voice became stronger as he went back in time and told me the tale."

Sam's gaze shot around the room to see Hunter, Brad, several of the detectives, and even Colt standing nearby. "I appreciate you talking to me, Mr. Mansfield. I'd love to hear the tale from your grandfather."

"He told me when he was a young man, Lloyd Young had married a girl named Edna. They had one son named Ralph. But it didn't seem to be a match made in heaven, according to what my grandfather said. Lloyd had a reputation as a drinker, probably tasting his whiskey too much, and was a mean drunk. When he got drunk, he wasn't too nice to his wife. My grandfather confessed that he cared a great deal for Edna. He even told her that if she wanted to escape Lloyd, he'd sell his farm, take her and Ralph with him, and go somewhere. But back in those days, a woman was expected to take whatever her husband handed out, even if he dealt it with a heavy hand."

"Do you happen to know if she ever had any broken bones?"

"Well, it's funny you should ask that. My grandfather mentioned that one time when Lloyd was drunk, he grabbed Edna and was yelling at her, and during that scuffle, he broke her arm. There may have been other times, but I think my grandfather was trying to tell me that Edna was in a bad situation."

Sam asked, "What happened?"

"He and Lloyd had a boatload of bootleg whiskey to get to Norfolk. Usually, they both went together, but on this trip, they had so much that there was only room in the boat for one. Lloyd said he'd take the batch and come back with all the money. While he was gone, my grandfather and Edna must've spent some... well, let's just say some time together. Lloyd came home early and found them together, with little Ralph just in the other room. Lloyd grabbed a shotgun and threatened to kill all of them. My grandfather calmed him down and tried to tell him he was just there to ensure Edna and Ralph were okay. He left but told me he decided that he and Edna would make the move to get away.

"But later that night, Lloyd came over half drunk and ranting about Edna not getting up. My grandfather didn't know what was going on, but he ran over to Lloyd's farmhouse and found Edna lying in the living room, blood coming from her head. He was upset and crying, but Lloyd told my grandfather that all he'd done was push her, and she tripped backward and hit her head. And, Detective, this brings us to where my grandfather felt like he needed to make his confession. As much as he cared for Edna, the only thing he could do for her was help Horace bury her. If the sheriff was informed and the whole story came out, then they'd both go to prison for bootlegging. So my grandfather and Lloyd went to the back of their farm property, dug a grave near the line between them, and placed Edna there."

Another heavy sigh sounded. "He cried when he told me the story. Tears ran down his wrinkled face, and the anguish was clear. He said he should have done everything he could to have saved her by taking her away earlier. And he regretted not going to the law immediately. He said he should have served his time for bootlegging, knowing that she would have been buried properly and remembered."

Sam's reaction to the story surprised him. His chest ached, and he lifted his hand to rub over the pain. "You never told anyone about what your grandfather said?"

"No, I never did. I'd made a promise on his deathbed and decided to keep that promise. Edna had no family, and I had no idea who I'd tell anyway."

Aaron asked, "Do you know when that was, Mr. Mansfield?"

"It must've been right around 1928."

"And no one asked about Edna? Wondered where she was?" Sam asked.

"My grandfather had mentioned Edna didn't have any family, and the story must've gone out that she ran off. Lloyd remarried a nice woman who raised Ralph as her own. Ralph took over the farm when Lloyd died."

"So that was probably Edna Young. I saw the family Bible with her name written in it and then a line drawn through it with no record of death."

"That sounds about like what my grandfather said Lloyd would've done. Instead of putting a death date, having to admit that he knew she died, he just probably drew a line through the Bible notation."

"And the Young farm?"

"I knew Malcolm Young growing up. We were about the same age, and even though our farms were next to each other, we weren't really close. There was no particular reason other than he had one set of friends, and I had another. He had a hankering to get out in the world. He went to college and became an attorney. He and his dad never got along real well, and his dad threatened to give the farm to someone else and cut Malcolm out."

"We know that Ralph Young sold the farm to developers around 1986."

"Yeah, the same developers bought the Mansfield farm. It was mine at that time, and I had no desire to keep it going. My wife and I had other jobs, and even though we were living in the farmhouse, we sold it all with the rest of the farm."

Taking a big chance, Sam asked, "Would you happen to know of a man being buried around there, also? Not at the same time as Edna, but maybe in the late 70s or early 80s?"

An audible gasp was heard. "Another body? Good Lord! No, Detective, I heard nothing about another body being buried there. If that happened, that would've been before all the land was sold."

Thanking him, Sam disconnected the call and then looked around at the others.

Everyone was quiet for a moment until, finally, Hunter shook his head and said, "Holy shit."

Brad looked at his partner and nodded. "That's

probably about the only thing you can say about that story."

Sam held Colt's gaze and said, "Of course, I'll need to mention this to Malcolm Young. If that is Edna, then she would be his grandmother. He may not care, but all I can do is try. Then I'll talk to Hank at forensics. While we might not definitively say that this is Edna Young, for remains that are that old, if no one claims them, I'll see if she can be buried at a local church with a graveyard."

Colt said, "That could be expensive."

"I understand. But it just doesn't seem right that she couldn't be laid to rest in a place where she grew up."

"I'll chip in," Aaron said.

"Me too," Hunter added, with Brad agreeing almost instantly.

"I think if we bring this up to others, you'll find that there will be local support," Colt said.

"Appreciate it," Sam admitted, suddenly overwhelmed. He pressed his lips together, battling the stinging in his eyes. Edna Young may not have found her happiness in marriage, but the Eastern Shore was her home. And it was a place where Sam had also found a home. A real home with Hayley, Eddie, and Hope.

After pulling himself together, he sucked in a deep breath. "Okay, so now I need to work on the next one… the young man found in my yard."

29

Sam placed a call to Hank at the forensic science agency. "I have some information for you on the first body found, and I'm seeking more information on the second."

"I thought maybe you'd called to let me know another one had been found," Hank quipped.

Grimacing, Sam worked to keep from snapping at the man who spent his days studying some gruesome sites. The skeletons were probably the easiest subjects Hank had looked at in a while. "No, I'm hoping there won't be anymore."

"Okay, what do you need from me?"

"I've come across some information from the farm that my property is now on. It seems a young woman, about thirty, who was in an abusive marriage in the early 1920s. She had a son, so she'd given birth. According to my source, she was accidentally killed. At least by the account I was given, it was noted as accidental. But her husband, who had been involved in bootleg whiskey, just buried her on the back of the farm. The woman had had a broken arm in adulthood, which I know fits with what you said."

"Sounds like you may have found an identity," Hank agreed.

"What would be the procedure for providing a burial for the remains?"

"Due to the age of the remains and the fact that she is not an active case, I have no problem releasing the remains to whoever can legally claim her. I would advise you to check with an attorney, and if that's what you want to do, it works for me. You will have paperwork to fill out once you've made that legal claim."

"Okay, thanks. I'll get back to you on that since, if she is who I think, her grandson lives on the Shore. Now, let's talk about the young man. Do you have anything new for me?"

"I have confirmed what I told you originally. Male. His age at death was probably between seventeen and twenty-two years old, and with testing of the bones, he probably died between forty and fifty years ago. Clothing remnants were found with him. Cotton, tan material, probably like khaki pants. Cotton, pale, blue material, probably his shirt. Dark brown hair. And an interesting notation that might help in identification. He had congenital, structural leg length discrepancy."

Sam sat up straighter. "Are you saying that his legs were different lengths?"

"Give the man a gold star," Hank said. "Yes, looking at the bone plates, our mystery man had a difference where his left leg was slightly less than four centimeters shorter than his right leg."

"Would he have limped?" Sam asked, gazing at Aaron, who was again staring at him.

"Most definitely. There were no shoes at the burial site. He could have had specially made shoes to accommodate the height difference. They would have been a bit expensive at that time and still might not have countered a limp."

"Thank you, Hank!" he said just before disconnecting. Standing, he grabbed his jacket and cell phone. Looking at Aaron, he said, "Let's go."

"What's going on?"

"Hayley has been talking to Lloyd Young's grandson, who was in college when his dad, Ralph, sold the farm back in the early 1980s. She saw a photograph of a young man and, when identifying him, found out his name was Will Rogers... he had a limp, just up and disappeared one day, and no one reported him missing because he was an orphan with no family."

Aaron leaped up. "Hell, Sam. But what are you thinking?"

Sam turned to see the other detectives and Colt. "Not going to do anything other than check on Hayley. She was returning to Malcolm Young's house this morning, and I just want to ensure she's okay. If he finds out she's been snooping... fuck, I just want to make sure she stays away from him."

"Go," Colt said. "Keep us informed. And don't lose your fucking head. Get Hayley safe, and we'll start the investigation into the missing Will Rogers as the possible remains are found in our county."

"Hello again," Hayley greeted as Anne welcomed her into their home again. "I'm sure you must be getting sick of seeing me."

"Not at all! Malcolm has been so thrilled with getting this DEPA fraternity alumni website up and running that he's spent hours going through some of our old photographs. I must admit that it's also brought back some memories for me."

"Oh, did you and Malcolm meet in college?"

"Yes." Anne nodded. "Looking at some of those pictures just reminds me how very young and sometimes naive I was back then."

A specter of sadness passed through Anne's eyes. "I think we can all relate to that," Hayley agreed. "In fact, after I met Malcolm and the other men here a few weekends ago, I was so impressed with their camaraderie that lasted all these years. I hardly keep up with anyone I went to college with."

"I know what you mean," Anne said. "I didn't join the Greek life when I was in college, but I was at a lot of events when the fraternity was involved."

"Did you and Malcolm meet your freshman year?"

"Yes. We even hung out together then, but it wasn't until we were sophomores that we started dating." Anne sighed, then offered a sweet smile. "It really is strange to think about all those times. Where did the years go?"

"Hello, Hayley!"

Hayley turned at the sound of Malcolm's booming greeting and smiled. "Well, I hope what I show you today will be the last mock-up until you're ready to move forward. I'll show you what I have, and you can decide if you like it, and if so, start getting the information you want me to finish putting on the pages as well as pictures."

"Well, I'll let you two talk," Anne said. "I have a book club meeting this afternoon." She winked and added, "Of course, it's a combination wine club and book club. We either sip wine and discuss a book that we love, or we forget about the book if it wasn't a great read and just drink."

She lifted on her toes and kissed Malcolm, and he smiled down at her. "Have fun and be safe," he said. "Call me if you drink too much, and I'll come get you."

Hayley smiled at their obvious affection. Once Anne left, she followed Malcolm into the beautiful family room and set up her laptop at a table to the side. After about thirty minutes, she was pleased at Malcolm's effusive praise of her work.

"Mrs. Brooks, the way you have this set up is perfect. I certainly know my basic way around computers, but my days of handling anything too complex is something I no longer care to do. But I'm so passionate about this project, and you've given me a website where I can easily add photographs, alumni member information, and updates. I can integrate names and phone numbers and even change a few things if needed." He aimed his beaming smile toward her. "And I hope I can come to you if I have any difficulties."

"Absolutely. I have no doubt that as you work with it, you'll find other things that you would like to be different. So whenever that happens, you can let me know."

"I'm just impressed with how much time you've been able to spend on this. I really appreciate it."

"Well, I found the subject fascinating. I do confess, though, that so many things have been going on in my life that it's been nice to focus on something else."

"I hope everything is okay?"

"I suppose you heard about that skeleton found in someone's backyard not too long ago?"

"Yes, I did. Because that was on the back of the old Young family farm, I even had a detective question me just to see if I knew anything about family history back then."

"Well, believe it or not, I live there too. In fact, my children were the ones who made the discovery!"

Malcolm jerked slightly, his eyes widening. "I... I don't even know what to say to that. My goodness!"

"And what hasn't hit the news yet was that additional skeletal remains were found there a few days ago. I can't believe that hasn't been reported on yet, but it'll probably come out today."

"Two in your yard? That means two on the old farm." He pressed his lips together and slowly shook his head. "That is... um... unexpected. Do the police have any idea about the identity of the other skeleton?"

She shook her head. "Not that I know of, but I'm sure they are investigating."

"Yes, I'm sure they are." He swiped at a bead of perspiration that started to roll down the side of his head and mumbled, "Anne must have the heat set too high."

Hayley turned back to her computer. "Would you like me to take some of the photographs and start uploading them?"

"Yes, I'll get some for you. Anne and I have been going through them."

He walked over, picked up a small box, and opened the lid. "You can start with these and choose from any of them. I've written the names of the people in the photographs on the back of them."

"Oh, that's so helpful! Speaking of names, I discovered the name of the student that you and the others couldn't remember. His name was Will Rogers."

Malcolm opened and closed his mouth several times, then finally uttered, "Oh. Yes, that sounds right. I... uh... had forgotten."

While she thumbed through a few of the photographs from the box, he asked, "I'm curious, though. How did you find out his name?"

"I had the opportunity to talk to Martin Worthy. I believe he was the sergeant at arms when you were pledging and later became the president. He had the same yearbook and remembered Will's name because of the actor and singer named Will Rogers. He also mentioned that Will had a limp because one leg was shorter than the other. He hoped that wasn't why he didn't complete the pledging process, but when I mentioned that you all said he disappeared, he said now that he thought about it, he hadn't seen Will again either."

"I didn't realize that my hiring you to work on a website gave you carte blanche to check into everything about the fraternity."

His sharp tone caused Hayley to lift her gaze from the photographs to Malcolm's face. His jaw was tight, and his blue eyes seemed more icy than welcoming. A strange sliver of unease moved along her spine. "In order to have an understanding of the fraternity, I looked up several of the past members. It's up to me to decide how best to present the information. And certainly making a call to someone is hardly doing anything, Mr. Young."

A muscle in his face twitched, and in her peripheral vision, she noticed his fingers clench and release. Now uncomfortable in his presence, she had the distinct feeling that she hadn't just stepped on his toes but may have stepped into something he didn't want her to know about. Plastering a wide smile on her face, she said, "Well, I'm going to keep working on the site, and I'll let you contact the members and have them send me pictures. I think it's going to be absolutely wonderful, Mr. Young."

She closed her laptop and, with another smile, started to walk toward the door. She didn't feel his presence right behind her for a few seconds, but then he caught up.

Opening his front door, his voice back to normal, he

said, "I am happy with your work, Mrs. Brooks. And please forgive my tone earlier. Fraternities have a close camaraderie, but like all groups, they can also have their petty, fractious behavior. I suppose your talking to Martin caught me off guard. I'd liked Martin well enough but found him to be a rather power-hungry president the year he was a senior. I suppose that left a little bad taste in my mouth."

Not one to usually be suspicious of people, she could feel Malcolm's disingenuousness pouring off him. She had no doubt he was more irritated that she'd learned about Will than anything to do with a feud with Martin. No longer willing to continue the conversation, she thanked him before walking down his front steps and waved goodbye. She sat in her car for just a moment, then pulled herself together and backed out of the driveway.

The lane to get to the Young's beachfront property was long and curvy, with woods on one side and farmland on the other. She had barely made it past the first curve when the rumbling of a pickup truck approaching quickly from behind caught her attention. "Okay, asshole, just because you're familiar with this road doesn't mean I am. Chill out!"

She couldn't tell much about the truck, but as it approached and nestled right behind her, she could see it looked very new. And very big. She increased her speed slightly, but it stayed right on her tail.

Her phone rang, and seeing it was from Sam, she hit her in-car phone connection. Before giving him a chance to speak, she complained, "Sam! There's an asshole driving like a maniac right behind me!"

"Where are you?"

"I just left Malcolm Young's house. I showed him the website, and he liked it, but then I thought he got kind of creepy when I mentioned I found out about Will Rogers."

"I'm coming toward you," he said. "Pull over and let the guy pass."

She put on her blinker and eased to the side of the road even though there was no shoulder. The pickup truck passed, and she couldn't see the driver through the tinted passenger window. She was right, though—it was a new, large pickup truck that looked like it had never been used for any work at all. And from the make and model, it was more of a status symbol.

"Okay, it passed, roaring by like it had somewhere terribly important to go to," she grumbled. "Anyway, why are you on your way toward me?"

"I knew you were going to Malcolm Young's house, and I wanted to make sure you were okay."

His words caused another snake of cold to slither down her spine. "Why would I not be okay?"

"I have some suspicions about Malcolm from forty years ago. I'm just at the beginning of an investigation, so that's all I'm going to say right now. But I'm still heading toward you because I just want to see you before I head back to the office."

"Okay, sweetheart, but I should be fine. Right now, I just... what the hell? What is he doing? Shit!"

"What? What's happening?" Sam yelled.

"That truck has turned around up ahead and is heading straight for me, weaving all over the road. Oh God, they're probably drunk!"

She heard voices over the phone and thought she recognized Aaron calling for all available units to respond to the road she was on.

"Hayley, can you get off the road? Can you turn down somewhere else?" Sam barked.

"There's nowhere. There's no other streets here—just farmland and woods!"

"I'm almost there, sweetheart. Just stay on the line with me—"

"Oh my God! No!" she screamed. The large truck bore straight toward her, and she could see Malcolm Young driving.

She jerked her steering wheel at the last moment, but his truck caught the tail end, sending her spinning off the road, not stopping until her car slammed into a tree. The airbag discharged, but her head had already hit the window. Her vehicle had come to a stop, but even dazed, she clawed at the airbag to get it out of her way. Coughing from the airbag powder, she opened her door and unhooked her seat belt. Her head pounded, and she swiped her hand over the wetness on her cheek, pulling it back to see it red with blood.

30

Sam's SUV careened around the curve, his horrified gaze landing on Hayley's car, smashed against the tree with a pickup just behind her. Before he could ask, Aaron was already on dispatch, ordering fire and rescue to the scene. Swerving to the roadside, he watched Hayley's door open. It appeared the truck driver had reached her and was attempting to pull her out as she tumbled to the ground.

"Shit! The man—that's Malcolm Young," Sam shouted. His heart pounded erratically in his chest as he watched Malcolm leaning over Hayley. Bringing his vehicle to a stop, he sucked in a deep breath, his mind blanking of all the hostage rescue work ever done, and could only focus on Hayley's bleeding face as she turned her gaze up toward Malcolm.

Aaron and Sam climbed from their vehicle and pointed their weapons toward Malcolm, who hadn't seemed even to notice they'd arrived.

"Malcolm Young," Aaron called out. "This is the sheriff's department. Put your hands up!"

Deputy cars arrived, and the approaching siren finally penetrated Malcolm's stupor even though his hand was still holding her arm firmly in his grip. "Get back!" he cried out. "I don't want to hurt her, but she can't know."

"It doesn't matter what you want. She's injured, and we need to get to her," Aaron called out. "Step away and put your hands up."

Sam didn't want to take his aim or his gaze off Malcolm, but he could see other deputies spreading out, their weapons raised, as well. "Malcolm," he called out. "There's no way out of this for you. She's done nothing to you. We need to get her help." His chest was quaking, and he had no idea that his words were also, but he must've struck a cord because Malcolm looked over at the approaching ambulance and then cut his eyes backward at Hayley.

"I'm sorry. I didn't mean for this to happen to you. But you… can't… I can't have you know. I can't have you tell."

Hayley appeared dazed, but she looked up at Malcolm, wincing at his grip on her arm. "I don't know what you're talking about, Malcolm."

"Will. I can't… it was so long ago."

"I was just looking at the man who looked like he loved being with you and your friends, and then he disappeared. I just wondered what could've made him want to disappear before the fraternity vote."

Malcolm's hand shook as he continued to hold

Hayley. "Fucking Will. This all comes down to fucking Will! He was ruining things forty years ago, and he's still fucking ruining everything!"

Aaron radioed to the others in a low voice, "Anyone got a clear shot?"

Sam gave an imperceptible shake of his head. At the moment, he didn't give a fuck if they all shot to kill as long as Hayley was protected.

Hayley swiped her hand over her face, but all she managed to do was smear more blood over her cheek.

Sam growled, "Malcolm, you've got no time to bullshit. Drop your hold and step away with your hands up. Whatever reason you think something is coming to bite you in the ass, it has nothing to do with Mrs. Brooks. Do not make this worse on yourself."

Malcolm suddenly appeared lost, shaking his head. "I don't want Anne to know. She can't know what happened."

Sam was done. He didn't give a fuck what Malcolm had done. He was looking to take the shot.

Hayley called out, "Anne was in love with him, wasn't she?"

At that, he shook her and snarled, "The man had a limp and was always smiling like he thought sunshine was going to shine out of his ass. Anne and I had gone out a couple of times when suddenly she met Will. He took one look at her and was smitten."

Talking softly into his radio, Aaron coordinated with the deputy who had managed to make his way around the backside of Malcolm's truck. "Moving into position."

"Did you mean to kill him?" Hayley asked.

At first, Sam thought Hayley was simply asking to give them time to get a clear shot lined up, and then realized she cared about Malcolm's answer.

Malcolm slowly shook his head. "We just wanted to scare him."

"I have a clear shot," one of the deputies radioed.

"Aim to wound," came the order.

A shot rang out, hitting Malcolm in the arm. Malcolm cried out as Hayley dropped backward to the ground and covered her head. Sam raced to her, scooping her into his arms. "I've got you, sweetheart. I've got you, sweetheart."

Sam stood just outside the hospital room, watching Hunter and Brad interview Malcolm. He hated leaving Hayley, but she insisted, and since she was only a few ER bays down from where Malcolm was being treated for the gunshot wound in his shoulder, he'd acquiesced to hear what the man had to say. Malcolm was shackled to the gurney and appeared so much older than he had the day that Sam had visited him in his home.

Malcolm sucked in a ragged breath and continued. "When I first met Will, I liked him. He was funny. Kind of a quirky sense of humor. He started pledging DEPA with us. I didn't think much about it. I didn't know if he could get in, but I didn't mind him hanging around us. I didn't see him, as you know... competition."

"Competition in what way?" Brad asked.

"In any way. Certainly not with Anne."

"Tell us about the relationship with Anne," Brad continued.

"She and I met the summer before college. We happened to be in the same group during orientation, and I couldn't imagine a more beautiful girl. She was perfect. She was smart, so pretty, but really kind." Malcolm's brow lowered, and he appeared to plead with the detectives to understand. "Really sweet. I don't think I'd ever met anybody so big-hearted in my life. Sure as hell not from my dad, and my mom was not really nurturing, either. But Anne? She was like an angel. We started going out but kept it light. I knew she was the kind of woman who wasn't easy. I wanted to give her the world, but slowly."

"And then Will came into the picture," Brad reiterated from earlier statements.

"He took one look at Anne, and I immediately saw he wanted her. I didn't blame him for that. Really. Who wouldn't have that reaction? But then Anne started spending some time with him and less time with me. I began to realize she felt something for him. I thought maybe it was just pity. But whatever it was, I wasn't about to have someone like Will Rogers, an orphan with no family, connections, money, or physical abilities, step in and play upon her sweet nature."

"So what happened?" Hunter asked.

Malcolm's throat worked as he swallowed deeply. "Ben, Reggie, Ted, and I took Will out one night, saying it was part of the fraternity pledge process. Drove outside of Richmond and then blindfolded him. We were in a... we ended up in a stupid graveyard somewhere. There was no plan. We... I grabbed a stick, and... we weren't hitting him hard, but just enough to make him swing around and try to get to us. But at one point, he was getting upset. And something in me just snapped. I began hitting him harder out of anger. He tried to pull off the blindfold, but his feet stumbled over tree roots in the area, and he fell, hitting his head on one of the large marble headstones."

Malcolm grew quiet, his vision off to the side, as though he'd taken himself back forty years ago and that night. "Christ, he didn't move. We just stood there, staring. Thinking he would get up. Laugh or call us names or something. But he didn't move. God... he didn't move."

Hunter and Brad gave him a moment to collect his thoughts, and then Brad asked, "What did you all do then?"

"We couldn't leave him there. Too much pointed straight to us. So Reggie grabbed a towel and wiped the blood off the tombstone, and we loaded him into the trunk of my car. We were all stunned and scared shitless. Ben kept asking, "Oh my God, what now?" And all I could think of was just to get rid of him. Suddenly, I thought about the family farm that was way out in the middle of nowhere on the Eastern Shore. When my dad died, I figured he'd give it to me, and I would always just make sure that that area stayed covered in grass. So we drove all the way out, went around the back way so we didn't go past my dad's house, and just started digging near the back of one of the fields, near some woods.

The ground was difficult to dig in with shovels, so we didn't go too deep. We covered him up, got back in the car, and drove back to campus. When it was done, we made an oath that what happened that night would stay buried on the Eastern Shore with Will's body."

"And when your dad sold the farm?"

Malcolm snorted and shook his head. "My father had never done anything for me except expect more no matter what I did. And then, because I didn't want to farm, he up and sold the whole fucking thing to a developer who wanted to put in houses. Sure, the money eventually came to me, but by the time I knew about it, fucking houses sat right in the area. All I could hope was that those bones would stay buried. And for forty years, they did."

Nodding his head, he finally seemed to focus on Hunter and Brad. "I did it all for Anne. And I can't bear the thought of her finding out."

"No, Mr. Young. You didn't do it for Anne. You did it for yourself. If you really loved her, you would've let her be with the man of her choice," Brad said.

At that, Hunter and Brad ended the interview, stood, and exited the room. The deputy, standing nearby, would stay close until Malcolm was released from the hospital and then transported to the county jail.

Sam stood, rage filling every cell in his body after having ridden to the hospital with Hayley in the ambulance while Aaron drove his SUV to meet them there. Luckily, Hayley had come out of the accident with nothing more than a mild concussion and a cut on her head that was stitched easily. Her biggest concern was fear of the kids getting off the bus and no one to meet them. Colt had called Carrie, who immediately drove to the duplex to meet the kids.

He didn't want to leave her, but she'd insisted that he go and find out what was happening with Malcolm. Now, Brad offered a chin lift before walking down the hall while Hunter stopped next to him, gripping his shoulders. Sam looked up to hold Hunter's gaze.

"My Belle was shot by some fuckin' drug runner," Hunter said.

Sam sucked in a gasp, not knowing that had happened. "How the hell did you get over that?"

Hunter shook his head. "You don't."

Sam's eyes jumped to his friend's, his gut clenching as though punched.

Hunter continued, "But you eventually get back to some kind of normal. Because while the image never leaves you, you'll bust your ass to make sure she doesn't keep reliving the nightmare over and over."

Sam reached out and clasped forearms with Hunter, then they moved together, each offering a comforting backslap. Nodding his thanks, Sam hustled down the hall, wanting to get back to Hayley's room. While still furious over Malcolm's actions against Hayley, he knew he would do anything to erase the memory from her mind.

Turning the corner, he caught sight of Anne sitting on a chair in one of the hospital lounges, tears streaming down her face as Brad talked to her. Anne seemed to be listening to whatever Brad was saying even though it was evident her heart was breaking.

Seeing Anne, Sam felt a weight of emotions hit him. The idea of how close Hayley came to being killed. Thinking of the young man who had worked so hard to attain what should've led to a better life, meeting a lovely woman interested in him, and losing it all to petty jealousy. And now Anne realized her husband was a murderer. And the pointless way Will had died, all because he'd dared to fall for Anne.

Aaron and Colt walked over and clapped him on the shoulders, jarring him out of his morose thoughts.

"Here are your keys," Aaron said. "I'll get a ride with Colt back to the station."

Colt held his gaze. "Take Hayley home. Hug your kids. Take time with them. Your cases will still be here another day. Now is time for family."

He had a feeling that was advice his boss had given himself when he met Carrie. Nodding his appreciation, he walked out of the hospital and headed home.

31

Hayley walked into her bedroom and stopped to cast her gaze around. Everything looked so familiar, yet her lips curved at the changes that were about to happen. In two days, the contractors were coming to take down the walls between the two sides of the duplex. It would be a messy job, and they would live in a building zone for weeks. But they wouldn't be in the house for the first part of the renovation because they were heading to Florida... after the wedding.

A full smile graced her face at the thought. The kids had two weeks off for the winter holiday, and they were spending Christmas in Florida, hitting both Disney World and Universal Resorts. Eddie practiced his wand flicking spells for Universal's Harry Potter World, and Hope pulled out every Disney princess outfit she had buried in her room. Of course, Hope claimed that her bridesmaid dress far outshone her princess costumes.

Another smile hit Hayley as she thought about the upcoming wedding. It was almost Thanksgiving by the time the fallout of Malcolm's crimes was exposed, her forehead cut had healed, and the stitches had been taken out. Sam had wanted to get married immediately, but she wanted a few weeks to pull together a simple wedding. She had secured the Methodist Church for the ceremony and the fellowship hall for the reception. Their friends were providing food for the reception, and she'd discovered a new bakery that was just opening and agreed to create a simple three-tiered wedding cake.

She had taken Hope on a shopping trip to Virginia Beach, where they found the perfect dresses to wear. Sam had gone with Eddie to find a new suit since he'd outgrown the last one.

Both her parents and Sam's parents were in town, and having already met years ago, they were off enjoying the kids at Sweet Rose's. Hope had been excited to try the new hot chocolate ice cream sundaes with whipped cream and sprinkles. Hayley could only imagine how bouncy Hope would be when she got home.

Edward's parents were expected to arrive later this afternoon. Her relationship with them was strong, and she made sure that they never felt left out of family events. They were her children's grandparents, and it warmed her heart to see how they had accepted Sam into the fold as not just their son's best friend but now the man who would become the father of Eddie and Hope. Life created changes in the pattern of relationships, but Hayley knew she was fortunate that their hearts remained connected.

Sam was at work, finishing some paperwork before he took two weeks off. Hayley had decided to resign from the marketing firm she worked for and open up her own web design and marketing business on the Eastern Shore. She worked from home, so she got to see the kids off to school each morning and was home when they got off the bus. Looking over at the table she'd set up in the bedroom, she imagined her own office once the house renovations were complete.

Her gaze then moved to the window, and she stared at the now-covered area that had formerly held two graves. One of a young woman who'd found love but was killed before she had a chance to leave the abuse and run off with a man who would take care of her. And the other of a young man who was on the cusp of finding love, but jealousy also ended his life too soon. Both were now buried in the Baytown Cemetery, courtesy of the generosity of the American Legion and friends who all pitched in to ensure a proper resting place.

So much tragedy and sadness from long ago met her gaze through the window. But then, she remembered how Eddie and Hope, along with their friends, would run, laugh, and play in the backyard. The space would also hold a lifetime of memories to cherish.

She walked to her dresser and pulled open the top drawer where she had lovingly placed the wedding picture of her and Edward. There were several other pictures of Edward throughout the house to remind the kids that he was always part of their lives. But now,

Sam's pictures far outnumbered Edward's. She accepted that fact... it was life.

Looking at the youthful couple staring back at her from the photograph, she sucked in a deep breath and then let it out slowly. "We had our whole lives ahead of us, didn't we, Edward? So much happiness. So much to look forward to, but it wasn't meant to be." She sighed. "I cherish every minute and every memory. And especially our children. I hope you'd be proud of where I am now. You loved Sam so much as a friend. Now, you can rest easy knowing that he will take care of the ones you held dearest to your heart." She kissed the photograph and then replaced it gently back into the drawer.

Sam stood at the front of the church, excitement and nerves coursing through his body. He gazed over the gathering, seeing the smiling faces of friends and family. But with a barely perceptible chin dip to acknowledge the support, his gaze stayed riveted to the back door. It opened, and his breath caught in his throat.

There stood Hayley, more beautiful than he'd ever seen. Her dress was the palest shade of pink, highlighting the subtle blush of her cheeks. The bodice was fitted, and the skirt was layers of a flowy material that fell to her calves. Sam had no idea what the dress was made of, but it made her look like an angel. Her hair was pulled back in the front with a clasp, allowing her wavy tresses to fall freely about her shoulders.

Her eyes met his, and time stopped. Or maybe time

just began. Her lips curved as she held his gaze and then dropped her chin to look downward at her sides at the children escorting her down the aisle.

His gaze followed her to see Hope at one side, wearing an almost identical dress, only in a slightly darker pink. Her hair was also pulled back in the front with a matching clasp. Her smile was wide and her eyes bright as she held her small bouquet of pink roses tightly in her hands.

Eddie appeared so grown-up in his suit on the other side of Hayley. He gave no evidence of nerves as he accompanied his mother down the aisle.

Once they arrived at the front, Eddie moved to stand near Sam while Hope stepped to the side to stand next to Hayley. His heart pounded as he took Hayley's hands in his, holding tight as he felt her fingers tremble slightly. Keeping his gaze on her, he whispered, "All good?"

Her beautiful smile widened. "All good," she whispered.

The wedding ceremony was not long, as the minister kept his words simple, focusing on the union of two people who had been through so much and grown stronger together. They exchanged vows, and then, with the exchange of rings, the minister pronounced them husband and wife.

She placed her hand lightly on his chest as his arm banded around her waist. Closing the distance, they met in their first married kiss, just as electrifying as the first kiss they'd shared. Separating, he was surprised when the organist didn't start the music for them to walk back down the aisle as they'd practiced the previous evening. He glanced quizzically toward Hayley, who simply smiled before stepping back to allow Hope to slip in front of her. He looked down at her sweet face gazing up at him.

Hope beamed and said, "I get to have a part, too."

He smiled, wondering what cute thing Hope was going to say or do. "Okay, princess. What would you like to say?"

Hope glanced up at her mom and receiving a gentle nod, she turned her attention back to Sam. "Mom said it was up to me to decide, and I didn't have to hurry. But I'd like you to be my dad. And my name can be Hope Alice Brooks Shackley if that's okay with you."

Sam's chest depressed as the air rushed out, and for a few seconds, he forgot to breathe. His heart threatened to burst out of his chest, but he realized all eyes were on him, especially the brown eyes of the pretty little girl who owned his heart. He knelt and took her hands in his. "To have you be the daughter of my heart is the greatest reward I could ever have. I pledge you my love and my protection as long as I live."

Hope's grin widened, and her whole body shook with excitement. He pulled her gently into his arms, then kissed the top of her head. Hearing a sniffle, he looked up to see Hayley swipe at a falling tear. Standing, he was about to take Hayley's hand when she inclined her head toward Eddie. Sam looked down, but instead of a wide smile on Eddie's face, he observed trepidation. The last thing he wanted was for Eddie to feel anxious in front of the other church members.

Sam wasn't surprised that Eddie seemed to be struggling, and he didn't want Eddie to feel like he had to make a name change. He placed his hand on Eddie's shoulder and knelt again to be close to his face. Whispering only to him, he said, "We're good, Eddie. I don't need anything other than knowing you're in my life."

Eddie pressed his lips together, then said softly, "I have something to say, too."

With his hand still on Eddie's shoulder, he nodded. "Okay, buddy."

Eddie glanced toward his mom, then turned and looked at Sam, keeping his eyes on him. "I remember my dad. Mom told me that because you and my dad were such good friends, that's how I got my middle name. So I feel like I've always carried both you and my dad with me."

Once again, the air seemed sucked from the room, and Sam nodded while trying to breathe. "You're right. Your dad was my best friend. And one of the greatest moments of my life was when he told me that they named you Edward Samuel Brooks. So you don't need to worry about anything else. You already have my name."

Eddie nodded, then quickly stopped and shook his head. "But I'd like to make a change, Sam. I'd like to have you be my dad now. But Mom said it would be okay if I'm Edward Samuel Brooks Shackley."

Sam would later wonder how his legs managed to hold his body upright. But for now, he could only concentrate on the way his heart seized, and the air became difficult to draw into his lungs. Unable to keep his emotions in check, he wrapped his arms around Eddie. "Being a dad to you and Hope while sharing that honor with the man who was your father and my best friend is more than I could have ever dreamed of." He stood and opened his arms, allowing Hayley to slip into his embrace, with Hope and Eddie pressed between them. "Having all of you is my greatest honor."

Finally, the pianist began, and as the four of them made their way down the aisle toward the back of the church, he glanced to the sides to see very few dry eyes. But for him, the moment of tears was over. And he was ready to celebrate their union.

After eating, visiting friends, drinking champagne, and dancing with their arms around each other, he took her to the Seaglass Inn for a wedding night before they left on their family trip to Florida. Eddie and Hope had already been taken back to the duplex by Sam's and Hayley's parents, who were going to spoil their grandchildren with one last night together.

After he and Hayley made love, they lay tangled together in the faint glow from the small lamp perched on the nightstand. The silk sheets wrapped around them, creating a soft cocoon. Hayley's eyes flickered and grew heavy as his hand drifted in languid strokes, tracing patterns over her back to help her find sleep.

He and Hayley had decided years ago that there was no way to know all the mysteries of the universe, certainly not why good men die before their time. Tonight, all that mattered was the connection that knitted their lives together in an intricate pattern of love. Hayley, Eddie, Hope, and him... family.

Embracing this humble truth, he finally surrendered to the inviting pull of slumber. Her peaceful face was the last image imprinted on his mind as he drifted off to sleep.

Don't Miss The Next Baytown Hero... Aaron's story!
In the Arms of Hero

ALSO BY MARYANN JORDAN

Don't miss other Maryann Jordan books!

Baytown Boys (small town, military romantic suspense)

Coming Home

Just One More Chance

Clues of the Heart

Finding Peace

Picking Up the Pieces

Sunset Flames

Waiting for Sunrise

Hear My Heart

Guarding Your Heart

Sweet Rose

Our Time

Count On Me

Shielding You

To Love Someone

Sea Glass Hearts

Protecting Her Heart

Sunset Kiss

Baytown Heroes - A Baytown Boys subseries

A Hero's Chance

Finding a Hero

A Hero for Her

Needing A Hero

Hopeful Hero

Always a Hero

In the Arms of Hero

For all of Miss Ethel's boys:

Heroes at Heart (Military Romance)

Zander

Rafe

Cael

Jaxon

Jayden

Asher

Zeke

Cas

Lighthouse Security Investigations

Mace

Rank

Walker

Drew

Blake

Tate

Levi

Clay

Cobb

Bray

Josh

Knox

Lighthouse Security Investigations West Coast

Carson

Leo

Rick

Hop

Dolby

Bennett

Poole

Adam

Jeb

Chris's story: Home Port (an LSI West Coast crossover novel)

Ian's story: Thinking of Home (LSIWC crossover novel)

Oliver's story: Time for Home (LSIWC crossover novel)

Hope City (romantic suspense series co-developed with Kris Michaels

Brock book 1

Sean book 2

Carter book 3

Brody book 4

Kyle book 5

Ryker book 6

Rory book 7

Killian book 8

Torin book 9

Blayze book 10

Griffin book 11

Saints Protection & Investigations

(an elite group, assigned to the cases no one else wants…or can solve)

Serial Love

Healing Love

Revealing Love

Seeing Love

Honor Love

Sacrifice Love

Protecting Love

Remember Love

Discover Love

Surviving Love

Celebrating Love

Searching Love

Follow the exciting spin-off series:

Alvarez Security (military romantic suspense)

Gabe

Tony

Vinny

Jobe

SEALs

Thin Ice (Sleeper SEAL)

SEAL Together (Silver SEAL)

Undercover Groom (Hot SEAL)

Also for a Hope City Crossover Novel / Hot SEAL…

A Forever Dad

Long Road Home
Military Romantic Suspense

Home to Stay (a Lighthouse Security Investigation crossover novel)

Home Port (an LSI West Coast crossover novel)

Thinking of Home (LSIWC crossover novel)

Time for Home (LSIWC crossover novel)

Letters From Home (military romance)

Class of Love

Freedom of Love

Bond of Love

The Love's Series (detectives)

Love's Taming

Love's Tempting

Love's Trusting

The Fairfield Series (small town detectives)

Emma's Home

Laurie's Time

Carol's Image

Fireworks Over Fairfield

Please take the time to leave a review of this book. Feel free to contact me, especially if you enjoyed my book. I love to hear from readers!

Facebook

Email

Website

ABOUT THE AUTHOR

I am an avid reader of romance novels, often joking that I cut my teeth on historical romances. I have been reading and reviewing for years. In 2013, I finally gave in to the characters in my head, screaming for their story to be told. From these musings, my first novel, Emma's Home, The Fairfield Series, was born.

I was a high school counselor, having worked in education for thirty years. I live in Virginia, having also lived in four states and two foreign countries. I have been married to a wonderfully patient man for forty-two years. When writing, my dog or one of my cats can generally be found in the same room if not on my lap.

Please take the time to leave a review of this book. Feel free to contact me, especially if you enjoyed my book. I love to hear from readers!

Facebook

Join my Facebook group: Maryann Jordan's Protector Fans

Sign up for my emails by visiting my Website!

Website

Made in the USA
Columbia, SC
29 June 2025